## *"Oh, my," she whispered, "it can't be—"*

Emma had thought she'd buried her feelings for Sam so deeply they could never be resurrected.

But she had been mistaken.

Just seeing him again had set her heart pounding, her palms sweating and her stomach turning somersaults. A longing unlike any she'd ever experienced had welled up inside her, and she had wanted—more than anything—to see him turn to her with outstretched arms.

But after the unforgivable way she'd treated him four years ago, she was probably the last woman on earth he would ever choose to hold close.

And that meant she couldn't risk giving herself away—not by word or deed. If he shunned her, she would be crushed.

And if he didn't?

She would give herself to him without a second thought....

Dear Reader,

February is the month of love…glorious love. And to commemorate the soul-searching connection between a man and a woman, Special Edition has six irresistibly romantic stories that will leave you feeling warm and toasty from the inside out.

Patricia Thayer returns to Special Edition with *Baby, Our Baby!*— a poignant THAT'S MY BABY! tale that promises to tug the heartstrings. Ali Pierce had one exquisite night with the man she adored, and their passionate joining brought them the most precious gift of all—a child. You won't want to miss this deeply stirring reunion romance about the tender bonds of family.

Cupid casts a magical spell over these next three couples. First, an intense bodyguard falls for the feisty innocent he's bound to protect in *The President's Daughter* by award-winning author Annette Broadrick. Next, *Anything, Any Time, Any Place* by Lucy Gordon is about a loyal bride who was about to marry her groom, until a mesmerizing man insisting he had a prior claim on her heart whisks her away…. And a forbidden desire is reignited between a lovely librarian and a dashing pilot in *The Major and the Librarian* by Nikki Benjamin.

Rounding off the month, celebrated author Robin Lee Hatcher debuts in Special Edition with a compelling story about a man, a woman and the child that brings them together—this time forever—in *Hometown Girl*. And finally, *Unexpected Family* by Laurie Campbell is a heartfelt tale about a shocking secret that ultimately brings one family closer together.

I hope you enjoy all our captivating stories this month. Happy Valentine's Day!

Sincerely,

Karen Taylor Richman
Senior Editor

Please address questions and book requests to:
Silhouette Reader Service
U.S.: 3010 Walden Ave., P.O. Box 1325, Buffalo, NY 14269
Canadian: P.O. Box 609, Fort Erie, Ont. L2A 5X3

# NIKKI BENJAMIN

## THE MAJOR AND THE LIBRARIAN

*Silhouette*®

**SPECIAL EDITION**®

Published by Silhouette Books

America's Publisher of Contemporary Romance

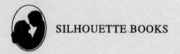

SILHOUETTE BOOKS

ISBN 0-373-24228-X

THE MAJOR AND THE LIBRARIAN

**Printed in U.S.A.**

**Books by Nikki Benjamin**

Silhouette Special Edition

*Emily's House* #539
*On the Whispering Wind* #663
*The Best Medicine* #716
*It Must Have Been the Mistletoe* #782
*My Baby, Your Child* #880
*Only St. Nick Knew* #928
*The Surprise Baby* #1189
*The Major and the Librarian* #1228

Silhouette Intimate Moments

*A Man To Believe In* #359
*Restless Wind* #519
*The Wedding Venture* #645
*The Lady and Alex Payton* #729
*Daddy by Default* #789

## NIKKI BENJAMIN

was born and raised in the Midwest, but after years in the Houston area, she considers herself a true Texan. Nikki says she's always been an avid reader. (Her earliest literary heroines were Nancy Drew, Trixie Belden and Beany Malone.) Her writing experience was limited, however, until a friend started penning a novel and encouraged Nikki to do the same. One scene led to another, and soon she was hooked.

When not reading or writing, the author enjoys spending time with her husband and son, doing needlepoint, hiking, biking, horseback riding and sailing.

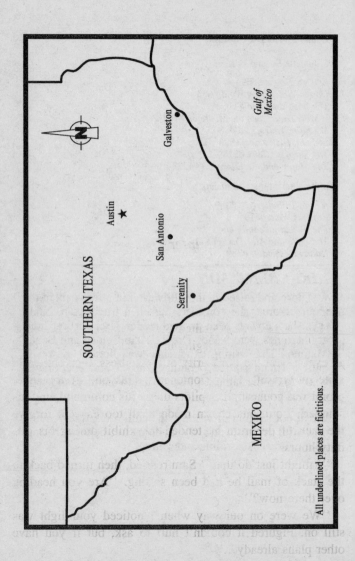

Gulf of
Mexico

Galveston

SOUTHERN TEXAS

Austin

San Antonio

Serenity

MEXICO

All underlined places are fictitious.

## Chapter One

"Hey, Sam, how about joining us for a drink at the officers' club?"

Major Sam Griffin, United States Air Force, glanced at the young lieutenant lounging in his office doorway, arched an eyebrow at the familiarity of his address, then smiled in spite of himself. Billy Fonteneaux was one of the more promising young fighter pilots under his command, and his southern Louisiana charm made it all too easy to forgive the lack of decorum he tended to exhibit during his off-duty hours.

"I might just do that," Sam replied, then turned back to the stack of mail he had been sorting. "Are you heading over there now?"

"We were on our way when I noticed your light was still on. Figured it couldn't hurt to ask, but if you have other plans already..."

"Actually, I don't," Sam admitted with a rueful twist of his lips.

Returning alone to his bachelor quarters to nuke a frozen dinner in the microwave wasn't exactly the kind of plan Lieutenant Fonteneaux's teasing tone had implied.

"So what do you say, Major? Have a beer with us, why don't you?"

"I can't make any promises," Sam hedged after a few moment's consideration. While the prospect of sharing a little lighthearted camaraderie with his junior officers was tempting, he preferred not to commit himself completely. "I have to clear up a few things around here first, then I'll see how I feel."

"Good enough, sir." Satisfied, Billy sketched a jaunty salute, then turned away.

As the lieutenant's footsteps faded down the hallway, Sam sat back in his chair, the stack of mail he had received that afternoon temporarily forgotten.

There had been a time when he wouldn't have thought twice about accepting Billy Fonteneaux's invitation. A time when he'd had a reputation for being the life of the party wherever he happened to be stationed. But that hadn't been the case for years now—almost four years, to be exact.

At thirty-five, he was still a relatively young man, and he wasn't tied down by a wife and children. But his younger brother's death had changed him in ways that were undeniable. Something had died inside him on that late June day as he'd sat on the roadside, cradling Teddy's lifeless body in his arms.

Don't go there, Sam warned himself.

There was nothing to be gained by resurrecting the past. What was done was done, and no matter how long he wallowed in his bitter, painful memories, that would never change.

Forcing his thoughts back to the task at hand, Sam sorted through the few remaining envelopes addressed to him. Nothing of any real importance, he noted. Bills from a couple of credit-card companies along with statements for his bank and brokerage accounts that he trusted would assure him he was still financially solvent.

He had hoped there would be a letter from his mother, but he'd quickly seen that there wasn't. Aside from the postcard she had sent over a month ago while visiting friends in Seattle, he hadn't heard from her in almost six weeks. Not all that unusual, really, and certainly nothing to be concerned about. Mail from the States to the air base in Italy could sometimes take awhile. And since she'd been away recently, she probably had quite a bit of catching up to do around the house.

Sam supposed he could call, but he was never quite sure what to say to her. Though he had never had reason to doubt his mother's love for him—quite the contrary, in fact—they had never been close. At least not as close as she and Teddy had been.

Sam had bonded more deeply with his father, perhaps because he and Caleb Griffin had been a lot alike—physically, as well as emotionally. Sam, too, had felt suffocated by life in small-town Serenity, Texas. And he, too, had found a way to leave, although not quite as dramatically or as devastatingly as his father had.

Once again, Sam caught himself venturing into a place he would rather not go. Forcing his thoughts away from the tragedy of his father's suicide twenty-five years ago, he vowed to write to his mother later that evening. By putting pen to paper, he could maintain the distance he needed and delay calling—

Tossing aside an application for yet another credit card, Sam frowned, then sat back in his chair, his gaze locked on the last envelope in his stack. The handwriting hadn't been familiar, so his attention hadn't been caught by it when he'd first glanced through his mail. But now, finally registering the return address, he experienced a sudden sinking sensation in the pit of his stomach.

"Emma Dalton, 1209 Bay Leaf Lane, Serenity, Texas."

Emma...shy, sweet Emma with her wild red curls, her bright green eyes and her lovely, lilting laugh.

She was the last person on the face of the earth Sam Griffin would have ever expected to send him a letter.

For years, she had been his brother's best friend. And sadly, secretly—for the most part—the only woman Sam had ever wanted. The one woman he could never have. All through high school and college, she had been Teddy's girl, then his blushing bride-to-be. And then, after he had taken Teddy from her—

*I hate you, Sam Griffin. I hate you, I hate you, I hate you....*

Reflexively, Sam crushed the envelope in his hand as he saw again the anger and pain flashing in her eyes, heard again the heartrending sobs shaking her slender body as she sank to the floor of the hospital waiting room, her cream silk wedding dress puddling around her.

Why had she chosen to contact him now of all times? The anniversary of Teddy's death was only a few weeks away. Was it something to do with that? But then, what could she possibly have to say to him after four long years of silence?

Sam wasn't sure he wanted to know.

Emma Dalton was a part of his past—one of the most devastating parts, to be exact. Surely he would be better off if that was what she remained.

What good could possibly come of allowing her to reenter his world? For years, he had done his damnedest to avoid even the mere thought of her. More and more often lately, he'd actually succeeded. Now...*this*...

He wasn't fool enough to think Emma's opinion of him had changed. And he certainly wasn't masochistic enough to feel he had to endure another round of her reproach. There was nothing she could say to him that he hadn't already said to himself a thousand times or more.

He would never forget what had happened to Teddy, nor would he ever forgive himself for it. He knew that he deserved Emma Dalton's animosity. He deserved it in spades. Of that he had never needed a reminder.

But he had finally come to realize all the mea culpas in the world wouldn't bring his brother back. That understanding, accompanied by acceptance, had gradually eased his anguish.

For one very long, very lonely moment, Sam fought the temptation to toss the unopened envelope into the trash can, grab his jacket, head for the officers' club and start working his way through a bottle of Scotch. By the end of the evening, he would be lucky to remember his name, much less all that had occurred four years ago. Unfortunately, that respite would be temporary at best, and with it would also come the possibility of grave repercussions.

Once already, he had come close to destroying his career as a fighter pilot by seeking solace in a bottle of booze. He wasn't about to risk doing it again. The air force was all he had left now. Which was only just, since the air force, with its promise of adventure, had been all he'd wanted from the moment he applied for an appointment to the academy in Colorado Springs.

Of course, that had been long before Teddy first introduced him to Emma. Then he had begun to realize the freedom he'd craved wasn't quite as satisfying as he had thought it would be....

Cursing under his breath, Sam shifted in his chair and smoothed the crumpled envelope.

How long had it been since he'd last thought of Emma—really *thought* of her? Months, he admitted. Yet, in a few minutes' time, and with nothing more than a plain white envelope addressed in her hand, she had slid under his skin all over again. And there she would stay, giving him no peace, if he threw her letter away without reading it.

He had no intention of suffering through any more sleepless nights than absolutely necessary. And there could be any number of reasons why she had written to him. Reasons that had more to do with the present than the past, he acknowledged. Reasons he had been too egocentric to consider initially.

Surely Emma Dalton had better things to do than send him a venomous letter four years after the fact. Yet he would lay odds she wasn't the type to seek out, impulsively, a man she had once claimed to despise, either.

Thanks to his mother, who had taken Emma under her wing after Teddy's death and mentioned her occasionally in her letters, Sam knew she still lived in Serenity and still worked at the town's library, where she'd recently been promoted to head librarian. She was still single, as well, but lived quietly in the small house she'd bought a couple of years ago.

A steady, responsible young woman making a decent, respectable life for herself despite the tragedy she had suffered. A woman who should, by all accounts, want nothing to do with the likes of *him*.

So *why* had she written to him out of the blue?

Realizing there was only one way to find out, Sam slit the sealed flap on the envelope and slowly withdrew the single sheet of stationery. He unfolded it reluctantly and saw that she had been brief—very brief—and almost painfully to the point.

Once again, Sam experienced a sick feeling in the pit of his stomach as he read the two short paragraphs rigidly written in her precise hand.

May 23
Dear Sam:

I am writing to advise you that your mother is ill. Specifically, she was diagnosed with a chronic form of leukemia several months ago. Since the initial treatment she received seemed to bring about a remission, she thought it best not to tell you. At that time she didn't want to worry you unnecessarily. She still doesn't. However, she recently suffered a relapse, and since the current prognosis is not good, I thought you should know.

I have been staying at the house with her and will continue to do so as long as necessary, so you don't have to be concerned that she's receiving proper care. But seeing you again would mean a lot to her. Since I realize you might not be able to get away on such short notice, I haven't told her that I've contacted you. She isn't expecting you, so she won't be disappointed if you can't make it. But please try to come home, Sam—for a few days, at least.

Sincerely,
Emma Dalton

Sam read through the letter a second time, wishing he could ignore the one thing Emma had left unsaid, yet knowing in his heart that he couldn't. Though she had refrained from spelling it out in so many words, he realized there was a very good chance that his mother was dying. And while she hadn't reached out to him herself—perhaps out of fear that she would be rebuffed by her wild, wayward son—he also knew that she needed him.

Unlike Emma, Margaret Griffin had never held him accountable for his brother's death. Instead, she had let him know time and time again that her faith in him was as strong as ever. And she had told him more times than he could count that she would always be there for him, just a phone call away—that if *he* needed *her* for any reason, she would come to him. As she had, traveling at least once a year to wherever he happened to be stationed.

She had understood how difficult returning to Serenity would be for him, and she had never expected it of him. Even now, faced with a life-threatening illness—her only remaining family half a world away—she hadn't asked him to come home. Not because she didn't want him there, but because she hoped to spare him what she knew as well as he would be a painful journey.

The mere thought of returning to Serenity with the anniversary of Teddy's death looming less than a month away filled Sam with trepidation. The sick feeling in the pit of his stomach increased, and his hands shook ever so slightly. Reactions more suited to the moments preceding a dog fight with enemy aircraft high above Earth. Reactions he had overcome when much more than his emotional well-being was at stake.

Drawing a deep, steadying breath, he set aside Emma's letter, then opened the center drawer of his desk and pulled out a calendar. His current tour of duty would be ending the following week. Though he'd had no specific plans, he had intended to take several weeks of leave before returning stateside.

Barring any unforeseen difficulties, he could be on a flight to San Antonio Thursday, Friday at the latest. Depending on the connections he was able to make, that ought to put him in Serenity sometime Saturday. He would also have time to request an assignment at one of the air bases in Texas so he would be reasonably close by when his leave was over.

Sam reached for the phone on his desk and began to dial his mother's number, easily calling it up from memory despite the length of time since he'd last used it. Halfway through, however, he stopped, then slowly cradled the receiver.

He didn't want to give his mother the chance to talk him out of coming, and he had no doubt that was exactly what she would try to do if he advised her of his plans. She wouldn't want to burden him, and in his present frame of mind, he would find it awfully hard to argue with her. In fact, allowing her to dissuade him would be too damned easy. Especially if she set her mind to it as he knew she would.

He couldn't let himself be drawn off course. Not if he had any hope of living with himself in the future. He owed his mother more than he could ever repay. Going back to Serenity wouldn't begin to cancel that debt, but it would be better than burying his head in the sand and pretending all would be well.

There was Emma to consider, too. Apparently, she had

already assumed a great deal of responsibility where his mother was concerned. Responsibility he had no intention of letting her continue to shoulder alone despite her all too obvious unwillingness to count on him.

*She isn't expecting you...won't be disappointed if you can't make it...*

Just as he had four years ago, Sam wanted to rise to his own defense. He wanted to call Emma and tell her—in no uncertain terms—how completely she had misjudged him. Granted he had made mistakes, and by God, he had paid for them dearly. But he had never meant Teddy any harm.

Why waste his breath, though? He doubted anything he had to say would change her mind. And what did her opinion of him matter in the general scheme of things?

Defending himself aside, Sam admitted he should still call Emma and let her know that help—such as he hoped he could be—was on the way if for no other reason than to ease her mind. Working a full-time job while caring for his mother on her own had to be a strain, not just physically but emotionally. Yet he pushed away from his desk without reaching for the telephone again.

Though he freely acknowledged he wasn't being fair to Emma, Sam decided it might be wiser to catch her unawares. He had no idea how she would react when they finally came face-to-face again. But forewarned would give her time to be forearmed against the kind of man she had chosen to believe he was.

There was no denying the part he had played in destroying her dreams. Yet for his sake, as well as his mother's, he hoped he and Emma could be allies rather than enemies. He had changed a lot over the years. He wanted a chance to prove it to her.

Of course, a truce could still prove to be impossible. But

then, at least *he* would be the one braced for battle. It wouldn't be much of an advantage, and certainly not one he intended to use against her unless absolutely necessary. But it would be better than nothing. And maybe, just maybe, it would save him from a whole new world of hurt.

Crossing his office, Sam grabbed his jacket, flicked off the light switch, then strode down the shadowed hallway, his footsteps echoing around him. With a mighty effort, he fought the urge to head for the officers' club, turning instead toward the housing complex. It wasn't company he was craving, but a good, stiff drink, and he knew—all too well—where that could lead. There were other, better ways to outdistance his demons.

Not quite twenty minutes later, changed into shorts, a T-shirt and running shoes, his warm-up complete, Sam set off at a steady pace, focusing his thoughts on nothing more than putting one foot in front of the other, eating up the first of what would be many miles as he blended into the twilight.

## Chapter Two

"Emma, come in out of the sun and have a glass of tea," Margaret Griffin urged.

Glancing up from the flower bed she had just finished weeding, Emma Dalton offered her old friend an appreciative smile.

"Sounds wonderful. I'll be right there."

She gathered her gardening tools together, then sat back on her heels, surveying her handiwork with a sense of pride and accomplishment. Early that Saturday morning, she had been determined to whip Margaret's much too long neglected front yard into shape. Now, nearly eight hours later—with only a short break for lunch during the worst heat of the day—she could happily say she had succeeded.

The scent of freshly mowed grass still lingered in the late-afternoon air. Once scraggly shrubs marched in neatly clipped rows along the railing that edged the wraparound porch. And the flowers in the beds—impatiens in various shades of pink and purple, bright-orange-and-yellow marigolds, hearty red geraniums, even a delicate smattering of white Gerber daisies—could finally be seen and appreciated.

As exemplified by her own riotously colorful yet neatly kept yard, Emma loved gardening. Working out of doors, close to the soil, with the sun shining overhead and a gentle breeze blowing never failed to fill her with a feeling of peace. That she seemed to have a green thumb helped, as well.

She had been itching to have a go at Margaret's yard for several weeks. But convincing her friend that *she* would be doing Emma a favor by allowing her to mow and clip and weed had taken some doing.

Margaret had insisted she'd imposed on Emma enough over the past few months. Emma, in turn, had argued that wasn't true. Whenever she had needed a strong shoulder to lean on, Margaret had always been there for her—even when she herself had been grieving. Helping Margaret cope with her illness had given Emma the chance to reciprocate. Not out of a sense of duty or indebtedness, but out of love.

Emma had never considered Margaret to be a burden, and she never would. Unfortunately, she had yet to get her to stop feeling as if she had become—in Margaret's words—little more than an old bother.

*Sometimes I think it would be easier on everyone if I went to sleep one night and didn't wake up again....*

Recalling her friend's offhand remark, Emma stared at the small shovel in her hand, not really seeing it. What would she do without Margaret? she wondered, overcome by a sudden sense of desolation. What *would* she do?

With a mighty effort, Emma shoved aside thoughts of

worst-case scenarios as she grabbed the trash bag full of weeds and pulled the drawstrings tight.

Granted, Margaret's most recent round of chemotherapy had left her frightfully weak, but she had rebounded with amazing fortitude. In fact, over the past three weeks she had regained much of her strength, and lately seemed to be almost her old self again.

She still tired more easily than before, but generally, her spirits were high. She kept herself busy—experimenting with new recipes, needlepointing a pillow cover and reading the cozy mysteries she enjoyed most. And she never, ever, uttered a word of complaint—

"Hurry, Emma, the ice is starting to melt," Margaret called out.

"I'll be just a minute more," Emma promised as she stood. "I want to put the tools away and dump the trash bag in the can around back."

Heading for the small, wood-frame garage at the end of the driveway, Emma wished she could have foreseen Margaret's extraordinary recovery. How that would have been possible, she didn't know. Even Margaret's doctor had expressed serious concerns about her prognosis. But at least she wouldn't have been in such a rush to write to Sam.

She shouldn't have done it. Shouldn't have jumped the gun in such a ham-handed way. First and foremost, because Margaret would have forbidden it had Emma asked her permission.

Margaret had made sure that she understood her son was not to be worried unnecessarily. And for the past six months—despite her own reservations—Emma had bowed to her friend's wishes.

Had she been Sam, she wouldn't have wanted to be kept in the dark. She would have rather been apprised of the situation without delay. But her loyalty had been to Margaret. Until that day three weeks ago when her doctor said she might not live to see the summer's end.

Margaret had been in a Houston medical center hospital undergoing treatment. Luckily, she had brought her address book with her, and Emma had found Sam's current F.P.O. number listed in it. Sitting beside her friend's bed as she slept, Emma had written to him as tears blurred her eyes, then posted the letter before she had time to change her mind.

Miraculously, Margaret's condition had improved within seventy-two hours, and Emma had begun to regret her hasty decision. Yes, there was a possibility the doctor could still be right. Margaret's recovery could be nothing more than a temporary respite. As often happened with a potentially life-threatening illness, she could suffer a relapse at any time. One that she might not survive.

But with Margaret almost her old self again, there no longer seemed to be any reason for Sam to come home. Not that he was going to. At least, not to *her* knowledge.

Three weeks had passed since Emma had sent her letter, and she had heard nothing in reply. He could have responded by mail, of course. That would take at least ten days. But considering the urgency with which she had written...

Emma had been sure he would call, if only to affirm that his mother's illness was as serious as she had implied. Beyond that, she hadn't known what to expect. But she'd been fully prepared for him to have some reason—some very good reason—why he wouldn't be able to make the trip to Serenity. And she would have understood.

There were too many painful memories for Sam in the small town where he'd grown up. Memories to which she had contributed in a ruinous way. She knew now that by blaming him for Teddy's death, she had been trying to assuage her own sense of guilt. Guilt that had sprung from her relief that *Sam* had been the one to survive that terrible accident on the narrow, winding road just outside of town.

*I hate you, Sam Griffin. I hate you, I hate you, I hate you....*

Hardly a day had passed since then that Emma hadn't wished she could recall those brutal words. But Sam hadn't given her a chance. He had stayed for his brother's funeral, but not in his mother's house. And after the service, he'd vanished, never—as far as she knew—to return.

Emma couldn't blame him. Not then, and certainly not now. Even with Margaret's health in question, she could understand why—torn as he had to be—he might choose to stay away. All that he had to look forward to here was more grief.

Yet again, Emma cursed her impulsiveness. She could have waited, *should* have waited.

"But you didn't," she muttered as she hung the gardening tools on their hooks, then disposed of the trash bag.

Doing her best to shake off the melancholy mood that had settled over her, Emma hurried back to the front yard. She pasted a smile on her face as she joined Margaret on the porch and accepted a tall glass of tea. Then, with a murmur of thanks, she sank into the old wooden rocking chair that matched her friend's. She took several swallows of the icy drink and sat back contentedly.

"Mmm, wonderful," she said.

She tossed her straw hat aside, took off her gold wire-rimmed glasses and set them on the little white wicker table, then tried to finger-comb some life into her damp curls. She was in desperate need of a shower, but first she wanted to relax a while and enjoy the gentle breeze wafting across the shady porch.

"You've outdone yourself, Emma. The yard looks just lovely. I'm going to be the envy of all my neighbors," Margaret stated proudly.

"Maybe not *all*. Mr. Bukowski looks like he's trying to give us a run for our money." Emma nodded toward the house across the tree-lined street where an elderly man puttered about, snipping and trimming his already well tended rosebushes.

"That old coot would sleep with his precious American Beauties if his wife would let him," Margaret retorted. "We won't count him."

"Well, then, I have to agree. Your yard definitely measures up now."

"Thank you, Emma. I really do appreciate all your hard work."

"Gardening never seems like work to me. Now scrubbing toilets and mopping floors—that's my idea of work." Emma shuddered delicately, then met her friend's gaze with an impish grin. "I'm so glad we found Mrs. Beal to handle those nasty chores for us."

"But you have a yard of your own to maintain," Margaret said, a look of concern shadowing her eyes. "I feel like I'm already taking advantage of you enough as it is."

"What nonsense." Emma waved a hand dismissively. "You've been paying Mrs. Beal to clean my house, as well as yours, while I've been staying here with you. Aside from cooking dinner occasionally and doing a few loads of laundry, I haven't really contributed that much until today. And, as I keep trying to convince you, I *love* gardening."

"You also have the responsibility of a full-time job," Margaret reminded her gently. "A job you love, too, but lately haven't been able to give the attention it requires because of my needs.''

''Actually, I've found a solution to that,'' Emma advised with studied nonchalance. ''Marion Cole and I have agreed to try job sharing for the summer. She came in one day last week asking about part-time work, but I don't have the funds to add anyone to the staff. So I'm going to let her have some of my hours. She's an experienced librarian, she's well liked by everyone in town and, with her husband out of work, she needs the money.''

''That's awfully generous of you, Emma. But…'' Margaret shrugged and looked away as she pulled a tissue from the pocket of her skirt.

''It's only temporary. Marion's fairly sure her husband will get a job offer from one of the companies he's interviewed with in Dallas or Houston. And I like the idea of having more free time this summer. We'll be able to drive down to Galveston for a few days before your next appointment with the doctor in Houston the way you wanted. I know how much you love the beach, and it's been ages since I've been there.''

Trying to ignore the fact that Margaret was dabbing at her eyes, Emma took another long swallow of tea, then rolled the cold, wet glass over her cheek as she looked out across the lawn.

Margaret had never been the type to show her emotions, but lately even the smallest act of kindness seemed to make her weepy. Much as Emma wanted to comfort her, she said nothing. Calling attention to Margaret's treacherous tears would only embarrass her friend unnecessarily.

Instead, she rocked quietly, allowing Margaret a few moments to gather herself. Without her glasses, everything beyond the porch railing blended pleasantly into a bright blur of colors, sometimes stable, sometimes shifting, depending on the slant of the breeze.

She didn't realize that the dark blue blob she glimpsed out of the corner of her eye was an automobile moving slowly down the street until it pulled into Margaret's driveway. Even then, Emma merely squinted at it lazily, sure that the driver, having made a wrong turn, intended only to back out and be on his way. The boxy sedan wasn't one she recognized as belonging to anyone she knew. And Margaret hadn't mentioned that she was expecting any visitors.

Unless—

"Well, who on earth could that be?" Margaret asked, her composure restored.

"I have no idea," Emma murmured, an odd sensation unfurling in the pit of her stomach.

The car's engine ceased its grumbling, but the driver seemed in no hurry to open the door and step out. Frowning, Emma reached for her glasses as Margaret stood, started toward the porch steps, then paused uncertainly.

"Oh, my…" she breathed, wonder in her voice. "It can't be—"

Adjusting her glasses, Emma rose from her chair, too. She knew what Margaret only suspected. Knew with terrifying certainty who sat behind the wheel of the dark blue sedan. And she wished—oh, *how* she wished—she could simply slip away. Her friend wouldn't understand, though. So she lingered in the shadows as the car door finally opened, and a breathless moment later, her heart slammed against her rib cage.

A tall, handsome man, neatly dressed in khaki pants and a white knit shirt, his short blond hair glistening in the sun, his eyes shielded by aviator sunglasses, stepped out of the car, closed the door quietly and started across the lawn.

"Sam...?" Margaret said, her voice barely above a whisper. Then she added joyfully as she moved down the porch steps and opened her arms to him, "Oh, Sam, you're home. You're home, son...."

Emma watched as he hesitated a moment, removing his sunglasses uncertainly. His surprise at how Margaret had aged in the months since he'd seen her last was evident, but only for an instant. Flashing the cocky grin Emma remembered all too well, he strode toward his mother, his long legs eating up the distance between them, and swept her into his embrace. As he hugged her close, however, his smile faded, revealing the true depth of his distress.

"Hey, don't cry," he chided softly. "I'll think you're not happy to see me."

"I *am* happy to see you, Sam Griffin, and you know it," she retorted. Smiling through her tears as she looked up at him, she put her hand against his cheek. "Happier than you'll ever know."

Still standing alone on the porch, Emma wished, once again, that she could slip away without being noticed. She felt uncomfortable intruding on Margaret and Sam's reunion. After being apart for almost a year, they deserved to have some private time together.

More disconcerting, however, was that Emma also felt afraid. Not only afraid of what Sam might say or do when he finally spied her lurking in the shadows, but also of what *she* might say or do. He wouldn't be happy to see her there. That she knew for sure. But would he show his displeasure in Margaret's presence?

She had just seen how easily he could hide his emotions when he wanted to. Yet she couldn't trust that he'd spare her in the same way he had his mother. She hadn't proved herself deserving of that care.

As for her... She had thought she'd buried her feelings for Sam Griffin so deeply they could never be resurrected. But she had been mistaken. Just seeing him again had set her heart pounding, her palms sweating and her tummy turning somersaults. A longing unlike any she'd ever experienced had welled up inside her, and she had wanted—more than anything—to see him turn to her with outstretched arms, as well.

Of course, after the unforgivable way she'd treated him four years ago, she was probably the last woman on earth he would ever choose to hold close. And that meant she couldn't risk giving herself away—not by word or by deed. If he shunned her, she would be crushed.

And if he didn't...?

Emma shivered as an altogether different kind of dread—a dread long nestled deep in her soul—reared its ugly head.

She would give herself to him without a second thought. And when boredom set in—as it surely would for a man like Sam Griffin—she would end up like her mother, grieving alone for a man who could only find happiness living dangerously close to the edge.

She couldn't do that, *wouldn't* do that. She needed safety and stability in her life, the kind of safety and stability she had found here in Serenity, first with Teddy, and then, on her own—

"Emma! Can you believe it? Sam's here," Margaret called out, interrupting her reverie.

Swiping futilely at her hair, Emma once again pasted a smile on her face and crossed to the porch steps.

"Yes, I see," she said, surprised at how steady her voice sounded, then risked a glance at Sam, barely meeting his penetrating gaze. With his iron jaw and eagle eyes, he had always had a tendency to look...severe. The expression she glimpsed on his face assured her that hadn't changed. "Hello, Sam. It's nice to see you again."

"It's nice to see you again, too, Emma," he replied, his tone matter-of-fact.

"Well, come on up to the porch and have a seat," Margaret urged. "How about a glass of iced tea?"

"Sounds good," Sam agreed as he started up the steps.

"I'll get it." Emma made the offer gladly, eager to have a reason to retreat, at least temporarily.

"Why, thank you, dear." Margaret patted her arm gratefully, then turned back to Sam. "You really should have given me some warning," she scolded.

"Then you wouldn't have been surprised..."

Relieved by Sam's bantering tone, Emma slipped into the house. She had no idea how he planned to explain his unexpected arrival. But for the time being, he didn't seem inclined to reveal the part she had played in it. That would mean he'd have to mention his mother's illness, as well, and he wouldn't spoil her happiness by doing that just yet.

Catching sight of herself in the hall mirror as she headed for the kitchen, Emma winced. The parts of her hair not plastered to her skull by the straw hat she'd been wearing stuck out in all directions. Her ratty T-shirt and shorts were sweat stained, bits of grass clung to her bare arms and her face was smudged with dirt and grime.

"Delightful," she muttered as she continued down the hallway, then laughed ruefully.

Had she put her mind to it, she probably couldn't have thought of a better way to put Sam off than she already had in her current state of dishevelment.

In the kitchen, she filled glasses for Margaret and Sam only, put them on a tray along with the tea pitcher and a fresh bowl of ice, then returned to the porch.

"Here you go," she said, interrupting their murmured conversation as she bumped the screen door open with her hip.

They glanced up at her, but she avoided meeting either of their gazes. Even when Sam stood and, his fingers brushing hers, took the tray and set it on the wicker table.

"You didn't fill a fresh glass for yourself," Margaret noted.

"I thought I'd let you two visit on your own while I get cleaned up," Emma replied as she turned to go back into the house. "I'll pop that casserole in the oven, too. Unless you'd rather eat a little later tonight…"

"Oh, no, Emma. The usual time will be just fine." Margaret touched Sam's arm. "How does King Ranch chicken sound to you?"

"Like a slice of heaven." He smiled at her with unabashed affection.

Feeling even more like a fifth wheel, Emma yanked the screen door open.

"Come out and join us as soon as you've had your shower," Margaret called after her.

"I will," Emma said, letting the screen door slap shut behind her.

Actually, she had no intention of hanging around now that Sam was home. She would shower, dress, then pack up her belongings, make her excuses and return to her own house a few blocks away. Her presence here was no longer necessary. Sam would be available if Margaret needed anything. And Emma could always return once he'd left again.

She put the chicken casserole Margaret had prepared earlier in the oven, then scurried upstairs to the guest room she had been using for the past three weeks. Margaret's bedroom was right next door. The bedrooms Sam and

Teddy had used as children were on the opposite side of the landing, their doors closed.

Emma supposed she should take a few minutes to air out Sam's room, but just the thought of invading what had always been his personal space made her uneasy. She could only hope Mrs. Beal had changed the linen and dusted recently. If not, Sam could do it himself.

Right now, all Emma wanted was to get away from him before she said or did something stupid. She could only pretend to be cool and calm in his presence for so long. Then anything could happen. Could, and with her luck, probably *would*.

## Chapter Three

"I wonder what's taking Emma so long," Margaret said, glancing at her watch for the third time in less than fifteen minutes.

Sam had been asking himself the same question as he eyed his own watch surreptitiously, and he already had a pretty good idea of what the answer could be. He'd seen how steadfastly Emma had avoided his gaze despite her courteous manner. As if she could barely stand the sight of him. Why, then, would she go out of her way to seek out his company?

He couldn't say as much to his mother, though. She would pretend not to understand. Just as she'd already pretended not to understand why he had expressed concern about her well-being. He couldn't come right out and tell her Emma hated his guts any more than he could come right out and tell her how shocked he was by her frailty.

She had aged to a frightening degree since he'd seen her last. But when he'd asked outright if she had been ill, she hadn't said anything specific about having been diagnosed with leukemia.

Instead, she had hedged, admitting only that she *had* been a bit under the weather the past few weeks, thus finding it necessary to ask Emma to stay with her. Then she'd also insisted—rather hurriedly—that she was feeling much better, especially now that he had finally returned to Serenity.

"It was time you came back," she had said. "But why now?"

"Because it was time," he'd replied, hedging in his own way.

He couldn't admit that Emma's letter had been the real catalyst without also revealing why she had written to him. And what would that do for his mother other than spoil the thrill of his homecoming for her?

There would be more than enough time in the days ahead to confront her about the true nature of her illness.

"Maybe I ought to check on her," Margaret continued. "Or, better yet, you could do that while I get started on the salad." She nodded purposefully. "Yes, that's a better idea. You can get your bags out of the car, take them up to your room, then make sure Emma didn't slip in the bathtub and bump her head."

Oh, now *that* was something he really wanted to do— intrude on Emma Dalton while she was taking care of her personal needs.

"She's probably just drying her hair," Sam said, the heat of a blush warming his face.

"Probably. But it would set my mind at ease to know

that nothing's happened to her. Of course, if you're going to be shy about it, I can climb the stairs myself.''

''Oh, no, you don't,'' he muttered, smiling ruefully as he glimpsed the merry twinkle in her faded blue eyes. ''As you pointed out, I have to take my stuff up anyway. I might as well check on her while I'm there.''

Margaret Griffin had always been much too good at getting her own way, and obviously, she still was. Though what she hoped to accomplish by sending him chasing after Emma he couldn't even begin to imagine. Or perhaps, more accurately, he *could,* but chose not to.

''Thank you, son.'' She smiled brightly as she retrieved the tray from the wicker table.

''You're welcome,'' Sam replied.

He held the screen door for her, then walked slowly down the porch steps and crossed the lawn to the car he had rented at the airport in San Antonio.

Had he honestly believed Emma had been delayed because of some mishap, he would have been more inclined to hurry. But likely as not, she had simply bypassed the front porch, going on to the kitchen instead.

No doubt Margaret would find her there, and the two of them would finish putting together the meal he'd been promised, leaving him to try to make himself at home in the one place he no longer felt he belonged.

The drive from San Antonio had been pleasant enough, but then he'd been away so long that the city itself, as well as the sprawling countryside on the outskirts, had seemed only vaguely familiar. As he'd entered Serenity, however, he had been bombarded by memories. Surprisingly, not all of them had been bad. And those that were... Well, they were also distant enough to have lost their edge.

Still, he had driven more slowly, prolonging the moment

when he would have no choice but to pull into the driveway of the aging, two-story Victorian house on Holly Street.

Sam had told himself he was simply reacquainting himself with his hometown, taking in the various changes that had occurred during his four-year absence—the refurbishing of many older homes and the building of new ones, as well as the revitalizing addition of shops and restaurants to the downtown area.

Yet he had known what he'd really been doing. In a roundabout way, he had been putting off what he had long believed would be the ultimate test of his fortitude.

Eventually, he was going to have to walk inside his mother's house, climb the steps to the second floor and face, once and for all, the emptiness—made even more awful by its permanence—of his brother's bedroom.

As Sam had drawn closer and closer, he had found himself wondering how his mother had faced the void Teddy's death had left day after day, year after year. And then, in a sudden flash of realization, he had mentally cursed himself for allowing her to do so all alone.

He had been so damned intent on distancing himself from *his* pain that, for the most part, he had blocked out all thought of hers.

Some son he had been, he'd thought as he finally turned into his mother's driveway.

And yet, she had never held his disregard against him. Not once in the four years he had stayed away. She had waited patiently for him to come to his senses—something he hadn't really done on his own, but rather, thanks to Emma's none too gentle nudging.

Hell, in her own subtle way, Margaret Griffin had even given him time to adjust to actually being home again before suggesting, at last, that they ought to go inside.

"So stop dragging your feet," Sam growled, grabbing his bags, then slamming the trunk lid and turning back to the house.

The place looked exactly the same as he remembered, at least on the outside. It also seemed to have held up fairly well. His mother had had the white clapboard and the dark red gingerbread trim painted within the past couple of years, and the yard appeared to be well tended—thanks to Emma, his mother had said.

He imagined little had changed on the inside, either. Which, while understandable, wasn't wholly heartening. Growing up there hadn't been a totally disagreeable experience. He and Teddy hadn't suffered for lack of love and affection from their parents or each other.

But Sam had suffered his most tragic losses while living within those four walls. And now the possibility of another equally life-shattering loss had brought him back again. Was it any wonder he had to force himself to mount the porch steps, open the screen door and enter the shadowed hallway?

"I've switched on the air-conditioning, so shut the front door, will you, please?" his mother requested from the door to the kitchen.

"Yes, ma'am," he replied, displaying the manners she had worked so hard to drill into him.

"Oh, go on." She waved a hand at him dismissively. "Don't be so fresh."

"I'm not," he protested, trying unsuccessfully to hide a smile.

"You *are*," she retorted, a smile of her own belying her grumpy tone.

"All right, I am," he conceded as he started up the staircase.

"Don't forget to check on Emma."

"She hasn't come down yet?"

Sam paused a moment, his brow furrowing. He didn't think Emma had come to any harm, and he doubted his mother did, either. She seemed much too placid for that. But then, what had she been doing up there for almost an hour? While she might have needed a little time to reconcile herself to his arrival, to his knowledge she had never been the type to hide from anyone, including *him*.

"Not yet, and she must know dinner's almost ready. See if you can hurry her along," Margaret instructed. "And don't dawdle yourself."

"I won't," Sam promised as he continued up the stairs.

From the little he had seen of the first floor, he had been right to assume most everything in the house had stayed the same. The sofa and chairs in the formal living room and dining room had been reupholstered, and the heavy velvet draperies on the windows had been replaced by curtains in a lighter, lacier fabric. Otherwise, the pieces of dark wood furniture stood in their respective places as stolidly as ever.

Yet Sam hadn't felt quite as uncomfortable as he had feared he would. Instead, he'd experienced a surprisingly strong sense of warmth and welcoming.

Probably due to the mouthwatering aromas wafting out of the kitchen, he told himself. But no matter. He was grateful for anything that eased his homecoming.

He paused again on the second-floor landing, his gaze drawn first to the hall bathroom straight ahead of him. Thankfully, the door was open and the light was off, indicating that Emma had finished in there. He didn't have to worry about finding her lying in a naked heap.

From the bathroom, his gaze swept farther down the hallway, taking in the closed doors of his and Teddy's bedrooms. With relief, Sam realized he wouldn't have to look inside his brother's room unless he chose—

A muffled thump brought his attention to the bedrooms on his left. The one with the door wide open was his mother's. The other, with the door partially closed, was the guest room where Emma must be staying.

Another thump, followed by a screech that sounded like a drawer opening, then an unintelligible mutter of words, almost made him smile. What on earth was she doing in there? Surely not rearranging things.

Drawn by his curiosity, Sam acted without really thinking. He dropped his bags on the floor, walked over to the guest room and nudged the door open a few inches.

The slight movement caught Emma's eye, and she looked up, obviously startled. Her gaze met his for an instant, then skittered away as she clutched what appeared to be a white sleeveless nightgown to her chest. From the expression on her face, Sam wasn't sure whether she was more angry or embarrassed by his intrusion.

"I'm sorry," he muttered. Shifting uncomfortably, he bumped against the door by accident, opening it even more. "I heard...noises in here and thought..." He hesitated uncertainly. "Actually, I'm not sure what I thought," he admitted.

Unable to stop staring, he noted that she'd cleaned up quite nicely. Her glorious red hair curled about her face in artful disarray, making her look incredibly young and innocent. But the pale yellow sundress she wore emphasized her femininity in a way that left no doubt she was all grown up.

"That's all right," she murmured, glancing at him, then away again.

As she lowered her gaze, Sam spied the open suitcase on her bed, and frowned.

"What are you doing?" he asked, though the neatly folded clothing already packed inside the bag made his question rather redundant.

"Now that you're here…" She paused, then tipped up her chin, her gaze finally meeting his head-on as she continued, "I thought maybe I ought to go back to my house."

So she had chosen to cut and run after all. Sam knew he should consider that a lucky break. If she went home, he wouldn't have to deal with her dislike on a full-time basis as he had been dreading he would. But oddly enough, what he felt was disappointment—deep disappointment.

While Emma hadn't greeted his arrival with any great joy, she hadn't gone out of her way to show any animosity toward him, either. Obviously he made her uncomfortable. Hell, *she* made *him* uncomfortable. But that didn't mean there was no hope for them.

Hope for what, he wasn't quite sure. Reconciliation, perhaps? He wasn't sure about Emma, but he wanted that, he realized. Wanted it and needed it. Only he couldn't come right out and say as much. At least not yet.

"Going back to your house?" He eyed her questioningly, trying to buy the time he needed to come up with a good reason for her to stay put. "Why?"

"Because you're here now," she repeated in a slightly exasperated tone.

"What difference does that make?" he asked, intentionally acting obtuse.

"With you around, Margaret's not going to need me anymore."

"I don't know about that," Sam countered, finally hitting upon a fairly good excuse for her to stay. "From what she said after you left us, she loves having you here. But she's afraid she's been taking advantage of you. If you rush off, she's going to think she was right, and she's going to be really upset."

"I've tried to tell her that wasn't so," Emma insisted, her brow furrowing.

"For her sake, I wish you'd stick around. And for mine," he admitted honestly.

"Yours?" She eyed him uncertainly, her confusion evident.

"My mother hasn't said anything about the leukemia yet. When I casually asked about her health, she mentioned— just as casually—that she'd been ill, but not how seriously. I didn't want to press her my first day home, so I didn't say anything about your letter. I know we're going to have to talk about it eventually, and we will. But until then…" He shrugged helplessly. "I'm afraid she won't ask for my help if she has a bad spell. And if I'm the only one here…" Again he allowed his words to trail away before adding, "At least she would have you to turn to if you stayed a while longer."

"How long are you planning to be here?" Emma asked, her frown deepening.

"A minimum of four weeks, longer if necessary."

"She has an appointment a week from Monday with her doctor in Houston. Since she won't be able to keep that a secret, I suppose I could wait until then to go home," she conceded, albeit reluctantly.

"I'd really appreciate it," Sam said.

"Well, I wouldn't want to upset Margaret."

With a look of resignation on her face, Emma tossed the nightgown on the bed, gathered an armful of clothes from the suitcase and turned back to the open dresser drawer.

Feeling as if he'd been summarily dismissed, Sam said nothing more as he backed out of her bedroom doorway and collected his bags.

"What's going on up there, you two?" Margaret called from the foot of the staircase. "Dinner's been ready for almost twenty minutes now."

"We'll be right down," Sam assured her.

"You said that once already."

"This time I mean it."

"What about Emma?"

"I'm on my way now," she replied.

Stepping out of her bedroom, she paused to exchange a wary glance with him, then started down the steps.

Sam eyed her thoughtfully a moment longer, then crossed to his bedroom, opened the door and dumped his things on the floor. He noted that his mother had changed the bed linens and curtains since his last visit home. But much to his dismay, the room still had the look of a shrine about it—a shrine to his boyhood. Fortunately, that could be remedied in the time it would take him to pack everything away in a couple of cardboard boxes.

By the time he reached the kitchen, Margaret was ready to serve. Since they were all hungry—or at least seemed to be if the way they filled their plates and set to eating was any indication—they managed to get through most of the meal without having to exchange more than the minimum of polite conversation.

Sam relished every bite of his mother's old-fashioned home cooking, helping himself to another serving of both the salad and the casserole. Emma ate heartily, as well, though she declined seconds. And though Margaret's appetite seemed somewhat diminished, she, too, finished everything on her plate.

"Sure you've had enough?" she asked when he finally sat back and pushed his empty plate away.

"More than enough," he replied, smiling gratefully.

"I hope you saved room for a slice of fresh peach pie." As his mother stood, she picked up his plate. "Emma baked it yesterday—homemade from scratch."

"There's vanilla ice cream, too," Emma added, helping Margaret clear the table.

"Sounds tempting, but I really stuffed myself with the King Ranch chicken."

"Then I'll make it a small slice," Margaret said.

"All right, but no ice cream...please."

"Coffee?" Emma appeared at his side, holding out a steaming mug. "It's decaf."

"Thanks."

Sam took the mug from her, but she turned away before he had the chance to add a smile.

"You know, I've been thinking..." Margaret began as she returned to the table with his pie.

"About what?" Sam asked, eyeing with chagrin the slice she had cut for him.

He had forgotten that his mother's idea of *small* would be twice the size he'd had in mind. But the first bite was so luscious, he doubted he would have any trouble finishing it.

"That car you rented," Margaret replied as Emma returned to the table with mugs of coffee for herself and his mother. "You don't really need it. You can use mine instead and save yourself a bundle of money."

"It's not that expensive. And returning it to the San Antonio airport would be a hassle. Someone would have to drive over in another car and give me a ride back. Someone other than *you*," he stated bluntly, hoping to ward off what he fully expected would be her next volley.

Whether she wanted to admit it or not, she wasn't up to making a long drive, especially on her own.

"Well, yes. Someone other than *me*," Margaret countered with a faint tinge of sarcasm, then faced Emma with a beguiling smile. "You wouldn't mind following Sam in my car and driving back with him, would you? Tomorrow. After church, of course."

Trying hard to mask his dismay, Sam glanced at Emma. She stared at Margaret for a long moment, a stricken look on her face, then bowed her head and gazed intently at the contents of her coffee mug, saying nothing.

"I'm sure she has a lot of things she'd rather do with her Sunday afternoon," he said.

"Oh, no," his mother said. "She's been wanting to go to San Antonio for ages. Haven't you, dear? To visit that nursery where they sell those Old Garden roses you like so much. You could stop at the needlepoint shop on the River-walk, too. Dolly called to say the canvas and yarn she ordered for me finally came in. I'm fairly sure both places are open on Sunday afternoon, so you could make a day of it. Unless you *do* have other plans…"

"Not really," Emma admitted. "But what about you? Don't you want to ride along with us, too?"

Sam couldn't help but hear the desperation in her voice. She didn't want to go off on her own with him any more than he wanted to go off on his own with her. But his mother seemed oblivious to that fact. *Seemed* being the operative word, since she had always prided herself on being highly perceptive.

What was she up to? he wondered. Surely not matchmaking. She, of all people, had to realize how impossible any union between him and Emma would be.

"I think I'll just stay here and take it easy," Margaret replied, then turned her gaze on him again, her eyes laser sharp. "So that's settled. We'll go to Mass at nine, have breakfast at the Serenity Café—they still make the best pecan pancakes in town—then you can hit the road."

"Only if Emma is sure she doesn't mind," Sam said.

"I don't." Without looking at either of them, she stood quickly, her jerky movements belying her words, and took her mug to the sink.

Sam could think of at least a hundred things he would rather do the following day, and he imagined Emma could, too. But she obviously wasn't any better at defying Margaret's wishes than he was. He could almost feel sorry for her, but he was already much too busy feeling sorry for himself.

Damn it, he should have let her go back to her house when he had the chance. Now he was going to be stuck with her all day tomorrow, and there wasn't anything he could do about it. What would she say to him once they were away from his mother's house?

And what in heaven's name would *he* say to *her?*

"Emma, dear, you look tired. And no wonder after all your hard work today. Why don't you make an early night of it. Sam can help me clean up the kitchen. Can't you, son?"

"Yeah, sure." He stood, his empty plate and mug in hand.

"You know, I think I'll do just that," Emma agreed, her relief evident. "See you in the morning." She gave Margaret a quick hug, then barely glanced his way and added, "Good night, Sam."

"Good night, Emma."

As he watched her leave the kitchen, Sam caught himself thinking about the frilly white nightgown she'd held against her chest when he'd intruded on her earlier.

Thought of her slipping into it, then climbing into the big, old-fashioned four-poster bed in the guest room, and wished—

"You wash and I'll dry," his mother instructed, diverting his attention not a moment too soon.

"Yes, ma'am."

Stepping up to the sink, he turned on the hot-water faucet, then reached for the liquid soap. Wordlessly, his mother moved to his side, reached up and curved her palm against the side of his face, surprising him.

"Have I told you how glad I am that you've come home?"

"At least once already," he assured her, putting an arm around her slender shoulders. "But I don't think I've told *you* how glad I am to be here."

"Are you really?"

"Yes, really."

Sam hugged his mother close, aware that he had spoken the truth. Despite everything that had happened there, coming back to Serenity had been the right thing to do. And he was glad he'd realized it before it was too late.

"I'm glad." She hugged him back, then eased away. "Now let's get this mess cleaned up so we can sit out on the porch awhile and talk. I want you to tell me all about those young pilots you've been training."

# Chapter Four

With each mile that spun by beneath the whirring tires of Margaret Griffin's stately Volvo, the dread that had first settled into Emma's soul the night before blossomed anew. She sat stiffly in the driver's seat, clutching the steering wheel with sweaty hands, her eyes locked on the dark blue sedan traveling at a sedate pace a couple of car lengths ahead of her.

Sam seemed in no more of a hurry than she was to reach their destination, but that inevitable moment would be upon them very soon. They had long since left the winding country roads outside Serenity for the four-lane freeway leading into San Antonio. Now they were less than a mile from the airport exit along which the car-rental agency's lot was located.

Emma couldn't remember the drive to San Antonio ever seeming to go by so swiftly. But a glance at the clock on the dashboard assured her they had been on the road the requisite hour and a half such a trip normally took.

Apparently, time could also fly when you *weren't* having fun.

Not that the drive had been unpleasant. Quite the contrary, in fact, since the weather was nice and the traffic light. What had her quailing wasn't the journey itself, but rather what awaited her at its end.

From the moment Margaret had first suggested she and Sam spend the afternoon together, Emma's stomach had been tied in knots. She could count on the fingers of one hand the number of times she had been alone with him. And she could recall in all too devastating detail the last of those blessedly rare occasions.

The memory of what had happened on that late June afternoon—only two days before she was supposed to marry Teddy—had seared itself into her mind and heart in such a painful way that any attempt to disregard it proved to be utterly futile. And though she knew better than to imagine there was any chance of a repeat performance, the mere thought of finding herself in a similar situation had been more than enough to unnerve her.

Sam, too, had seemed just as dismayed as she was by his mother's proposal, which—in a perverse way Emma refused to contemplate too closely—had not only annoyed her, but offered her a small measure of consolation, as well. At least she hadn't been the only one thrown for a loop.

Yet there had been little either of them could say to dissuade Margaret from the course she had set. Arguing with her would have been a waste of time. She'd had right on her side, and she'd known it.

Allowing Sam to pay for a rental car when he could use

hers would have been foolish. And since Margaret really wasn't up to making the drive to San Antonio on her own...

Of course, she could have ridden along as a passenger and served as a buffer of sorts, Emma thought as she pulled to a stop behind the sedan just outside the rental agency's office.

Actually, she had been counting on Margaret to do just that up until the moment they had finally said their good-byes outside her house. The chance to spend some time with Sam had to have appealed to her. And hadn't she often said how restful she found it to ride in a car?

Not that she had seemed in need of a nap. In Emma's opinion, she had been in fine fettle that morning. Standing proudly beside her son, she had sung the hymns during the church service in a vibrant voice. Then she'd polished off a tall stack of pancakes at the Serenity Café with obvious relish.

Her decision to take to her bed once they'd returned to her house hadn't rung true. And Emma had been hard-pressed not to remind her of her oft-stated disapproval of sleeping the day away. Especially when she'd caught the mischievous twinkle in her eyes. A twinkle Emma sincerely hoped Sam hadn't seen.

Bad enough that *she* had an idea of what Margaret seemed to have had in mind when she'd sent them off alone. She didn't want Sam getting wind of his mother's machinations, as well. Too much had happened for them to be friends, much less anything more...intimate.

For Margaret's sake, they could try to tolerate each other in the days ahead. But expecting either of them to do more than that would be like asking for the moon. Or, more accurately, expecting any more of *Sam*.

In all honesty, Emma had to admit it wouldn't take much

for her to succumb to his masculine appeal. After all, she had spent the past four years mourning his absence, as well as Teddy's, albeit in a very different way. But she knew without a doubt that she had destroyed any feelings he might have had for her. Otherwise, he would have never stayed away so long.

Only his concern for his mother had brought him back to Serenity—his very obvious and deeply felt concern.

As Emma shut off the Volvo's engine, Sam—looking cool and confident in navy shorts and a chambray shirt with the sleeves rolled to his elbows—stepped from the sedan. He glanced back at her a moment, his expression unreadable thanks to the mirrored sunglasses he wore, lifted a hand in acknowledgment, then turned toward the rental agency's entryway.

With a pang of longing that was almost laughable under the circumstances, Emma watched him pull the door open and disappear inside.

She had always prided herself on her ability to face facts head-on. And she had certainly never considered herself a masochist. So how could the mere sight of one man—especially the one man who had every reason to spurn her—still have such a devastating effect on her?

Her reaction to seeing him just now had been only slightly less unsettling than the reaction she'd had when she'd seen him yesterday afternoon and again when she'd first come upon him early that morning.

At Margaret's request, he had dressed in uniform for the church service. Seeing him standing tall and handsome in the living room, Emma had felt her breath catch in her throat. She had halted in the doorway, staring at him as a rush of emotion engulfed her. The urge to walk up to him, put her arms around his waist and rest her head on his shoulder had been almost overwhelming.

Until he had glanced at her, his chin up, his blue eyes cold and distant.

Then she had wanted to turn on her heel and run as far and fast as she could. Her pride alone had held her still. Lifting *her* chin, she had somehow managed not only to hold her ground, but to meet his icy gaze with her own brand of hard-won reserve, as well.

She had stayed on in his mother's house because the argument he'd made in favor of it had been a valid one. But she hadn't been about to let him intimidate her.

Now Emma wondered if that might have been the wisest course of action, after all.

Had she simply walked away, she wouldn't be sitting here, her heart racing, waiting for Sam to finish his business. She wouldn't be dreading the moment when he joined her in the close, quiet confines of his mother's car. And she certainly wouldn't be making herself crazy trying to decide what she *could* say to him, what she *should* say to him and what she actually *would* say to him in the hours ahead.

He would probably want to discuss his mother's illness. But there was only so much she could tell him about that. Then what? she wondered.

In an effort to pull herself together, Emma grabbed her purse, exited the Volvo and locked the door, then walked into the rental agency. A sideways glance assured her Sam was still waiting to speak to an agent. He stood third in line, his head bent, studying the rental contract. Moving quickly, she went on to the ladies' room without attracting his attention.

When she caught sight of herself in the mirror, she grimaced. The expression on her face was one more suited to a woman on her way to her execution.

She couldn't afford to let Sam see her looking so grim. Not when he was capable of cloaking himself in such utter dispassion. That would give him even more of an edge than he already had. If she was to have any chance of getting through the afternoon without making an idiot of herself, she was going to have to try to level the playing field. And she could only do that by at least *pretending* a nonchalance equal to his own.

She took several deep breaths as she dried her hands on a paper towel, then refastened the banana clip holding her curls away from her face. Forcing herself to think no further than the present moment, she faced the mirror on the wall by the door, smoothed a hand over her narrow, calf-length denim skirt and adjusted her white, sleeveless blouse.

It would do no good to anticipate the worst. In fact, she would only be buying trouble. Better to paste a smile on her face and hope for the best. No matter how blasé Sam might seem, he couldn't be looking forward to the next few hours, either.

As she left the ladies' room, Emma saw that Sam had finally made it to the counter. Pen in hand, he was signing a paper while the young female agent stood by, eyeing him appreciatively.

Emma imagined he garnered lots of looks like that from women everywhere he went. Why, *she* would smile at him that way, too, if she thought it would do her any good.

Realizing that she was frowning again, Emma went on to the car. She unlocked the passenger's door and slid onto the seat. Reaching over, she stuck the key in the ignition, started the car and turned up the air-conditioning in readiness for Sam's arrival. Then she took out a map of San

Antonio and the article about the nursery she wanted to visit, and tried to pinpoint its location.

From the corner of her eye, she saw Sam leave the rental agency. He crossed to the driver's side of the Volvo, opened the door and leaned inside.

"Sure you wouldn't prefer to drive?" he asked. "You know your way around here better than I do."

"Not really," she admitted, glancing up at him, then away again. "I don't get into the city all that often, and the traffic near the downtown area can get kind of hairy." She gestured at the map spread open in her lap. "I'd just as soon navigate. Unless you'd rather not…"

Realizing that she was rambling, Emma allowed her words to trail away. She stared at the map, her grip on it tightening until the edges crumpled in her hands.

"No problem. I don't mind driving," Sam replied, his tone matter-of-fact. Slipping behind the steering wheel, he adjusted the seat to accommodate his height. "Where would you like to go first—the nursery that specializes in Old Garden roses or the needlepoint shop down on the Riverwalk?"

"You know, we could just…head back to Serenity," Emma ventured, looking out the windshield.

Beside her, Sam turned in his seat so that he faced her, but he said nothing. Acutely uncomfortable, Emma hastened to fill the silence stretching between them.

"I mean, you just got into town after traveling for several days, and here you are, on the road again. You must be exhausted. Now that we've taken care of the car business…" She waved a hand at the rental-agency office. "I can always go to the nursery another day, and the needlepoint shop can send your mother's supplies the way they've always done in the past."

When several moments passed and Sam again made no comment, Emma finally turned to look at him. The darkened lenses of his sunglasses made his expression hard to read, but there was a grim twist to his lips as he eyed her quietly.

"I don't mind going to the nursery and the needlepoint shop as we planned," he said at last. "But if you want to go back to Serenity, Emma, just say so, and we'll go back."

"*We* didn't plan to go to the nursery and the needlepoint shop, Sam," Emma argued as calmly as she could. "Your mother planned that for us. So why go through the motions if we don't want to?"

"I've already said that *I* don't mind," he reminded her reasonably. "But I also said if *you* do, we can head back right now." He shifted in his seat again, released the parking brake, put the car in gear, then added almost as an afterthought, "Of course, if we get back earlier than expected, she's going to wonder what made you change your mind. And more than likely, regardless of what you say, she's going to hold me responsible for spoiling the day."

"She wouldn't do that," Emma protested.

"I'm afraid she would." Sam pulled to a stop at the rental agency's exit and glanced at her again. "She warned me two, maybe three times before we left to mind my manners and behave like a gentleman so you'd have a nice time. She said you deserved a day away, and she wanted me to make sure that it was as pleasant as possible."

Emma groaned inwardly as she bent her head over the map again. She could almost hear Margaret saying the words. And she now knew without a doubt that she'd been right about that mischievous twinkle in her friend's eyes.

She wished she had kept her mouth shut. Her only intention had been to spare Sam, and in all honesty herself, from several hours of strained silence punctuated by odd intervals of stilted conversation. But all she had actually succeeded in doing was putting both of them in an even more untenable position.

Had she just gritted her teeth and gotten with the program, they could have pretended to make the best of the situation. Now they each knew that the other would rather be anywhere but there. Margaret wanted to give Emma a respite of sorts, and she had elected Sam to do the honors in the hope that something more might come of their spending time together.

And something most certainly would. Only not what Margaret had in mind. Sam would consider her even more of a cross to bear. And *she* would have to work even harder at acting as if she didn't have any feelings for *him* one way or another.

"Well, then, I supposed we ought to go to the nursery first," she said, hoping her cheerfulness didn't sound as false to him as it did to her. "Unless I'm mistaken, it's not far from here." She looked at the street sign, then back at the map. "Turn right here, go down to the second intersection and turn left."

"Emma, if you really want to go back, we can," he offered. "Just because my mother gets a notion in her head doesn't mean we have to go along with it. This is supposed to be *your* day, after all."

"I know. But I *do* want to check out the roses at the nursery, and we're already here."

"Well, then, let's go." He turned out of the agency lot as she had directed, then glanced at her questioningly. "Left at the second intersection?"

"Yes, then down about two miles or so. According to

the article I clipped out of the paper, the nursery should be on the right.''

They covered the relatively short distance in virtual silence. Sam seemed perfectly at ease. He leaned back in the driver's seat, his shoulders relaxed, his long, lightly tanned legs stretched out in front of him as he gripped the steering wheel in a loose hold, his attention focused on the road ahead.

Emma, on the other hand, sat rigidly in her seat, hands clasped knuckle white in her lap, so tense she could hardly draw a breath. She willed herself to say something inane, but the longer she waited, the more impossible it became. She could barely swallow around the nervous flutter in her throat, much less speak.

Sam had given her no reason to feel so uncomfortable in his presence. He hadn't said or done anything to disparage her. Nor had he given any indication that he would.

He had argued for her staying at his mother's house when he could have sent her packing. And he had just gone out of his way to make sure they did what *she* wanted now. All with the deference of a true gentleman.

As if the last time they had been together she hadn't screamed at him like a madwoman, spewing out her hatred—

"This must be it," Sam said, jerking her back to the present as he flicked on the turn signal and slowed the car. "Wimberly and Sons Nursery?"

"Yes, Wimberly and Sons Nursery," she murmured, scrambling to gather her wits about her.

He seemed to have put the past behind him. Unless she succeeded in doing the same, the next few weeks were going to be unbearable.

Sam found a parking space under a leafy oak tree and switched off the engine.

"I won't be long," Emma said, reaching for the door handle.

"Take your time. I'm not in any hurry." He, too, opened his car door.

Emma wasn't sure what she had expected him to do while she prowled around the nursery's spacious grounds. Even with the windows rolled down, it was too warm out for him to sit in the car. But he could have gone off on his own in search of something that might catch his interest— the goldfish pond, perhaps. Instead, he seemed quite content to trail after her.

At first, she was overly conscious of his presence close behind her. Gradually, however, as the beauty of the flowering rosebushes for sale captured her interest, she finally began to relax.

"I never realized there were so many different varieties of roses," he said after a while.

"And they're all so lovely," she replied, trailing her fingers over the velvety pale yellow petals of an especially lush blossom.

"Are you looking for one bush in particular?"

"Several, actually. I have only modern hybrids in my garden at home. Now that they're established, I want to add some Old Garden roses. They bloom only once in late spring or early summer, but they're known for their wonderful fragrance. That makes their petals an especially favorable addition to potpourri," she explained, then gestured to a long, wide plot set slightly apart from the others and marked aptly enough, Old Garden Roses. "Ah, here they are."

Emma eyed the various containers carefully, and soon

saw that the bushes she wanted were all available at prices she could afford.

"You've found what you were looking for, haven't you?" Sam asked, a hint of amusement in his voice.

"Yes, I have. But how did you know?"

She glanced at him curiously, but he was still wearing his sunglasses, making it all but impossible for her to determine exactly what he might be thinking.

"The way your eyes lit up. Like a kid on Christmas morning."

Emma felt her cheeks flush with embarrassment.

"That obvious, huh?"

"Yes, that obvious," he replied in a kindly tone. "Why don't I grab one of those little red wagons and help you load up, or will you need more than one?"

"One will be enough," she assured him with a wry smile.

For just an instant, the ghost of an answering smile tugged at the corners of his mouth. Then he turned away to claim a wagon for her.

Feeling oddly lighthearted for the first time since the previous afternoon, Emma went about selecting the new additions to her garden. Two of the Great Maiden's Blush bushes, known for their ivory coral-centered blooms. Two of the Leda bushes—a smaller, more compact shrub than the Maiden's Blush featuring shell pink flowers picoteed with crimson. And two of the Tuscany bushes bearing semidouble dark red blooms.

Sam lifted the large, heavy containers into the wagon for her, then pulled it up to the counter where a clerk tallied her bill. Emma gladly wrote a check, her thoughts racing ahead to the following afternoon—the soonest she would be able to start putting her new rosebushes in the ground.

At the car, Emma spread the tarp she had brought over the floor of the trunk, then stood aside while Sam loaded the containers. Luckily, all six fit quite nicely. And thanks to the deep well, Sam was able to close the lid without crushing the tops of the bushes.

"Are you sure they'll be all right in there?" he asked with obvious concern.

"They may look delicate, but they're hearty enough and healthy enough to survive a lot worse than a few hours in the trunk of a car. So don't worry. They'll be fine," she assured him as he helped her into the car.

"My mother told me that you really enjoy gardening," Sam continued as he settled into the driver's seat and started the engine.

"Yes, I do, although I'm not sure why. Probably because my mother enjoyed it, and I was the only one around to help her. Everywhere we lived before she died, she always planted something. Usually flowers, but sometimes herbs and vegetables, too...if we moved into a house with a big yard. Even when there was a good chance we wouldn't be around long enough to see the results of all our hard work. I remember asking her once why she did it. She said it was the only way she could put down roots. All she ever really wanted was to live in one place and have a home of her own, but she never did."

"You moved around a lot when you were a kid?" Sam asked.

At first, Emma was surprised by his question. She had always assumed he knew as much about her background as Teddy had. Now she realized that wasn't necessarily so.

Sam had gone off to the Air Force Academy in Colorado Springs a year before she and his brother became friends. Granted, he had seen her with Teddy on the rare occasions when he'd been home on leave. But he'd probably had more important things to discuss with his younger brother than the shy little redhead Teddy had taken under his wing.

"Until my mother died," she replied. "My father had a hard time hanging on to a job. He was always looking for something better, somewhere else. My mother insisted on trailing after him even though she hated always having to start over in a strange place. She loved him so much, and I suppose he loved her, too. But he was never there for her when she really needed him. After a while, the loneliness got to be too much for her and she started drinking."

Pausing for a moment, Emma stared out the window, recalling a time when her home had been anything but the haven she craved. Clasping her hands in her lap, she drew a breath and pushed back the painful memory of her mother lying on the floor in a drunken stupor.

"She died when I was twelve," Emma continued matter-of-factly, determined to head off any show of sympathy from Sam. "We were here in San Antonio at the time, but my father was getting ready to move on again. He claimed he couldn't look after me on his own and dumped me into a foster-care program. I was lucky enough to be placed with the Gruenwalds in Serenity, and except for the years I spent at the university in Austin, I've been there ever since. Putting down roots of my own, I suppose."

"And you're happy living in such a small town?"

"More than happy," Emma stated succinctly.

Nothing on earth could tempt her to relive—ever again—the constant upheaval of her childhood years. That was why marrying Teddy had been so important to her. He offered her the kind of stability she needed, and now, although she didn't have the family she'd always wanted, she had a home of her own. And lonely though it sometimes was, she had long ago convinced herself that was all she really needed.

"Funny, isn't it?" Sam mused as he shifted into gear and pulled out of the nursery's lot. "The place used to give me claustrophobia. In fact, I couldn't wait to get away."

"I know..." she murmured, then barely caught herself before she added that was what Teddy had told her once. She wasn't ready to bring him into their conversation yet. Instead, she added, "My foster sisters at the Gruenwalds' felt exactly the same way. I'm the only one of the four of us who stayed in Serenity. Jane lives in Seattle with her husband and son—my little godson. Megan lives in San Diego with *her* husband and son. And last I heard, Kathleen was living in New Orleans. Of course, that was almost a year ago. She's always liked to move from place to place, so she could be anywhere by now."

"Jane is the one who stayed with you last year, isn't she? My mother mentioned her in her letters. She also said the two of you went up to Seattle to visit them about six weeks ago."

"That's right. We did."

"Point me toward the needlepoint shop, then tell me about Jane and your trip to Seattle."

Emma guided Sam back to the freeway and told him which exit to watch for. Then, glad to have something neutral to talk about, she explained briefly how Jane, and eventually her husband, Max, had come to stay with her in the months before the birth of their baby.

What a time that had been for the two of them. But thanks to the power of their love for each other, Jane and Max had solved their problems.

As Emma had six months ago, she wished that could be true for everyone, herself included. Of course, she didn't say as much to Sam. That could open the door to questions she didn't want to answer. So she gave him the facts, then went on to talk about the lovely time she and Margaret had had in Seattle.

"So you liked it there," he said.

"I *loved* it there. It's one of the most beautiful places I've ever been."

"But you absolutely, positively wouldn't ever want to live there?"

"Well, no..." Emma began, then hesitated as she looked out the window.

Actually, she *had* considered that possibility while she was there, imagining more than once what it might be like to live in one of the high-rise condos within walking distance of Elliott Bay and the Pike Street market or to ferry over from a little cottage on one of the islands as Jane and Max did. Though their house was anything but a cottage—

"You don't sound so sure."

"Well, it *was* awfully nice there. I guess I wouldn't mind it too much," she admitted.

"I imagine roses would grow rather nicely there," Sam said, the barest hint of teasing in his tone.

"Rather nicely, indeed." Emma gazed out the window thoughtfully, then added, "Still, I was really glad to get home again."

"Most people usually are. Especially when home is where their heart is." He paused for only a moment, giving her no time to reply, and when he continued, he changed the subject without seeming to miss a beat. "Looks like we're getting close. Where do you think we should park?"

Relieved that Sam didn't expect any reply to his comment, Emma directed him to a small parking lot down a side street near one of the entrances to the Riverwalk. From there, it was only a short walk to the needlepoint shop. Picking up Margaret's supplies took less than ten minutes since the clerk had the package ready and waiting.

Emma assumed they would go straight back to the car again, but out on the Riverwalk Sam halted, looking around at the milling crowds as he tucked the brown paper bag under his arm.

"I don't remember this place being so busy. At least not on a Sunday afternoon," he said.

"San Antonio has become a popular tourist town. Companies from around the country have also begun holding conferences here. Lots of shops and restaurants have opened up along the river over the past few years."

"Do you mind if we take a walk along here? Maybe stop and have a cup of coffee?" He gestured toward the famous-name coffee bar on the other side of the narrow river channel, accessible by an old stone bridge about half a mile away.

What Emma really wanted was to quit while they were ahead. So far, they had managed to get along rather well, all things considered. But she didn't want to push her luck. Leaving now, they would still have almost two hours together.

But Sam seemed so eager to see the sights. And he hadn't given her any grief about the lengthy amount of time she'd taken at the nursery. Acknowledging that fair was fair, after all, she mustered as much enthusiasm as she could.

"Coffee sounds good," she said, smiling up at him.

He seemed to hesitate, as if he sensed her reluctance, then nodded once, choosing to accept her response without argument. Together they joined the other people on the walkway, strolling along side by side, saying nothing.

Emma tried to enjoy the hustle and bustle around her, but as they made their way up one side of the river, then down the other, her thoughts turned to the one thing she should do that day. The one thing she should have done, *would* have done four years ago if only he had given her the chance.

As she had admitted to herself many times in the past, she owed Sam an apology for the way she'd behaved at the hospital the day Teddy died. Yet she had allowed one chance to slip away yesterday evening when he had come upon her in her bedroom. She'd been flustered then because he'd taken her by surprise. But now she was as calm and collected as she'd probably ever be in his presence.

Telling herself that she was waiting for some cue from Sam, she had studiously avoided any mention of that particular part of their past so far. But he had seemed just as intent as she was to avoid the subject.

She *could* put off saying what she had to say until the drive back to Serenity. But maybe it would be better to do it somewhere more…open. Somewhere like the coffee bar just ahead. Sitting among strangers, she wouldn't be as likely to say more than was absolutely necessary as she would when alone with him in the car. Nor would she be tempted to reveal the deepest secret of her heart. A secret that would surely appall him.

Whatever had come over them that afternoon two days before her wedding, it obviously hadn't had the same significance for Sam as it had for her. But there was no reason he had to know that. And he wouldn't. Not as long as she kept her wits about her, said only what she had to say and no more.

That shouldn't be too hard, should it?

Her heart pounding and her palms sweating, Emma plodded along, the grip of dread lodged in her chest tightening its hold with each step she took. She had to hide her feelings from Sam. *Had* to, no matter what. Otherwise, she would end up making a fool of herself, and that she simply could not bear.

## Chapter Five

Sam could all but feel the tension building in Emma as they wandered along the stone walkway edging the narrow river channel. At first, he had been puzzled by her sudden change in mood. Then, too late, he'd realized that he should have let well enough alone.

They could be in the car now, heading back to Serenity, their time together almost over. But they had been having such a nice time—much nicer than he had anticipated—and he hadn't wanted to risk losing the new affinity they'd found for each other. Instinctively, he had known that once they returned to his mother's house, they wouldn't be able to ignore the shadows haunting their past quite so easily.

Sam hadn't been any more enthusiastic about the trip to San Antonio than Emma. For her sake, however, he had been determined to make the best of it. Even without his mother saying so, he had seen that Emma needed a break.

She had taken a great deal of responsibility upon herself. More than she should have had to handle alone. And Sam had hoped that during this brief respite, he could convince her she wouldn't have to struggle on her own any longer.

There was little enough he could say or do to change her low opinion of him. But he had thought that by spending a little time with him she would see he had some redeeming qualities. Maybe then she would be able to treat him more as a friend than an enemy.

After all, he was not only ready, but also willing to do whatever she deemed best for his mother. Only with her compliance, however, would he be able to lend the full measure of support she needed.

Since his mother insisted on being so secretive about the true nature of her illness, he needed to have Emma on his side. And up until the moment he suggested they linger on the Riverwalk, he had believed that would be possible.

Granted, they had avoided certain potentially painful topics of conversation. Topics one of them would have to broach eventually. But as if by mutual agreement, they had each sought out neutral ground that afternoon. Or rather, *he* had, asking first about the roses that had given her such obvious delight, then her friend Jane and the trip Emma had taken to Seattle to see her.

He had made only one blunder, but luckily it hadn't resulted in any serious repercussions. He hadn't known about the kind of life Emma had lived before she'd come to Serenity, and he had revealed his ignorance without stopping to consider how she might be affected by his probing. But she had spoken of her childhood so pragmatically that he need not have worried about upsetting her.

Instead, oddly enough, Emma's responses to his questioning had unsettled *him*. Why should he care if she never wanted to leave Serenity? She certainly deserved to have the home she had worked so hard to make for herself.

He should have been happy for her, not...disconcerted. Nor should he have pressed her into admitting that—despite her claim to perfect contentment—she *had* been tempted by the thought of living in Seattle. Just because *he* had always craved wider horizons than his hometown offered didn't mean she had to, as well.

And just because *he* had wanted more time alone with her didn't mean he'd had the right to assume the feeling was mutual....

Sam knew that the camaraderie they'd been sharing had vanished at almost the same moment he suggested they stay in San Antonio a while longer. He had glimpsed the flash of consternation that had crossed her face just before she forced herself to smile up at him agreeably. After that, he had sensed her growing uneasiness and with it, a kind of grim determination.

As if she had made a decision to go forward with something she found distasteful. Something no doubt he, too, would rather not contemplate.

Unfortunately, there had been no going back. He could only walk along beside her and wait for whatever was to come, losing more ground with each step he took as she slowly, surely, distanced herself from him once again.

Desperate to avoid any type of showdown, Sam was fully prepared to pass by the coffee bar without suggesting a second time that they stop.

But as they drew closer to it, Emma asked offhandedly, "Still want to stop for a cup of coffee before we head home?"

"Do you?" he countered, hoping she would give some sign that she had only mentioned it to be polite.

"Sure," she replied, glancing up at him with another strained smile.

"All right, then."

Trying for an upbeat manner—why buy trouble, after all?—Sam reached around Emma and opened the door, then gestured for her to enter ahead of him.

A cool draft of air washed over him, carrying with it the deep, rich aroma of dark roasted coffee, tantalizing his senses. With luck, maybe a steaming cup of the daily blend would be just the bracer he needed for whatever lay ahead. Thankfully, that late in the afternoon the place wasn't crowded, so they shouldn't have to wait too long to be served.

They joined the short line at the counter, standing side by side without speaking, the murmur of other, barely audible, conversations floating around them. Reluctantly, Sam took off his sunglasses and stowed them in his shirt pocket.

Years ago, he had learned how much easier it was to hide his true thoughts and feelings behind a pair of dark lenses. But he also knew that some people considered wearing them indoors to be in poor taste, and he didn't want to give Emma any reason for embarrassment.

"What would you like?" he asked as the line moved forward.

"Um, a mocha cappuccino sounds good."

She glanced up, meeting his gaze, and Sam saw a flicker of surprise in her eyes. Then she turned her attention to the menu board behind the counter, a blush tingeing her cheeks.

He wondered what about him had her behaving so self-consciously. As far as he could tell, he was as neatly tucked and zipped as he'd been all day. And he was trying just as hard as ever to project a nonthreatening air.

He knew he could sometimes seem forbidding. But he only adopted that manner as a means of self-preservation. Of course, he was finding it almost impossible to let his guard down around her. Apparently, from the look she'd just given him, he wasn't being as successful as he'd thought he was at disguising that fact without his sunglasses.

Whoever said that the eyes were the windows of one's soul had been right. Unless you were skilled in the art of duplicity, you could all too easily give the game away.

Sam had always hated lies, especially lies of the heart. Yet with Emma, he had always felt the need to…deceive. And he couldn't imagine how that would ever change— today, tomorrow or any of the days that followed.

Revealing his true feelings for her had always been and would always be completely out of the question. He had slipped only once—on that June afternoon two days before she was to marry his brother—and look what had happened. He simply couldn't expose himself to the anguish he believed would be inherent in slipping again.

"What about you?" Emma asked, interrupting his reverie as they inched closer to the head of the line.

"I'm going to have a cup of the house blend." He gestured toward the glass case filled with pastries. "Would you like something to go with your cappuccino?"

"How about an almond biscotti?"

"You got it."

Sam ordered for both of them, adding a biscotti for himself, as well, and paid the cashier. Together they moved around the counter to pick up their order. Emma paused to add a packet of sweetener to her frothy drink, then they crossed to a table by one of the windows overlooking the Riverwalk.

As they settled into chairs across from each other, Sam caught a glimpse of Emma licking daintily at the whipped cream atop her cappuccino, and almost dropped his own steaming cup in his lap.

There had been nothing provocative about her action, at least not intentionally so. Yet the swell of desire that rolled through him left him decidedly weak in the knees. He could remember—as if it had been yesterday—the taste and texture of her tongue. Could almost feel the velvet swirl of it against his own—

"So, tell me, has life as an air-force fighter pilot been everything you imagined it would?" she asked with a bright smile, effectively curbing his lascivious daydreams.

Sam wasn't sure exactly what he had thought she'd been mulling over on their walk, but his career had not been on the list. While it might be of interest to her, it certainly wouldn't have put that wrestling-with-demons look on her face that he'd seen earlier.

"In some ways. Actually, in most ways," he admitted. "I love to fly and I've seen quite a lot of the world." He dipped his biscotti in his coffee, took a bite, chewed and swallowed, then added, "Guess I can't ask for more than that."

Under other circumstances, Sam would have elaborated. But the way Emma fidgeted with her coffee cup as her gaze roved around the room, he knew she wasn't really paying attention. Obviously, she had something else on her mind. Something he would just as soon she spit out. He would rather have the other shoe drop and get it over with than engage in a round of well-mannered but meaningless conversation.

"No, I guess not," she agreed, her gaze focused on

something outside the window. "I just wondered if maybe you ever…missed being…home."

"Sometimes," he said.

True enough, but he would have been even more honest if he had said *most* times lately. Especially late at night, alone in his bed, when he thought of her there in Serenity.

"Yet you haven't been back for four years now." She hesitated, glanced at him, took a swallow of her cappuccino, then shoved her cup away. "Even considering all that happened when you were home last, that's a long time to stay away."

Suddenly aware of where Emma was leading, Sam said nothing. He wasn't about to amble down that particular stretch of memory lane. Not if he could help it. Instead, he glanced at his watch, then reached for the brown bag holding his mother's needlepoint supplies.

"It's getting late," he said. Pushing back his chair, he nodded toward the door. "We'd better go."

"Not yet," Emma replied, her voice firm.

The touch of her hand on his arm surprised him into meeting her gaze. Behind the lenses of her gold wire-rimmed glasses, her green eyes held steady, revealing her resolve.

She was going to say what she had to say regardless of how he tried to put her off. He could let her do it here in the relative privacy of the coffee bar or out on the sidewalk with crowds of people pushing past. But she was going to say her piece, one way or another.

Easing his arm from her hold, Sam sat back in his chair again and eyed her coldly. He refused to offer her any encouragement, verbal or otherwise. Talking about Teddy's death, as he was sure she meant to do, couldn't possibly help either one of them. Nothing would change how his brother had died. Nor could the part he had played be erased.

For one long moment, Sam thought maybe Emma would reconsider. As if cowed by his mutinous glare, she clasped her hands atop the table and lowered her gaze. He found himself wanting to lean forward, to cover her hands with his, and comfort her. But he couldn't afford to aid her in even that small way.

Finally, she drew a breath and looked up at him again. The sorrow he saw in her eyes clawed at his heart, leaving him feeling raw...wounded. She was going to tell him again just how completely he had destroyed her life. She was going to say that even now she still hated—

"I owe you an apology, Sam. An apology I should have given you four years ago," she began, her voice barely above a whisper. "I'm so sorry for the things I said to you that day at the hospital after...after Teddy died. So very, very sorry. I had no right to accuse you the way I did. And I had no right to...blame you for my...grief. I knew the accident wasn't your fault, but I...but I..." Blinking back tears, she turned her face away.

Sam stared at her, too shocked to speak. She was apologizing to *him?* But why? *Why?* She'd had every right to blame him. Every right in the world because he *had* been responsible.

"I should have never been so cruel," she continued. "But that day, I just couldn't—"

"Stop, Emma. Stop berating yourself." In one swift movement, Sam stood, pushing against his chair so forcefully that it teetered behind him and would have crashed to the floor if he hadn't grabbed it. Working hard to keep his voice even, he added quietly, "You don't owe me an apology. You had every reason to blame me and you still do."

She stared at him wide-eyed and shook her head.

"No, Sam, that's just not true. The accident wasn't your fault. I knew it. *Everyone* in Serenity knew it. That truck ran the stoplight—"

"Technically, no, Teddy's death wasn't my fault. But I was to blame, Emma. Believe me, I *was* to blame." He glared at her angrily. "*That* is why I stayed away. Coming back here, facing what I'd done to Teddy and to you... I couldn't—"

"But, Sam—" Emma began, fully prepared to argue further.

"There are no *buts*, Emma. *None,*" Sam cut in, then gestured toward the door impatiently. "Come on. Let's get out of here."

She stared at him, obviously shocked by his heartless tone. Then, her lips thinning into a narrow line, she stood, too.

"Yes, let's."

She picked up her purse and walked away from the table, her spine stiff, her shoulders straight, her chin tipped up dangerously.

Good, she was angry, Sam thought. Better that than weepy. Had he made her cry, he wasn't sure what he would have done. Probably something stupid like take her in his arms and try to kiss away her tears.

There were things he would rather she never knew about the moments before Teddy was killed. Things he would have been all too easily tempted to reveal unless he remained aloof.

He could understand why she felt she had fences to mend. But her anger at him that day at the hospital hadn't been the major reason why he'd stayed away. He could only hope he had made that plain. Then she wouldn't feel responsible any longer, and in turn, wouldn't bring up the subject again, forcing a showdown they would both end up regretting.

Outside at last, Sam dug his sunglasses from his pocket and put them on again gratefully. With the onset of early evening the sun had shifted, casting the riverside walkway in shade, but he didn't care. At that moment, any barrier against Emma's probing gaze was better than none, no matter how odd he appeared in the bargain.

The number of people jostling past them seemed to have doubled in the time they had been in the coffee bar. Concerned that they might be separated in the crowd, Sam took Emma by the arm. Predictably, considering her mood, she tried to pull away, but he held on to her gently but firmly.

"I don't want to lose you among all these people," he said as he looked down at her.

"Heaven forbid *that* should happen," she retorted sarcastically. "You might have to drive home alone."

"And leave you here on your own? Never," he vowed in a matter-of-fact tone. "I'm responsible for your safekeeping, at least for today. And I take my responsibilities seriously."

"I'm a big girl, Sam. I've been on my own for years. Why should today be any different? You haven't had any reason to be concerned about my well-being in the past, and I can't see that you have any reason to be now."

"You're wrong, Emma. I've been concerned about you for a long time," he admitted, unable to let her think of him so ignobly.

"Well, you have a really strange way of showing it." She glanced up at him, looking more puzzled than angry now. "Staying away for four years—"

"Maybe so, but it was the best I could do," he cut in, hoping to throw her off track again.

"But that doesn't make any sense to me," she persisted, her voice gentling. "If you cared—"

More sure than ever that the time had come to nip this particular line of conversation in the bud, he responded in the tone he reserved for those under his command most in need of a dressing-down.

"It doesn't have to make sense to *you,* Emma. Not as long as it makes sense to *me.*"

"What kind of answer is that?" she demanded, her anger coming to the fore again.

"The only one you're getting."

"Well, it's just not good enough."

"Tough luck, huh?" he drawled, not the least bit proud of himself for speaking so callously.

He couldn't see that he had any other choice, though. Knowing that she cared about him enough to question his real reason for staying away stirred the stark, hungry need for her he'd buried deep in his soul. But revealing that reason would do her no good. And he would much rather have her angry at him than cause her more pain.

"You...you jerk."

Her face flushed, she yanked her arm free and started up the steps that led away from the river.

Making no response to her caustic comment, Sam followed after her. Though he noted with relief that the street-level sidewalk was much less crowded, he lengthened his stride to keep up with her. But he didn't attempt to touch her again.

Since they were no longer in any danger of being separated, he hadn't any reason to hold on to her. But he also knew that if he maintained physical contact with her much longer, he might just do something stupid like haul her against his chest and kiss away her willfulness. When she got an idea into her head, she could try the patience of a saint, and he had never been part of that breed.

As she had so succinctly pointed out a moment ago.

*You…you jerk.*

She had that right…in spades.

Forced to hurry to keep ahead of him, Emma said nothing more. But Sam doubted he had heard the last from her on the subject of Teddy's death. Sooner or later, she was going to bring it up again. Probably not on the drive home. The outraged look he'd glimpsed on her face all but guaranteed she wasn't going to speak to him again that day even if her life depended on it. But eventually the piper would demand to be paid.

Had they not veered into dangerous territory, Sam would have used the hour-and-a-half drive back to Serenity as he'd originally planned—to ask her what she thought about his mother's condition. Under the circumstances, however, that would have to wait another day or two. And maybe by then his mother would have told him herself.

Any further conversation with Emma now could lead back to places he would rather not go. Especially when she was furious and he was on the defensive. A volatile combination, that. One he would have to try to avoid at all costs in the future. Even if it meant staying well out of her way.

Sam didn't much care for that option. Not after the pleasure he'd had in her company earlier. But then, how real had that actually been when he'd had to guard almost every word he said?

After what seemed like an eternity, they finally reached the lot where they'd left his mother's Volvo. With a weary sigh, he opened the car door for Emma. She slid onto the passenger's seat without acknowledging him—verbally or otherwise. And she continued in that vein all the way to Serenity.

Which was exactly what Sam wanted, not to mention what he fully deserved. Still, her icy, angry silence hurt. Sharp edged, it hung between them, cutting into his heart more deeply than he would ever admit to anyone, including himself.

## Chapter Six

Emma couldn't sleep. No matter how hard she tried. And she *had* tried. For almost three hours now, according to the ticking clock on the nightstand.

She had to get some rest or she would never make it through the day ahead. She was scheduled to work a full eight hours at the library, during which she had to catch up on a mountain of paperwork, as well as familiarize Marion Cole with her new duties. Otherwise, she wouldn't be able to begin scaling back on her own hours as soon as she had planned.

Although that didn't seem quite so urgent now that Sam was home...

With a groan of frustration punctuated by a string of muttered curses that would have appalled everyone who knew her, Emma tossed aside the light blanket covering her and slid from the bed. Wearing only her long, sleeveless, white cotton nightgown, she padded barefoot to one of the windows overlooking the front yard and leaned her forehead against the glass.

Regardless of where she had attempted to direct her thoughts since she'd first switched off the bedside lamp, *he* kept leaping out of the shadows of her mind. She didn't like it. Not one little bit. But what could she do? He hadn't been home a full forty-eight hours yet, and already he'd managed to get under her skin.

Sam...oh, Sam, you're making me crazy and you don't even know it. Or maybe you do, but you just don't care.

What an emotional roller-coaster ride the afternoon had been for her. Though she had started out anxious and uncertain, she had actually found herself enjoying his company after a while. But then, her attempt at an apology rudely thrown back at her, she had ended the day angry, frustrated, hurt and confused.

Her anger had been paramount on the drive home. The kind of white-hot anger she'd had to clamp her teeth on. Otherwise, she would have spewed out invectives that she would have never been able to take back.

It was only as they'd entered the outskirts of Serenity that she had calmed down enough to realize she'd played right into Sam's hands. By choosing to give him the silent treatment instead of forcing a confrontation when she'd had the chance, she had done exactly what he'd wanted her to do. She had allowed him to thwart her attempt to talk about the past with a few well-chosen words uttered in a brook-no-argument tone of voice guaranteed to haul almost anyone up short.

He must have known that aside from tossing her out of the car, there wasn't much else he could do to stop her. He had been stuck with her in a way he would probably never be again if he could help it. And she had been too furious at his high-handed behavior to realize it until too late.

They had been turning onto Main Street, just a few blocks from home, when Sam had given the game away. He had asked, ever so casually, what she wanted to do with her rosebushes—drop them at her house or take them to his mother's.

Nothing in his mild tone of voice or his calm, courteous manner would have led anyone to believe there had been an altercation between them only a couple of hours earlier. But why should it? *He* had gotten his way.

And that had outraged Emma all the more.

Through gritted teeth, she had told him she would just as soon go straight to his mother's house. Though it would have been easier on the rosebushes to take them to her house, she didn't want Sam anywhere near there. She didn't want to have one single, solitary memory of him invading the most private of all her places, either inside or out.

He had nodded deferentially, saying nothing more. A few minutes later, when they had reached their destination, he had ignored her murmured protest, unloading the bushes and setting the containers in a safe yet easily accessible spot in his mother's backyard.

Somehow, Emma had mustered a smidgen of gratitude— enough to offer him a curt "Thank-you" before she turned on her heel to go into the house. She hadn't gotten far. In a matter of moments, he had caught her by the arm, halting her hurried steps.

"Emma, wait…" he had begun as she'd glared at him.

She had meant to pull free of his hold, as well, but something in his eyes made her hesitate. He had taken off his sunglasses again, and without them he couldn't hide his emotions quite so easily. For just the space of a heartbeat, he had looked down at her, his expression anguished.

"Why, Sam?" she had asked, layers of meaning laced through what should have been a simple question. *"Why?"*

He had frowned, his uncertainty evident. Then he had gazed off into the distance, his jaw clenched, withdrawing from her yet again.

"I wish I could tell you," he'd muttered cryptically, releasing her arm and brushing past her.

She had stormed after him, determined to get a straight answer. But as she had rounded the corner of the house, she'd seen Margaret standing on the front porch, smiling happily. Rather than spoil her pleasure in their safe return, Emma had opted to call a truce—at least for the time being. And Sam had gone along without a qualm.

During the light supper Margaret had prepared, they'd taken turns answering her questions about their afternoon together. Emma doubted that they had fooled her into believing they'd done more than tolerate each other's company. But she had seemed satisfied with their responses. And after they'd finished their meal, she hadn't argued when Emma, pleading weariness, excused herself and went up to her room.

In retrospect, Emma admitted that hadn't been the wisest thing to do. A long walk around the neighborhood, even in the growing twilight, would have been a much better idea. At least then she might not have been so restless. And for a little while, she would have had other sights and sounds to occupy her mind.

Alone in her room, Emma hadn't been able to do much more than pace while she tried, unsuccessfully, to ward off thoughts of Sam. Thoughts that had caused the worst of

NIKKI BENJAMIN                                    81

her anger to dissipate while heightening her initial, but temporarily forgotten, confusion.

What had Sam meant when he'd said she had been right to blame him for Teddy's death? And more importantly, why had he insisted that he'd been responsible?

There was no way the accident that had taken his brother's life could be his fault. Emma knew that, as did everybody in Serenity—just as she had told him.

The pickup truck that had slammed into the passenger's side of the rental car Sam had been driving was traveling well above the posted speed limit when the driver ran the stoplight. Sam had had the right-of-way through the intersection just outside of town, and evidence at the scene had shown that he'd tried to swerve out of the way, not to save himself, but in a vain attempt to save Teddy.

Teddy, who apparently hadn't been wearing his seat belt.

Emma still found that vaguely puzzling. Teddy had always been so safety conscious, telling everyone who rode in the car with him—front seat or back—to buckle up. For him to forget had been odd, even on his wedding day. But she had never considered Sam to be the blame. After all, Teddy had been an adult, responsible for his own actions.

Her thoughts whirling more tumultuously than ever, Emma pushed away from the window. In the moonlit darkness, the walls of her room suddenly seemed to close in around her, making her feel claustrophobic.

She had been locked up in there on her own much too long. If she didn't get out for a little while, she knew she would never settle down enough to sleep. Of course, at two-thirty in the morning, she couldn't leave the house. Even in a small town like Serenity, that wouldn't be smart. But she could go down to the living room, stretch out on the sofa and try to read for half an hour or so.

Both Margaret and Sam were probably sound asleep, so neither of them would know she was still up and about. And she could think of nothing else that might work.

With a weary sigh, Emma put on her glasses, then slipped into the long white cotton robe that matched her gown, grabbed the book she'd left lying on the bedside table and crossed the room.

She had left the door slightly ajar so that she could hear if Margaret called out during the night. Now she peered out into the hallway through the narrow crack, checking to make sure Sam wasn't still awake.

His door was only partially closed, but no light at all filtered out into the hallway. He, too, must have wanted to be sure he'd hear his mother if she needed anything. Emma appreciated his concern, but she also hoped he was a deep sleeper. She didn't want him to hear her creeping down the stairs, and decide to investigate.

As quietly as she could, Emma slipped out of her room, relieved that the door hinges didn't squeak. She glided down the stairs, making her way easily, guided by the tiny night-light in a wall socket in the entryway. She halted at the bottom of the stairs, straining to hear any sounds, but only the tick of the mantel clock in the living room disturbed the silence surrounding her.

Relieved, she walked into the living room, sat on the sofa and switched on one of the lamps. As her eyes adjusted to the light, she tucked her legs up under her and opened her book.

Ten minutes later, having reread the same paragraph half a dozen times, Emma tossed her book aside. Frustrated, she looked around the living room for something—*anything*—to occupy her mind.

As luck would have it—*her* luck, at any rate—her gaze

lit upon the row of framed photographs lining the fireplace mantel. She had pored over them so often, both here and at home, where she, too, had copies, that she could conjure up the details of each one without a closer look. Yet she was drawn to one in particular. The one Margaret had taken of Sam and Teddy the week Sam had been home for the wedding. It had ended up being among the last photographs of the two brothers together.

Against her better judgment, Emma crossed to the fireplace, lifted the silver frame from the mantel and tilted it to catch the light from the table lamp.

Sam and Teddy had always been so different, not only in appearance, but in personality, as well. Yet tall, blond, wildly handsome Sam, with *his* yearning to fly jets all over the world and shorter, darker, more average looking Teddy, with his yearning to settle down in his hometown, teach English at the local high school, marry his sweetheart and raise a family had also been undeniably close. And that closeness, as well as the deep and abiding affection that had fostered it, had been evident in the way they had looked at each other as Margaret snapped the shutter.

The first time Teddy had introduced her to his older brother, home on leave from the Air Force Academy, Emma had been aware of the very special bond between the brothers. But she hadn't resented it. Sure enough of her own special place in Teddy's heart, she hadn't had a need to establish priority by saying or doing anything to come between them. And years later, when she'd finally had the courage to admit to herself how she felt about Sam, she had been even more cautious of her words and actions.

One teasing comment or one laughing glance could have all too easily hurt the very people who had welcomed her so willingly into their hearts.

Emma had loved Teddy. Loved him like the brother she'd never had, as well as the best friend he had become. That they would marry eventually had been taken for granted by everyone they knew. Even Margaret had talked of the day when she would finally, *officially,* have the beloved daughter she had always wanted.

Yet Emma had insisted on waiting to set a date until after college, then after graduate school and *then* after they'd had time to get settled in their respective jobs. She hadn't wanted to give up the promise of a safe, secure life—the life Teddy had been prepared to give her. But in her heart of hearts, she had known there was something lacking in their relationship. Something she had grown more and more aware of each time her gaze rested on Sam.

Sam, who made her heart pound and her senses sing. Sam, who rarely had more than six words to say to her, who hardly ever glanced her way, who, more often than not, left a room whenever she entered.

Except that once, just two days before her wedding—

With a low moan, Emma set the framed photograph on the mantel and turned toward the kitchen. She would drink a glass of milk. A tall, cold glass of milk. That should help to soothe her restive spirit. Then she would brew a steaming cup of chamomile tea for good measure.

Hoping to keep herself busy until the one memory she had to avoid at all cost finally faded, Emma filled the kettle with water, set it on the stove and put a tea bag in a mug. Then by the dim glow of the stove light, she took the milk carton from the refrigerator and poured a glass full.

She had swallowed only a sip or two when she heard a noise at the back door. Startled, she set her glass on the counter and backed toward the hallway.

Who in the world could be out there at three o'clock in the morning?

The sharp rasp of a key turning in the lock told her all she needed to know. *Sam.* He was the only one besides herself who had a key to his mother's house.

Though what he had been doing outdoors at that hour she couldn't imagine.

Unwilling to have him catch her there, Emma spun on her heel and headed out of the kitchen as the latch clicked open. Only when she had made it to the narrow hallway did she hesitate, a new and frightening thought crossing her mind.

What if it wasn't really Sam? What if a stranger—bent on burglary—had jimmied the lock? They could all be in danger if she ran up to her room without being sure.

Halting just far enough up the hallway to see without being seen, Emma held her breath and waited as the outside door creaked open. Relief of a kind washed over her as she saw that it *was* Sam. But it was followed closely by the same dismay she'd experienced a few minutes earlier.

She didn't want him to stumble upon her lurking in the hallway. Yet she couldn't seem to move away. Instead, she hovered in the shadows, hardly daring to breathe as she stared at him.

He wore only a pair of gray knit shorts, a white T-shirt hanging from the waistband and a pair of well-worn running shoes. His blond hair clung damply to his forehead, and sweat glistened on the taut, lightly tanned skin of his broad, bare chest and flat belly. And though he wasn't breathing hard, in the pale glow of the stove light he looked exhausted.

As if he had run until he simply couldn't run any farther, Emma thought, pleating the fabric of her robe with nervous fingers. Apparently, she hadn't been the only one unable to sleep.

To some extent, that fact surprised her. And while she had never been a believer in misery loving company, in an odd way it also gave her some small comfort. Seeing her again hadn't seemed to affect him, but now she wondered if that was really true.

Of course, he could have something else on his mind, Emma reminded herself sternly. He could be worried about his mother's illness. Or he could be pining for someone else. Someone he cared for deeply. For all she knew, he could—

With a start, Emma realized that Sam had pulled his T-shirt free and was using it to mop his face and chest as he moved away from the kitchen door. The longer she lingered in the hallway, the greater her risk of detection. And she really didn't want him to catch her spying.

He would ask questions that she'd have to answer, and she just wasn't in the mood to defend her actions. Still, she couldn't seem to tear her gaze away from the enticing ripple of muscles in his chest and thighs as he prowled around the kitchen.

When he paused by one of the counters, his attention drawn to the half glass of milk she'd left there, Emma knew her time was up. Yet she held her ground a few moments longer, watching as he ran a finger down the side of the glass, then glanced toward the hallway where she hid.

She spun around as soundlessly as she could, hurried through the living room and on to the staircase in the entryway. She was in such a rush that she didn't think to lift the hem of her robe as she started up, and as a result, she managed to climb only a few steps before her right foot tangled in the fabric, throwing her dangerously off balance.

Stumbling, Emma grabbed for the banister and upset her equilibrium even more. She swayed wildly for a second or two. Then, feeling herself falling backward, she uttered a low cry.

She fully expected to land in a heap on the entryway floor. Instead, she thudded against a hard, warm body. Sam's hard, warm body, she realized as his arms went around her, first steadying her, then slowly, gently turning her to face him.

As if drawn by a magnet, Emma looked up at him, her eyes meeting his. Time seemed to stop, then to spin backward, whirling her inexorably toward that June afternoon just two days before her wedding....

Arms loaded with towels fresh from the dryer, she had been on her way upstairs when she'd tripped on a step and fallen straight into Sam's arms. Their eyes had met—just as now. And in the lengthening silence, his hold on her had tightened, shifting her closer until her breasts brushed against his chest.

She should have protested. Should have made a joke of it and eased away from him. Should have, could have...

Instead, she had gone very still, waiting, waiting...until he muttered something unintelligible, bent his head and kissed her deeply, completely, engaging all her senses for the space of several gloriously long moments. Then, and only then, had he released her, setting her aside so unceremoniously that she'd sat down hard on the steps as he stalked to the front door, flung it open and stormed out of his mother's house.

After that, they had never been alone together again. Nor had they exchanged any words until the moment when they'd come face-to-face in the hospital emergency room. But Emma had sensed *his* waiting. And she had seen it in his questioning gaze the few times she'd caught him watching her.

He had expected her to do the honorable thing and call off the wedding, but she hadn't had the courage. She had been terrified of the feelings he'd stirred in her. And she had wanted, needed, the safety and security that Teddy offered her too much to walk away.

She had been so foolish. So very, very foolish. And they had all paid the price in one way or another—Teddy most dearly of all.

"Emma, are you all right?" Sam demanded, his voice harsh, bringing her back to the here and now.

She drew a breath, the musky, masculine scent of him teasing her senses. Unlike four years ago, he held her away, his hands on her shoulders. But she could still feel the heat radiating off his body.

She wanted to close her eyes and curl against him. Wanted to press her lips to the pulse beating madly at the base of his throat—

"*Emma.*" He shook her once, just hard enough to get her attention without hurting her, then repeated slowly, "Are you all right?"

"I...I don't know," she murmured, staring at him in confusion.

Why was he being so curt with her? Didn't he remember how it had been between them that day? Didn't he want—?

"Did you hurt yourself when you tripped?" Sam pressed, his tone suddenly matter-of-fact. "Your ankle, maybe? Or your knee?"

"No," Emma admitted.

"So you're all right?"

"Yes. I'm...I'm just fine."

He let go of her then and took a step back. Left without his support, she swayed slightly, and he quickly caught her again, this time grasping her by the elbows.

"I thought you said—" he began almost angrily.

"I *am*," she countered, wrenching free of his hold.

To Emma's dismay, a sudden rush of tears blurred her vision. Wanting only for him to be gone before he sensed her distress, she hung on to the banister with one hand and swiped at her eyes with the other.

"Well, you don't look like you are," his said, his voice gentling as he reached out and caught an errant teardrop on his fingertip.

"Oh, Sam…"

Touched by his unexpected tenderness, her tears flowed more freely. Embarrassed, she turned her face away.

"Don't cry, Emma. Please don't cry."

Stepping forward, he put his hands on her shoulders and tried to draw her close.

Emma could think of nothing she wanted more than to be held in his arms. But not out of pity. *Never* out of pity. Sadly, that seemed to be all he had to offer her, though. Otherwise, why would he have waited so long to draw her into his embrace?

"Don't," she ordered angrily, straightening her shoulders, her eyes meeting his. "Just…don't."

Sam reared back as if she had slapped him with the flat of her hand, then released her. But he didn't turn away from her. He continued to hold her gaze, instead, his bewilderment apparent.

What a pair they were, Emma thought, standing on a dimly lit staircase in the wee hours of the morning, eyeing each other warily, unable to overcome the tendency to strike out rather than soothe. With good cause, all things considered. But surely they could agree to some sort of truce.

"Sam, I'm sorry. Really, I—"

"No, I'm the one who should apologize. The way I spoke to you this afternoon and again just now—"

The high-pitched whistle of the kettle Emma had left on the stove interrupted them.

"Oh, I forgot." Startled, Emma looked away. "I was going to make a cup of tea."

"I'll get it," Sam offered.

"No, let me," she insisted, brushing past him, glad of the sudden distraction.

She held the hem of her robe out of the way and hurried down the steps. Then, unable to ignore the demands of common courtesy, she paused in the entryway and glanced back at him.

"Would you like a cup, too?"

He seemed to hesitate, then shook his head, his reserve back in place.

"No, thanks. I think I'll go on up to bed."

As she watched, he turned away and continued up the stairs, finally disappearing into the darkness.

Overwhelmed by an unexpected sense of sadness, Emma made her way to the kitchen. What might they have said to each other if the whistling kettle hadn't interrupted? Now she would never know, but perhaps it was just as well.

Whatever feelings Sam had had for her once, evidently they hadn't survived the years they'd been apart. And the kiss they had shared—*their* kiss—obviously that had only been an aberration. One he seemed intent on never repeating again.

He had proved that on the staircase, hadn't he?

*Yes, undeniably.*

At the stove, Emma switched off the kettle. She didn't want tea, after all, she realized. But she did finish the glass of milk she'd poured. Then she trudged wearily back to her room. With luck, she might get three hours of sleep before her alarm went off. But luck hadn't been on her side lately, and she knew better than to expect that to change anytime soon.

She tossed her robe over the armchair by the window, took off her glasses and set them on the nightstand and crawled into bed. She drew the blanket to her chin, closed her eyes and willed herself to relax.

Almost immediately, the gush and splash of the shower running in the bathroom next door echoed all around her. Groaning audibly, she rolled onto her stomach and pulled her pillow over her head as a vision of Sam, standing naked under the steamy spray, danced through her mind.

Somehow, she was going to have to find an excuse to move back to her house until he left Serenity. She loved Margaret dearly and would continue to do whatever she could for her. But she wasn't going to be of any help to anyone, herself included, unless she got some rest.

The kind of rest she knew she would never find as long as Sam was nearby.

# Chapter Seven

Sam had been sure the long, evenly paced run he'd taken through the deserted streets of Serenity would be just exhausting enough to allow him to sleep. But then, he hadn't considered the possibility that Emma would be up and around when he finally crept back to his mother's house.

Even when he'd spied the half-finished, still-cold-to-the-touch glass of milk on the kitchen counter, he hadn't thought of Emma first. Rather, he had been concerned about his mother, fearing she might be suffering through a bad spell brought on by her illness.

Only when he had reached the entryway and seen Emma on the steps had he realized his mistake. He had halted in midstride, as unwilling as she obviously had been to initiate a confrontation. Then she'd tripped on the hem of her robe, and he'd had no choice but to save her from a nasty fall.

Just as he had done four years ago...

Cursing under his breath, Sam shut off the shower, grabbed a towel from the rack and scrubbed none too gently at the droplets of water trickling down his body. Talk about bad luck. He couldn't have chosen a worse thing to have happen if he had tried.

As he'd caught her in his arms, he had been inundated by a wellspring of unwanted memories. Memories that had brought with them a pain so sharp he had almost cried out.

He had never thought he would hold her in his arms again. Had never thought he would feel her melt against him, her heart fluttering as wildly as his, her eyes filled with a longing that surely matched his own.

He'd had no right to hope for such a moment, and so he hadn't. When it came out of nowhere, it astonished him. But swiftly, surely, dismay had followed, halting him before he could compound the mistake he had made that June afternoon so very long ago.

Sam hadn't been able to stop himself then. He'd had to try, just once, to let Emma know how he felt about her. As he had told himself that day, he had made one last-ditch effort—born of desperation—to stop her from marrying his brother before it was too late.

Though kissing Emma hadn't been his very *last* effort. That had come on the winding road outside Serenity when he'd finally had Teddy all to himself—

Cursing again, Sam hung his damp towel on the rack, then pulled on clean shorts and a T-shirt. He had always prided himself on his self-control, but four years ago he had acted on impulse twice in three days. And in one way or another, he had destroyed everyone he'd ever held dear.

He couldn't go back and change that. But at least tonight he had managed to rein in his lustful urges before he did any more damage.

Four years ago, he had wreaked more than his fair share of havoc in Emma Dalton's life. Now, in spite of everything he'd done, she seemed to have found a small measure of peace and happiness. He wasn't going to spoil that by inflicting himself on her again.

He could have kissed her tonight. Could have teased and tempted her with ease. He had seen the willing look in her eyes and had felt her yearning as she'd swayed against him. But he had caught her unawares, her defenses down. He had taken advantage of that situation once before, only to have her turn away from him. He wasn't about to make the same mistake twice. No matter how he ached to claim her as his own.

More than once while he had been with Emma Sunday afternoon, Sam had allowed himself to consider possibilities—all sorts of possibilities. But over and over again, he had reminded himself that there was too much standing in the way of their having any kind of future together.

His own lack of integrity topped the list.

He had no right to hope for a reconciliation where Emma was concerned. Not as long as he kept from her the truth about what had happened the day Teddy died. He couldn't allow her to believe he had been blameless, then try to be a part of her life.

But neither could he come right out and tell her what he'd done. She would loathe him as much as he loathed himself for revealing—in a way—what she herself had chosen to keep secret.

There could have been only one reason for *that*. Their kiss hadn't meant anything to her. Not compared to what Teddy had had to offer her. They had been together for years. *He* had simply stolen one kiss, then imagined she had been touched as deeply and completely as he was.

Unable to face himself in the bathroom mirror, Sam ran a comb haphazardly through his damp hair, then switched off the light. He eased the door open as quietly as he could, glanced up and down the hallway, assuring himself that Emma wasn't anywhere nearby, and hurried back to his bedroom. Only when he was safe inside with the door shut did he draw a calming breath. One late-night encounter with Emma Dalton was about all he could bear.

Sam didn't expect to get any sleep during what remained of the night. But for want of anything better to do, cooped up in his bedroom, he stretched out on the narrow twin bed and pulled the old patchwork quilt up to his waist. Lying on his back, one arm under his head, he turned and gazed out the window.

He knew it wouldn't be much longer until the sky began to lighten with the coming dawn. And soon after that, he could get up and start another day.

Mentally he reviewed the list of small repair jobs that needed to be done around the house. Those would keep him busy, at least for a while. He could begin with the garbage disposal that wouldn't grind and take it from there....

What seemed like only a short time later, Sam awoke with a start. Bright sunlight spilled through the window and spread across the bedroom floor. He had slept, after all. Much more deeply and, according to the alarm clock on the bedside table, a good deal longer than he'd expected he would.

Unfortunately, he didn't feel the least bit refreshed by the rest he'd had. Instead, he was so groggy it was all he could do to stumble down the hallway to the bathroom. And that, in turn, made him grouchy.

Much to his relief, neither Emma nor his mother was still upstairs at that late hour of the morning. Since they had left their doors open, he could see that both of their rooms were empty, the beds neatly made.

Good thing, too, he thought as he stalked out of the bathroom a short time later, tissue paper dotting the razor nicks on his cheek and chin. He was in no mood for feminine wiles, whether intentional or not.

Dressed in khaki shorts, a faded navy blue sweatshirt with the sleeves ripped off and a battered pair of leather deck shoes, Sam finally headed for the kitchen.

The house was as blessedly quiet downstairs as it had been upstairs, and there was no sign of Emma or his mother in the living room, the dining room or the kitchen. However, the front door was open, which likely meant at least one of them was out on the porch.

He helped himself to coffee from the pot on the counter and a cinnamon roll slathered in icing from the bakery box on the kitchen table. Then, much as he would have preferred to be alone, he retraced his steps.

He hadn't come to Serenity to sulk in solitude. He had come to find out exactly how ill his mother really was, then make sure she was getting the care she needed. He couldn't do that unless he confronted her or Emma, face-to-face, and insisted one or the other of them answer his questions in a forthright manner.

So far, he had allowed his mother to avoid the subject rather than spoil her pleasure in his homecoming. But she had to realize he knew she wasn't quite as hale and hearty as she pretended to be. No matter how brightly she smiled or how busily she bustled about, she couldn't hide her fatigue or her fragility. He had seen the way her hands trembled when she thought she was alone. And he had glimpsed the weariness in her eyes on the rare occasions when she forgot herself and met his gaze head-on.

He knew she was only trying to protect him, but he wasn't a child anymore. Hard as it had to be for her to accept, their roles had changed in a way neither of them had ever anticipated. Now he was responsible for her well-being. And, without the least bit of resentment, he intended to fulfill that duty to the very best of his ability.

They might not have been as close as they could have been in the past, but Sam had never doubted the depth of her love for him. She alone knew the whole truth about the moments leading up to Teddy's death, and still she had refused to blame him. Though he had yet to be as forgiving of himself, her belief in him meant more than he could ever say.

As he opened the screen door, Sam spied his mother sitting in one of the rocking chairs out on the porch. He also noted that she was alone. His footsteps on the porch floor drew her attention from the book open on her lap. She glanced over her shoulder and smiled up at him, her cheerful expression not quite masking the fatigue shadowing her eyes.

"Well, sleepyhead, it's about time you rolled out of bed. I was beginning to wonder if you were all right. Then I figured maybe the jet lag had finally caught up with you."

"Something like that," he hedged as he sat in the rocking chair across from her. Setting his mug on the table between them, he bit into his cinnamon roll. "Mmm, good…"

Her smile fading, his mother gazed at him thoughtfully.

"I hate to say it, but you don't look like you slept twelve hours," she murmured after a moment.

"I didn't," he admitted, licking icing from his fingers, then reaching for his mug.

"So you had a restless night, too?"

"You had trouble sleeping?" Sam eyed his mother with concern. "Were you—?"

"Not me. I slept like a log," she cut in. "But when she came down to the kitchen earlier Emma mentioned she was up half the night."

"Oh, really?"

Avoiding his mother's increasingly avid gaze, Sam took another sip of his coffee. He had no intention of mentioning his early-morning rendezvous with Emma on the stairs. And though he wanted to ask where she had gone—since she seemed to have left the house—he wasn't about to let on that he cared. Considering the way his mother had thrown them together yesterday afternoon, he knew better than to offer her even the tiniest bit of encouragement.

"I wanted her to stay home from work, but she insisted on going in," Margaret explained. "Said she had a lot to do before we left for Galveston on Friday."

"You and Emma are going to Galveston on Friday?"

Unable to hide his surprise, Sam swung around and stared at his mother. Telling himself avoiding Emma's company was one thing. The prospect of actually having to do without it was something else altogether.

"Oh, you're going, too," she assured him blithely. "I've rented a house right on the beach so we can all be together, but still have lots of room to spread out."

"Nice of you to let me know," he muttered, irked with himself, as well as with his mother's high-handed manner. Apparently whatever *he* thought about a weekend on the island wasn't of interest to her. "Any idea how long we're going to be there, or are you planning to reveal that information at a later date?''

"Until Monday," she stated matter-of-factly, ignoring his sarcasm. "We'll have to be on the road by eight-thirty. I have an appointment with my doctor at the medical center in Houston at eleven. There's a slim chance that I'll have to spend a few days in the hospital undergoing another round of chemotherapy. Otherwise, we can drive back to Serenity that afternoon."

Sam gazed at his mother wordlessly, his earlier annoyance forgotten. He had wanted to talk to her about her illness, but he hadn't been prepared for such pragmatism on her part. He hadn't any idea how to respond.

"Unless I'm mistaken, Emma has already mentioned that I have a chronic form of leukemia and the prognosis isn't good," she continued. "I went into remission for a few months, but since the end of April..." Smiling slightly, she shrugged, then reached across the table to take his hand. "That's the real reason why you came home, isn't it?"

"Yes." Clasping her hand tightly in his, Sam turned away as an unexpected rush of tears blurred his vision. "Emma wrote to me a few weeks ago. I came as soon as I could."

"I'm glad Emma told you. It was unfair and very selfish of me to ask her to keep my secret so long. And I'm really glad you've come home." She squeezed his hand reassuringly, then continuing in a conversational tone, changed the subject. "Galveston Island has always had a special place in my heart. Probably because that's where I met your father. And because we always had such fun there—your father and I and you and Teddy—the summers before Caleb...died. I wanted to go back once more with you and Emma. I love you both so much, but we haven't spent much time together, the three of us. We need to do that, Sam, and I can't think of anywhere better than the beach.''

"You make it sound so…final. As if…as if you've given up hope," he protested.

Surely the chance that she would benefit from additional treatment wasn't as insignificant as she seemed to believe.

"There's always hope, Sam. But I'm not fooling myself and I won't fool you, either. Unless my condition has improved considerably in the past four weeks, chemotherapy could do me more harm than good. And if I only have a few months left, I want to have the strength to make the most of them." She gave his hand another squeeze, then changed the subject yet again. "Now…let me get the brochure the real-estate agent sent. The pictures of the beach house I've rented are just lovely." Standing, she reached for his mug. "More coffee?"

"Yes, thanks," he replied, his voice rough.

"And another cinnamon roll?"

"Sure."

Watching as she moved toward the door, her steps surprisingly brisk, Sam realized that she had made peace with whatever the future held for her. But he wasn't quite that accepting. Until he had proof to the contrary, he wasn't about to believe that nothing more could be done for her.

He would talk to Emma first, he decided, rubbing the moisture from his eyes with his fingertips. As close as she was to his mother, she had to know a lot more than she'd revealed in her letter. Then he would contact his mother's doctor and hear what he had to say. And he wouldn't stop there, either. He would read every article he could find about chronic leukemia and the various treatments for it. Emma could help with that—she was a librarian, after all.

At the very least, she would be able to guide him in the right direction.

"Here you go." His mother joined him again, two steaming mugs and a plate of cinnamon rolls on the tray she carried.

"You should have told me you planned to transport half the kitchen," Sam chided, taking the tray from her and setting it on the table. "I would have gladly given you a hand."

"I'm not completely helpless yet," she retorted with a testiness he remembered well from his boyhood.

"I wasn't implying you were. But I don't expect you to run yourself ragged waiting on me, either."

"I know." She smiled fondly as she offered him the brochure she'd mentioned. "That's why I enjoy doing it."

Shaking his head in exasperation, Sam took the brochure from her and eyed the contemporary glass-and-wood-and-stone house set back behind the dunes edging the beach.

"Very nice," he murmured approvingly as he reached for his mug.

"Emma thought so, too," Margaret said. She settled into her rocking chair, helped herself to one of the cinnamon rolls, then added, "You know, along with satisfying my yen for the beach, I think going to Galveston will also be good for the two of you. You need to spend a little time together somewhere besides Serenity. Getting away from here for a few days will give you a chance to put the past behind you and make a fresh start."

"I'm not sure that's possible for us regardless of where we are," Sam stated, edging his words with an attempt at finality.

From the moment he'd made the decision to return to Serenity, he had wondered how Emma would respond to his presence there. But no matter how he'd tried, he hadn't been able to convince himself that she'd be happy. So far, it seemed he'd been right.

"Anything's possible, Sam. Unless you're the one who's given up hope."

"Not any more than you. But I'm not fooling myself, either. Not after what I did..."

"Despite what Emma said to you at the hospital, she's never blamed you for Teddy's death."

"Only because she doesn't know the whole truth."

"Then tell her," his mother insisted none too gently. "You didn't act with malicious intent. You simply said what you believed you had to say to your brother that day. There was no way you could have anticipated how he would react. I'm sure Emma is capable of understanding that."

"And if she's not, she'll end up despising me more than ever," Sam countered angrily.

He wished he had as much faith in Emma's compassion as his mother did. Then he wouldn't hesitate to try to set things straight between them. But he hadn't the courage to count on gaining her forgiveness—at least not yet.

"I don't think that will happen," Margaret said.

"But there's no guarantee, is there?"

"There are never any guarantees in life. Sometimes we just have to believe...."

Aware of the futility of arguing with his mother any longer, especially when she had right on her side, Sam rocked slowly back and forth, nibbling on a cinnamon roll and sipping his coffee. Maybe he *had* given up too easily. Maybe he should trust that Emma was capable of giving him the benefit of the doubt. Maybe...maybe he should go soak his head.

Better yet, he could get started on the repairs he wanted to make. *That* would get his mind off Emma.

But the sunny summer day held him in its thrall. Aside from the twitter of birds in the trees, the buzz of insects over the flowering shrubs and the occasional whoosh of a car passing by, all was quiet. Quieter than he remembered, but then most of his mother's neighbors were elderly—

"I was wondering…" his mother began, interrupting his reverie.

"What?" Sam prodded reluctantly when she seemed to hesitate.

"How much longer do you think you'll be stationed in Italy?"

"Actually, my tour of duty there is officially over. I'm being transferred back to the States. In fact, I've done all the paperwork already. I've requested an assignment at one of the air bases in Texas. I should find out exactly where I'll be stationed within the next week or so."

"You didn't have to do that." She turned to him, her eyes filled with concern.

"I know," he assured her, aware that she wouldn't have wanted him to make such a request on her account. "But I've been away a long time. I meant it when I said I was ready to come home for a while."

"I'm glad you feel that way." Smiling again, she patted his hand.

"I do," Sam replied, realizing he spoke the truth.

He had spent years trying to avoid the pit into which his father had fallen, feeling trapped in a small town, weighed down by a growing sense of futility. He had realized—too late—that everything he wanted was in Serenity, after all. And then, the circumstances surrounding his brother's death had sent him into exile once again.

But he had a duty to his mother—a duty he'd been determined to fulfill. That had made it impossible for him to stay away. Now, having finally come home, he couldn't imagine leaving again, especially for good. Not when his mother could be terminally ill.

And not when he hadn't yet accepted that all had been lost with Emma. As his mother had said, anything was possible. But what chance would he have of making things right between them from half a world away?

More than anything, Sam now knew he wanted that chance. He had already admitted more times than he cared to count that there was too much standing between him and Emma and a future together. Yet he couldn't seem to totally discount that possibility, either. And he wouldn't... couldn't. Not until he found the courage to be truthful with her. And surely that would come with time.

Filled with a sudden, inexplicable sense of exhilaration, Sam pushed out of his rocking chair.

"I thought I'd take a look at your garbage disposal and see if I can get it running again," he announced. "Then I'm going down to the hardware store to buy some new washers for your faucets."

"Oh, Sam, I'd really appreciate that."

"While I'm busy, why don't you decide whether you want the wooden fence across the backyard up or down. Unless there's something else you'd rather I do first, I'll work on that tomorrow."

"But you're supposed to be on vacation," Margaret protested.

"That starts Friday when we leave for Galveston. Until then, try to think of all the work around here you'd like to have done and let me play handyman."

"Well, if you insist..." she demurred.

"Absolutely."

She considered him thoughtfully for several moments, then grinned at him, a wicked gleam twinkling in her eyes.

"Well, in that case, I'd better get a pad of paper and a pencil."

## Chapter Eight

After the sleepless night she'd had, Emma wasn't sure how she made it through Monday, but she did. Necessity coupled with sheer determination helped a lot. She couldn't go off to Galveston on Friday with a clear conscience unless she did her utmost to make sure the Serenity Public Library ran smoothly in her absence.

Luckily, Marion Cole proved to be quite capable. Not only was she eager to learn, but she also caught on quickly. And with her cheerful personality, she got along well with the other members of the library's small staff. Emma soon realized she couldn't have found anyone better suited to help out over the summer.

With Marion running interference for her, Emma was also able to make a sizable dent in the new book orders that had piled up while Margaret had been in the hospital. By the time five o'clock rolled around, however, she felt like a zombie. It was all she could do to gather her things together and walk out to her car.

The lingering heat of the day dragged at her, increasing her weariness even more, and made the short drive to Margaret's house—a distance she often walked in nice weather—seem interminable. What she really wanted was to go back to her house, but she knew that would cause Margaret more concern than it would be worth. Thanks to her friend's efforts, she and Sam would be thrown together again anyway at the beach house Margaret had rented on Galveston Island.

They had talked about a long-weekend getaway, but with Sam's return Emma had assumed the trip would be postponed for a while. Having been presented with a veritable fait accompli, she'd had no choice but to go along with it enthusiastically. Especially since she'd been too weary to put up any kind of argument.

But she had promised herself that once they returned from the island, she would go back to her own home until Sam left again. She could hold off that long for Margaret's sake, but only for Margaret's sake.

At the Griffin house, Emma paused in the kitchen only a few minutes to tell her friend that she wanted to lie down for an hour or so before dinner. On her way upstairs, she saw no sign of Sam, for which she was grateful. She changed out of her skirt and blouse into soft knit shorts and a T-shirt, stretched out on her bed and ended up sleeping straight through till morning.

She awoke just before seven, feeling more refreshed than she had in weeks. As she blinked the last vestiges of sleep from her eyes and stretched luxuriously, she realized someone had come in during the night and covered her with a quilt. Margaret, Emma assumed. She had been sleeping too soundly to know for sure, but she doubted Sam would come within five feet of her unless ordered to under pain of death.

Shoving away all thoughts of him almost as swiftly as they came to mind, Emma crawled out of bed resolutely, headed for the bathroom with only the slightest glance at Sam's open bedroom door, showered and dressed for another day at the library. She still had a lot left to do. Allowing herself to be sidetracked emotionally, even for a few minutes, was a waste of much-needed time.

In the kitchen, Margaret sat alone at the table, dressed in a denim skirt and bright red shirt that set off her silvery hair. She looked up from the morning paper, smiled and gestured toward the coffeemaker on the counter.

"I just brewed a fresh pot."

"Thanks—for the coffee and for looking in on me last night." Emma helped herself to a mug, then put a slice of bread into the toaster. "I must have been more tired than I realized."

"You're welcome—for the coffee. But it was Sam who checked on you. When you didn't come down to dinner, he offered to go up and make sure you were all right. When he came down again, he said you were fast asleep."

"I must have been," Emma muttered, momentarily flustered by the thought of Sam entering her bedroom and covering her with the quilt, all without her knowledge.

Just doing his duty—looking after her at his mother's insistence, she told herself, recalling how resolutely he'd distanced himself from her on the staircase Sunday night.

"You should have something more than that," Margaret said as the toaster popped. "Especially since you missed dinner last night."

Though no easy task, Emma brought herself back to the present moment.

"You're right," she admitted, patting her growling stomach as she crossed to the refrigerator. "A piece of toast just isn't going to be enough this morning. How about some scrambled eggs?"

"No, dear. Don't fix any for me. I had a bowl of cereal earlier with Sam. Then he took off for the lumberyard north of town."

"The lumberyard?" Emma eyed her friend questioningly as she whisked eggs and milk together in a small bowl.

"He's going to replace those rotten boards in the fence across the backyard for me today. Yesterday, he repaired the garbage disposal, put new washers in all the faucets that have been leaking and ran something called a snake down the drain in my bathroom so it won't keep clogging up."

"He's been busy, hasn't he?" Emma commented, stirring the egg mixture into a pan on the stove.

"And he will be the next few days, as well. He insisted that I make a list of things I need done around here, and I did just that. Told me to let him play handyman, so I figured, why not? No sense letting him sit around getting bored."

"No sense at all." Smiling, Emma spooned her scrambled eggs onto a plate, added the slice of toast and joined Margaret at the table.

"I've got enough to keep him busy around here for the rest of the week. But when we get back from Galveston, he's going to have some time on his hands. Maybe he could give you a hand with some of the work you've been wanting to do around your place. Painting and wallpapering goes much faster when you have a little help."

"Oh, I couldn't ask him to do that," Emma protested,

hoping she didn't sound as dismayed by the idea as she felt.

She had already decided she didn't want Sam anywhere near her house. Not even for the few minutes it would have taken to unload her rosebushes Sunday evening. How could she possibly have him there for days on end while they worked closely together hanging new wallpaper or painting the woodwork? Talk about letting him invade her space. She would never be able to forget him—as she knew she must—if she allowed him into her home in such an…intimate way.

"Nonsense," Margaret replied, waving her hand dismissively. "He appreciates everything you've done for me. He's said so several times already. He certainly wouldn't mind doing something for you in return. Especially something you've had to postpone because I've needed your help."

Try as she might, Emma couldn't think of a way to respond as she wanted without sounding churlish. She had never expected any kind of payment from her friend, but Margaret was a proud woman. Emma knew she had worried about taking advantage of her. And now she obviously saw a way for her son to cancel the debt she seemed to feel she owed.

"Well, let's see how things go next week," Emma finally said as she finished her breakfast. "We may end up spending several days in Houston, you know."

"Perhaps," Margaret murmured noncommittally.

Emma glanced at her sharply, but suddenly Margaret seemed engrossed in the day's headlines.

Had she begun to lose hope? Emma wondered, gathering her dishes and crossing to the sink. She had seemed so much better the past week or two—more so after Sam's arrival. Had she actually been feeling worse than she'd let on? Or was she simply afraid of going through another round of treatment after the problems she'd had last time?

Emma knew better than to press for answers. Margaret believed in putting on a brave face regardless. And she would never say anything that might cause those she loved what she deemed to be needless worry.

Pausing by the table on her way out to give her friend a quick hug, Emma decided she had better ask Sam what he thought. He was her son, after all. Maybe she had confided in him in a way she didn't feel she could with *her*.

"Full day again today?" Margaret asked, reaching up to give her hand a squeeze.

"I'm taking off at three this afternoon. Thought I'd let Marion work a few hours on her own while I'm within shouting distance—so to speak. And I really need to get my rosebushes in the ground, too."

"Ah, yes. Can't let them sit in those containers too long, can you?"

"Not at this time of year," Emma agreed. "And the sooner they're planted, the better they'll do next spring." She slung her purse strap over her shoulder, then added, "Call if you need anything and Sam's not back, okay?"

"I will, dear. Have a good day."

"You, too."

Since Tuesday was the day the library hosted a series of story hours for children of various ages, there was lots of activity throughout the morning and early afternoon. The previous summer, Emma's friend Jane Hamilton had taken over the read-aloud duties while staying in town. This year, Emma had hired a couple of college students, home for the summer, and so far, thanks to their boundless enthusiasm, they had been a big hit with the children, as well as with Emma. Though she still had some supervising to do, they had helped to lighten her workload considerably, much as Jane had done.

As she returned to her office on the second floor of the library, Emma wished Jane were still living in Serenity. With her friend close by, she would have had an easier time asking her advice about Sam. But Jane was in Seattle, happily married and mothering her young son.

Burdening her from a distance with a problem that had no real solution—at least as far as Emma could see—didn't seem fair. Especially when Jane had gone through such a hapless time herself only a year ago.

Hundreds, perhaps thousands, of women dealt successfully with the effects of unrequited love, Emma reminded herself. She might feel like the only one facing heartache on a daily basis, but she wasn't. And she had dealt with so much grief already. As long as she put her mind to it, she could deal with her feelings for Sam, as well.

She had no doubt he was just as eager to stay out of her way as she was to stay out of his, and that would certainly work to her advantage. Since she was going to be away over the weekend, she had good reason to spend time at her house the next few days, battening down the hatches. And the house on Galveston Island was huge. They would hardly have to cross paths at all except at mealtimes.

By three o'clock, Emma was on her way home, confident that Marion would be able to cope on her own during what was usually the quietest time on a summer weekday. Eager for fresh air and exercise after her long, deep sleep, she had walked to work that morning, and she enjoyed the walk back to Margaret's house equally despite the increased afternoon heat.

Half a block away, Emma slowed her pace and scanned the front yard for any sign of Sam. Margaret's Volvo was parked in the driveway, so he was probably home. Emma hoped he was still working on the back fence. That would make it easier for her to slip into the house, change clothes, load her rosebushes into her car and get away without a hassle.

Not that she expected Sam to go out of his way to cause her any problems. But just running into him would leave her feeling…flustered.

Emma let herself into the cool, quiet house, made a detour to the kitchen to see if Margaret was there and found it empty. After a glance out the window into the equally empty, but newly fenced, backyard, she quickly headed upstairs.

She paused at the partially closed door to Margaret's darkened bedroom, noting that her friend was napping peacefully on the bed as she had been doing most afternoons lately. Otherwise, Emma had the upstairs all to herself.

Relieved, she wasted no time changing into faded denim cutoffs and a lemon yellow tank top. She slathered sun lotion on her face, arms and legs, grabbed her straw hat, purse and keys and hurried down to the kitchen again.

She couldn't help but wonder where Sam had gone, especially without the car. She doubted he would be out running at that time of day. Maybe he had walked into downtown Serenity for the same reason she had that morning— for the fresh air and exercise.

Telling herself she didn't care where he was or what he was doing as long as he wasn't anywhere around the house, Emma left a note for Margaret detailing when she would return, then exited through the back door.

The containers holding her rosebushes should still be lined up along the side of the house. All she had to do was pull her car into the driveway behind Margaret's, load them into the trunk and she could be on her way.

Only the containers weren't where Sam had left them Sunday evening, Emma realized as she rounded the corner of the house. Halting in midstride, she stared at the grassy spot, a grimace tugging at the corners of her mouth. Surely they hadn't been stolen. Theft wasn't unknown in Serenity, but who would want her rosebushes besides old Mr. Bukowski? And he would never stoop to stealing them. Maybe Sam had moved them for some reason.

Uncertain what to do, Emma looked up and saw Sam leaning against his mother's car, arms crossed over his chest, watching her. He was dressed in worn khaki shorts and a dark blue, sleeveless sweatshirt that had seen better days. As usual, his mirrored sunglasses hid his expression.

She hesitated, a sinking sensation in the pit of her stomach. Recalling her talk with Margaret that morning, she had a pretty good idea of why he was there.

"Ready to go?" he asked as if their meeting were not only prearranged but also mutually agreeable.

Emma didn't appreciate the casual way in which he assumed his assistance would be welcome. But how could she turn down his offer—such as it was—without being rude? Obviously, her rosebushes were already loaded into the trunk of Margaret's car. And he had a determined-to-do-my-duty look about him that warned her arguing would be a waste of breath. By sheer force of will, he would end up getting his way, and she would come across as a thankless wretch.

So go along graciously, she told herself. Let him help with the rosebushes without making a big deal of it. She had already given him too much power over her as it was. And no matter how much she would have preferred to keep him away from her house, allowing him to dig a few holes in her back garden certainly wouldn't traumatize her for life.

Yet she couldn't just…give in.

"As soon as I find my rosebushes," she quipped with a slight smile, choosing to play dumb.

"They're in the car." Straightening, Sam gestured toward the Volvo's trunk, then opened the passenger's door for her. "I'll drive you over and give you a hand with them."

"That's not really necessary," she began in a last-ditch effort to dissuade him. "I know you have a lot to do around here—"

"I want to talk to you about my mother," he cut in. "And I thought it would be…easier at your house."

"Was she feeling bad today?" Emma asked, making no effort to hide her sudden concern as she walked toward him.

"Not really. But there's a lot she isn't telling me about her illness. I figured maybe you could fill in some of the blanks."

"Of course," Emma agreed, feeling foolish as she slid onto the car seat.

Talk about jumping to all the wrong conclusions. He wanted to ask about his mother's condition somewhere where they could speak freely—nothing more, nothing less. She should have suggested it herself, but she had been so self-involved…

"You'll have to give me directions to your house," Sam said, sliding in beside her and starting the engine.

"It's not far. Just about three blocks. Turn left at the corner, go down to Bay Leaf Lane, then turn right."

They made the short drive in silence, arriving at her house within a few minutes.

"Where are you going to plant the rosebushes?" Sam asked as he pulled into her driveway.

"In the back garden by the gazebo. Let me open the gate, then I'll help you carry the containers into the yard."

"Why don't you get your gardening tools while I do the heavy lifting," he suggested instead.

"All right," she agreed after a moment's hesitation.

She could manage the containers as easily as he could, but they would finish the planting much sooner by dividing the tasks. And the less time they spent together, the better for her fragile peace of mind.

While Sam transferred the containers from Margaret's car to Emma's back garden, she gathered the necessary equipment from the little shed behind her garage. With the two shovels she had, they could each work on digging the holes, then Sam could help her set the bushes in the ground.

"Now what?" he asked as he set the last container on the grass edging the garden.

"Have you planted rosebushes before?"

"No."

"Well, it's fairly simply. The holes should be about twenty-four inches wide and eighteen inches deep—large enough to accommodate the container. We want to give the bushes plenty of room to grow and we don't want to crowd the roots."

"Okay. Where do I start?"

"How about here?" Emma indicated one of several sparsely planted sections alongside the steps of the gazebo.

Sam nodded agreeably.

''Let me know when you're finished, and I'll tell you where to dig next. I'll be working on the other side of the steps.''

Sam nodded again, then dug into the dry soil with obvious ease.

They worked quietly for several minutes, Sam doing most of the digging since he was stronger and faster. Considering the heat, even in the shaded area where they were working, Emma was more grateful for his help than she had anticipated.

When all the holes had been dug, she showed him how to remove a bush from the container, loosen the soil at the bottom of the root ball, then plant the bush with the top of the root ball at the same level as it had been in the container.

Sam followed her instructions with care, handling the rosebush gently. Emma knelt beside him in the grass, watching as he set it in the hole, then scooped the loose soil around it.

The caressing way in which his long, lean fingers moved under the thorny stems caught and held her gaze.

Around them, birds twittered and insects buzzed. A slight breeze ruffled her curls and cooled her heated skin. Her thoughts drifted lazily, and suddenly, unaccountably, she found herself imagining Sam's clever, capable hands deftly skimming over *her,* stroking her—

''How's that?'' he asked, interrupting her reverie with a questioning glance.

''Fine. Just…fine,'' she replied as she stood quickly and took a step back, desperate to put some distance between them.

What in the world had come over her? He had been planting a rosebush, for heaven's sake. But she'd had something entirely different on her mind—something that likely would have appalled him if he'd been able to read her thoughts.

"Why don't you plant this one here," she said, gesturing to one of the remaining containers, then to the spot where she wanted the bush to go.

Still looking somewhat bemused, Sam nodded.

As he set to work, Emma lugged another of the containers to the opposite side of the garden and began to work the root ball loose, mentally chastising herself all over again.

Really, she had to get a grip.

They finished the planting, exchanging no more than a few words. Emma kept waiting for Sam to ask about his mother, but he seemed interested only in the task at hand.

When all the bushes were in place, Emma set out the water sprinklers and turned them on while Sam gathered the gardening tools and took them back to the shed.

Emma wished she could simply send him home now, but she couldn't bring herself to be that crass. He had spared her a lot of hard work—not without his own good reasons, of course. Still, he had to be as hot and tired as she was. The least she could do was offer him a cold drink and give him one last chance to ask about his mother. Even if it meant inviting him into her house as she would have to do so he, too, could wash the dirt from his hands.

"How about a beer?" she asked as he joined her by the garden's edge.

He glanced at her, his surprise obvious, then nodded once.

"Sounds good to me."

"Just let me get my keys and we can go inside."

Leaving him by the back porch, Emma hurried out to

Margaret's car and retrieved her purse from the front seat. As she joined him again, she noticed that he'd tucked his sunglasses in the pocket of his T-shirt.

She met his gaze for a moment, then looked away uncomfortably as she fit her key into the lock and opened the door. Whether intentional or not, his scrutiny made her feel as if she were lacking in some way.

"There's a bathroom in the downstairs hallway," she said, gesturing toward the doorway on the far side of the kitchen. "In case you want to get cleaned up."

"That would probably be a good idea." Smiling slightly, he moved past her.

"I need to get a couple of things upstairs, then I'll meet you back here, okay?"

"Okay."

"The beer is in the refrigerator. Just help yourself."

Feeling oddly breathless, Emma trailed across the kitchen after him. He seemed so at ease, as if he'd been there a hundred times before. And belonged...

She should have offered to bring him a beer, then let him wash off at the faucet outside, she thought ruefully, just a tad too late.

Oh, well, they didn't have to linger long. They could drink a beer, talk a bit about Margaret, then he could go on home while she erased all trace of his presence as quickly as she could. Or at least tried, she amended as she took the stairs two at a time, the sound of water running in the bathroom below echoing in her ears.

## Chapter Nine

Emma hadn't wanted his help with her rosebushes. Sam had known that as surely as he knew his own name. But he had refused to let her put him off. He had wanted to talk to her away from his mother's house, and Margaret's suggestion that he give her a hand with her planting had presented the perfect opportunity.

Now, standing at the sink, washing his hands, Sam eyed himself in the mirror and acknowledged that she hadn't wanted him in her house, either. Again, however, he had chosen to stand fast. Not only because they had yet to talk, but also because he had wanted, needed, to see the place she had chosen to call home.

He had heard the hesitation in her voice when she invited him to have a beer. And he had sensed her apprehension as she unlocked the door, then stood aside so he could cross the threshold.

Yet she hadn't seemed *afraid* of him. He wouldn't have taken her up on the offer if she'd given that impression. Instead, she had seemed vaguely troubled, as if she hadn't been sure exactly what to expect of him.

Nothing hurtful, he had sworn as he slowly made his way through her bright, cheerful little kitchen, taking in the warm, homey feel of it. At least not if he could help it. He just wanted something to take away with him—some small, special memories of the place where she lived so he could think of her there months from now in the loneliness of the night.

Perhaps she had reason to be uneasy, Sam mused, a wry twist to his lips as he rinsed the soap from his hands, then splashed cool water on his face, washing away the dusty film of sweat that coated his skin. How rational was it to obsess over a woman he had yet to believe he could ever have?

Unless he took a chance and told her the truth...

Would Emma understand as his mother had insisted? *Could* she?

With a muttered curse, Sam dried his face and hands on a fluffy dark green towel that exactly matched the tiny ivy leaves in the patterned wallpaper. Then he opened the bathroom door, stepped into the hallway and paused.

Sounds came from overhead—as good a sign as any that Emma was still upstairs. That meant he had a few more minutes to himself. Not to snoop, he told himself as he turned toward the living room doorway. Just to...look around.

Floral-print fabric in shades of rose and blue covered the cushioned sofa, a deep, comfortable-looking chair and an ottoman. Cherry-wood end tables topped by brass lamps, a matching coffee table and wardrobe, doors open to reveal a television, small stereo, books and several framed photographs, completed the furnishings. A lovely Oriental carpet, also in shades of rose and blue, added warmth to the highly polished hardwood floor. And old-fashioned, wide-slatted wooden blinds, slanted to let in the late-afternoon sunlight, covered the windows.

The room suited Emma—feminine, but not frilly. The blend of soft colors and sturdy wood made it livable. Pretty as the furnishings were, a man could still feel at ease there. At home, Sam thought, drawn into the room despite his intention not to leave the doorway.

He prowled around slowly, savoring the ambience Emma had created. He could stay there forever, he admitted. Quite happily, as long as he had Emma by his side.

At the wardrobe, he paused, eyeing the silver-framed photographs curiously.

One was older, taken when Emma was nine or ten, he guessed. She stood between a lovely, fragile-looking, unsmiling woman with curly red hair similar to hers and a tall, dark man with a wild, rakish grin—her parents, more than likely.

Another, featuring a tall, handsome couple, the man holding a baby in his arms, had been taken more recently—her friends Jane and Max Hamilton, he supposed. There was also one of Emma holding the baby—their son, Emma's godson.

Grouped together on another shelf were three photographs that caused Sam's breath to catch in his throat. All were of Teddy and *him*: one taken years ago at the swimming pool in the park outside of town, one of them with their mother at the rehearsal dinner the night before the wedding and one of them dressed in their tuxedos, a picture

he remembered Margaret taking the following morning just
before they'd left for the church.

Of all the photographs Emma must have of Teddy, why
had she chosen to display those that included *him,* too? Sam
wondered. Was it her way of constantly reminding herself
of his role in his brother's death?

No, she wouldn't do that. Not when she had made such
a point of telling him she'd never really blamed him for
what had happened.

Looking at the photographs more closely, Sam noted that
in the older one he and Teddy appeared to be quite happy.
Their smiles were carefree and...genuine. By contrast, their
smiles seemed oddly strained in the other pictures.

Understandable for him, Sam mused. He had been on the
verge of watching the woman he'd only just admitted he
loved exchange vows with his younger brother. But Teddy
should have been grinning broadly.

Had *he* been in his brother's position, Sam knew he
wouldn't have been able to contain his jubilation. Yet
Teddy looked more like a man doing his dreaded duty than
a man about to have his dream come true.

In the days before the wedding, Sam had been so
wrapped up in his own problems he hadn't really paid much
attention to Teddy's behavior. Thinking back now, he re-
called how quiet his brother had been. Granted, they had
engaged in their usual horsing around, but Sam hadn't been
the only one who'd done so halfheartedly. And several
times, Teddy had gone off alone without telling anyone.

Had he had doubts about marrying Emma? Doubts he
had chosen not to voice for fear of hurting her?

They had been such close friends for so many years, yet
they certainly hadn't been in any hurry to marry even after
they'd graduated from college. Though Sam hadn't been

home much during those years, it had seemed that everyone around town assumed they would…eventually. He certainly had, and he knew his mother had, as well.

Had Teddy and Emma been weighed down by those expectations? Expectations that had kept each of them silent rather than risk causing the other anguish?

That would explain why Emma had made no move to stop the wedding after the mad, passionate kiss they had shared. And now that Sam thought about it—really *thought* about it—that could also explain his brother's erratic behavior that fateful morning as the two of them set out for the church.

Teddy had been the one to suggest they take a more roundabout route, and Sam had agreed willingly enough. He had been in no hurry to watch Emma walk up the aisle and into his brother's arms. And self-involved as he'd been, he hadn't questioned Teddy's rather odd request.

Thinking back to that sunny summer day, Sam admitted he wouldn't have been able to get to the church quickly enough had he been in his brother's place.

Teddy's foot-dragging should have alerted him to a possible problem. Instead, it had merely set the stage for the tragedy that followed. And Sam had all too willingly played his part, initiating the conversation that had driven his brother to make the fatal mistake that had ultimately cost him his life.

"Are you sure you want to go through with the wedding?" Sam had asked, only half-teasingly. "Sure you want to tie yourself down to a wife and family without ever having gone anywhere or done anything except teach high-school English in your hometown?"

"What do you suggest I do, Sam? Leave Emma standing at the altar? I couldn't do that to her."

"Well, I could always take your place. I'm already dressed for the occasion...." Any lingering trace of light-heartedness had vanished from his voice.

"You're serious, aren't you?"

"Yes."

Teddy had eyed him without rancor, nodded once and unbuckled his seat belt.

"Then let me out of the car up there, just past the intersection. I'll catch a ride back to the house, clear out my stuff and be gone before the service is over."

"Teddy, don't be silly. Emma loves you."

"Not the way she—"

*Not the way she should?* But Sam would never know what Teddy was going to say. Before Teddy had been able to finish, a pickup truck had sped through the intersection, failing to stop at the stoplight, and plowed into Sam's car. The sudden impact had sent Teddy hurtling through the windshield and onto the pavement.

Had Sam been paying attention to his driving, he might have been able to swerve out of the way. Or, even more important, had he simply kept his mouth shut, Teddy would have been saved by the seat belt he'd have still been wearing—

With a start, Sam heard the floorboards creaking overhead, warning that Emma was more than likely on her way downstairs. Not wanting to be caught where he hadn't been invited, he turned away from the photographs in the wardrobe and hurried back to the kitchen.

He had just time enough to help himself to a bottle of beer and slouch into one of the ladder-back chairs by the antique gateleg table in the bay-windowed alcove. Emma bustled through the doorway, a file folder full of papers in one hand.

"Sorry I took so long. I wanted to give you as much of the information I've been collecting on leukemia as I could, but I didn't have it all in one place." She plopped the folder on the table, then crossed to the refrigerator and took out a beer for herself. "Ready for another?" she asked, eyeing his bottle.

"Not yet."

She had also taken time to wash her face and comb her hair and—to his disappointment—change into a less revealing T-shirt while she was upstairs, he noted as he took a long swallow of the frosty brew.

"Thanks again for helping with the rosebushes." She sat across from him, drank from her bottle, then set it aside with a slight smile. "Mmm, good."

"Tastes the best after hard work on a hot day, doesn't it?"

"Or with a plate of tamales and cheese enchiladas." She hesitated, finally adding, "I think I might have a bag of tortilla chips and a jar of salsa in the pantry if you're hungry."

"Not really, but you go ahead."

"No, I'm not, either."

She reached for her beer again as the silence stretched between them uncomfortably.

Sam knew he was getting very close to wearing out his welcome. He had held off asking about his mother as long as he could. Not because he dreaded what Emma might have to tell him. He had already come to terms with the seriousness of his mother's illness. But once Emma had answered his questions, his reason for having her all to himself would no longer exist.

"You mentioned you've been collecting information on

leukemia?'' he began at last, gesturing toward the file folder on the table.

"Whatever I could find about the disease itself and the options for treatment. I wanted to be able to understand what the doctors were saying and also be able to question them intelligently."

"Thanks for taking the time to do that."

"Since Margaret insisted she didn't want you to know, I thought someone should look out for her."

"I would have done it if I'd known," Sam said, holding her gaze.

"Yes, I know you would have. And I know now that I should have contacted you sooner. But I kept thinking she would get better, and I didn't want to worry you needlessly, either." Her tone defensive, Emma looked away.

"I'm not faulting you, Emma. You were only trying to do what you thought was best for everyone, especially my mother. I'm just glad I'm here now so I can give you a hand. You shouldn't have had to deal with her illness on your own for as long as you did."

"I didn't mind. Really, I didn't." She faced him again, smiling slightly.

"I know." Touched by the benevolence of her gaze, he wanted to reach out and smooth a hand over her hair. Instead, he pushed away from the table, stood and crossed to the refrigerator. "I think I'll have another beer, after all. How about you?"

"Yes, please."

"Is the offer of chips and salsa still good? I'm going to need a little something to sop up the alcohol or I won't be able to walk a straight line."

"It most certainly is."

Crossing to the pantry, Emma retrieved the bag of tortilla

chips and jar of salsa while Sam opened the beer bottles at the sink.

"Why don't I give you a summary of the information I've collected," she suggested when they were seated at the table again. "Then you can read through everything on your own later."

"Sounds good to me," Sam agreed, grabbing a handful of chips and dipping into the salsa.

"Basically, Margaret was diagnosed with a chronic form of leukemia that occurs primarily in older adults. The onset was gradual, as is usually the case. At first, her doctor thought she had a touch of flu. She was running a low-grade fever, she was achy all over and she didn't have much of an appetite. When those symptoms lingered for several weeks and she also started complaining about feeling weak all the time, he assumed she'd contracted a bacterial infection while her defenses were down.

"He prescribed several different rounds of antibiotics, and eventually she seemed to start feeling better. When she had a relapse just before Thanksgiving, he finally ordered a series of blood tests. The results came in, and he immediately made arrangements for her to see a specialist in Houston.

"She went through one round of chemotherapy then. That relieved her symptoms, and she seemed to go into remission. But the symptoms recurred again about two months ago. Since the original treatment she received produced only a very temporary improvement, her doctor ordered another round of chemotherapy using a different combination of drugs that ended up making her even more ill than she had been.

"At her age and in her weakened condition, there are only a limited number of options when it comes to treat-

# FREE BOOKS! FREE GIFT!

## PLAY BANGO!

### AND CLAIM 2 FREE BOOKS AND A FREE GIFT!

**BANGO**
5 19 32 54 73
6 17 41 50 6
13 22 FREE 52 5
5 24 44 46
8 21 35 47 75

**BANGO**
9 19 44 52 71
4 20 32 50 68
11 18 FREE 53 63
7 27 36 60 72
3 28 41 47 64

★ **No Cost!**
★ **No Obligation to Buy!**
★ **No Purchase Necessary!**

**TURN THE PAGE TO PLAY**

# PLAY BANGO!

## AND GET THREE FREE GIFTS!

**It looks like BINGO, it plays like BINGO but it's FREE**

## HOW TO PLAY:

1. With a coin, scratch the Caller Card to reveal your 5 lucky numbers and see that they match your Bango Card. Then check the claim chart to discover what we have for you — FREE BOOKS and a FREE GIFT. All yours, all free!

2. Send back the Bango card and you'll receive 2 brand-new Silhouette Special Edition® novels. These books have a cover price of $4.25 each in the U.S. and $4.75 each in Canada, but they are yours to keep absolutely free.

3. There's no catch. You're under no obligation to buy anything. We charge nothing — ZERO — for your first shipment. And you don't have to make any minimum number of purchases — not even one!

4. The fact is, thousands of readers enjoy receiving books by mail from the Silhouette Reader Service® months before they are available in stores. They like the convenience of home delivery and they love our discount prices!

5. We hope that after receiving your free books you'll want to remain a subscriber. But the choice is yours — to continue or cancel, any time at all! So why not take us up on our invitation, with no risk of any kind. You'll be glad you did!

## YOURS FREE!

**This exciting mystery gift is yours free when you play BANGO!**

It's fun, and we're giving away
# FREE GIFTS
## to all players!

**PLAY BANGO!**

SCRATCH HERE! →

**CALLER CARD**

## YES!
Please send me all the free books and the gift for which I qualify! I understand that I am under no obligation to purchase any books as explained on the back of this card.

YOUR CARD ↘

**BANGO**

| B | A | N | G | O |
|---|---|---|---|---|
| 38 | 9 | 44 | 10 | 38 |
| 92 | 7 | 5 | 27 | 14 |
| 2 | 51 | FREE | 91 | 67 |
| 75 | 3 | 12 | 20 | 13 |
| 6 | 15 | 26 | 50 | 31 |

### CLAIM CHART!

| | |
|---|---|
| Match 5 numbers | 2 FREE BOOKS & A MYSTERY GIFT |
| Match 4 numbers | 2 FREE BOOKS |
| Match 3 numbers | 1 FREE BOOK |

**335 SDL CPNM**

(SIL-SE-02/99)
**235 SDL CPND**

Name: _____
(PLEASE PRINT)

Address: _____ Apt.#: _____

City: _____ State/Prov.: _____ Postal Zip/Code: _____

## The Silhouette Reader Service® — Here's how it works:

Accepting free books places you under no obligation to buy anything. You may keep the books and gift and return the shipping statement marked "cancel." If you do not cancel, about a month later we'll send you 6 additional novels and bill you just $3.57 each in the U.S., or $3.96 each in Canada, plus 25¢ delivery per book and applicable taxes if any.* That's the complete price — and compared to the cover price of $4.25 in the U.S. and $4.75 in Canada — it's quite a bargain! You may cancel at any time, but if you choose to continue, every month we'll send you 6 more books, which you may either purchase at the discount price or return to us and cancel your subscription.

*Terms and prices subject to change without notice. Sales tax applicable in N.Y. Canadian residents will be charged applicable provincial taxes and GST.

If offer card is missing write to: Silhouette Reader Service, 3010 Walden Ave., P.O. Box 1867, Buffalo, NY 14240-1867

**BUSINESS REPLY MAIL**

FIRST-CLASS MAIL   PERMIT NO. 717   BUFFALO, NY

POSTAGE WILL BE PAID BY ADDRESSEE

SILHOUETTE READER SERVICE
3010 WALDEN AVE
PO BOX 1867
BUFFALO NY 14240-9952

NO POSTAGE
NECESSARY
IF MAILED
IN THE
UNITED STATES

ment, and unfortunately, even a minor complication can be life threatening. A bone-marrow transplant is out of the question. She's just not strong enough. Even the chemotherapy she's received is of questionable value when it comes to actually prolonging her life. Considering how sick she was the last time, I can understand why. And I can't say I blame her for not wanting to go through more of the same.''

"But if she's no longer in remission and she doesn't agree to additional treatment, then how long can she survive?" Sam asked, his brows furrowing.

"That would depend on how quickly the disease progresses from the chronic to the acute stage. A drug called interferon has been known to delay that happening in some people without unbearable side effects. But there's no guarantee she won't have an adverse reaction—one she might not survive.''

"So, damned if she does and damned if she doesn't, right?''

"Something like that," Emma admitted, eyeing him sadly. "And it has to be her decision. She's the only one who can choose between taking the risk involved in whatever treatment her doctor recommends or letting the disease run its course over the next year or so.''

"That's all the time she would have left?" Sam hardly recognized the sound of his own voice.

"Give or take a few months.''

He looked away, barely able to contemplate the consequences of either alternative. After a few moments, he asked, "What do you think she should do?''

"I think she should do whatever feels right to her,'' Emma murmured.

At the touch of her hand on his arm, Sam met her gaze,

then shook his head helplessly. He had thought he was prepared for the worst, but he'd been wrong.

"I saw what she went through in the hospital a few weeks ago," Emma continued. "I'm not sure I want to see her suffer through something similar again. I don't want to lose her that way. I don't want to lose her at all...ever. She's all the family I have left."

"I know how you feel. She's all the family I have left, too." He covered her hand with his and gave it a gentle squeeze. "But I want her to be as comfortable as possible for whatever time she has left. Quality of life has always been so important to her."

"I guess we'll just have to trust her to know what's best."

"Maybe I'll come across something in your notes. Or better yet, maybe her doctor will have good news for us next week."

"I hope so." Emma smiled again, then withdrew her hand from his hold to brush the moisture from her eyes.

With their shared closeness severed by her seeming retreat, Sam glanced at his watch, then reached for the folder.

"I suppose we should be getting back," he said.

"You go on," Emma urged. "I have a few things I want to do around here."

"Anything I can help with?" File folder in hand, he stood.

"Thanks for offering, but I can manage on my own." Without meeting his gaze, she pushed away from the table.

Sensing that she wanted to be alone, Sam took the car keys from his pocket, set them on the table, then headed toward the door.

"I'll leave the car here for you. That way, you won't have to walk back on your own."

Emma seemed about to protest, but didn't.

"Okay, fine," she agreed instead. "I won't be too much longer."

"See you at dinner, then?"

"Yes, see you then."

Relieved by her reply, Sam stepped onto the back porch, pulling the door shut behind him. He had been afraid she would find an excuse to stay there overnight, and then to move back permanently. She had every right to. He was more than capable of caring for his mother on his own.

But he wanted Emma close by for as long as possible. Wanted to know that—deep in the night darkness—she was only a few steps away. Even though he couldn't yet allow himself to go that short distance.

## Chapter Ten

Once Sam had left, the silence that settled around Emma suddenly seemed…forlorn. Just as she had feared, he had filled her private, personal space as it had never been filled before, his vibrant masculinity casting a warm glow on the surroundings they had shared. And now the cluttered little kitchen she had always considered cozy echoed with the emptiness of an abandoned warehouse.

Sitting at the table again, Emma stared out the bay window, her gaze focused on the bright colors of her flower garden, and called herself a fool for allowing Sam's presence—or rather, the lack thereof—to affect her so noticeably.

For heaven's sake, they had been there together no more than thirty minutes, discussing his mother's prognosis as pragmatically as they could under the circumstances. They hadn't talked of anything that could be considered personal.

And the only physical intimacies they had shared had been the touch of her hand on his arm, then his hand covering hers—gestures meant only to comfort and console.

Maybe that was what she was missing more than Sam himself, Emma decided. Having a shoulder to lean on in a crisis—any shoulder, even temporarily—was something she had sorely missed since Margaret had become ill.

Though Jane and Max Hamilton had stayed in Serenity until the end of January, Emma hadn't wanted to cause them any concern. They had been so wrapped up in each other, their infant son and their newfound happiness that she had chosen to keep the worst of her fears for her friend to herself, not only then, but again when she and Margaret had visited them in Seattle several weeks ago.

Here at her house with Sam, however, she had finally been able to speak freely about Margaret's illness, and thus shift some of the burden she had been carrying alone for so many months. Just as she could continue to do. Sam hadn't disappeared completely. He was still close by. And he would be for a few weeks, at least.

She had no reason to feel so bereft just because she sat alone in the one place where she had more often than not been alone—by choice—for the past couple of years.

Why, Jane and then Max, too, had stayed with her for months, and while she had missed them when they returned to Seattle, having her little house all to herself again had been almost a relief. The place hadn't been any less empty then as it was now.

It wasn't as if she couldn't have had company on a regular basis, either—masculine company. For a small town, Serenity had a fair number of single men. Several had indicated an interest in her over the years. But she hadn't encouraged any of them. They were nice; they just weren't...Sam.

"So, snap out of it," Emma muttered as she pushed her chair away from the table.

She had the home she had always wanted, and she had made it her own as best she could. She had never yet been lonely there, and she wasn't about to start now.

She had long ago accepted the fact that she would probably spend the rest of her life alone. Much as she wanted a family of her own, she refused to settle for second best. And what other choice did she have when the man she loved obviously didn't love her in return?

"And just as well, too," Emma added, stowing the bag of chips in the pantry and the jar of salsa in the refrigerator.

She needed the security that came with putting down roots, the kind of roots she had finally been able to put down in Serenity, Texas. And by choice born of *his* needs, Sam lived as rootless a life as any man possibly could.

Even if he had feelings for her, how could they ever have a life together without one of them making a sacrifice that could so easily lead to bitterness and regret?

Emma didn't want to end up like her mother, and from what Teddy had told her years ago, she knew Sam had a fear of ending up like his father. Love could conquer only so much. And where she and Sam were concerned, love—mutually deep and abiding love—didn't seem to be a part of the equation.

With a soft sigh of resignation, Emma rinsed out the beer bottles and tucked them into the recycling bin under the sink. She had learned long ago that some things in life just weren't meant to be. Why couldn't she accept the fact that spending the rest of her life with Sam happened to be one of those things?

As she turned away from the sink, a glance at the clock on the wall warned that she had only an hour until she was expected back at the Griffin house for dinner. Time enough to sort through her clothes and choose a few things for the long weekend in Galveston, water her indoor plants and run a dust cloth over the furniture in the living room, dining room and upstairs bedrooms.

With Mrs. Beal, the housekeeper Margaret had hired to look after both houses, off on her own vacation the entire month of June, a little damage control seemed to be in order.

Unfortunately, she wouldn't have enough time to do the one thing she had consistently put off doing since Jane and Max had left in January. Heading up the stairs, her gaze snagged on the closed door of the room they had outfitted as a nursery for their baby.

Max had generously offered Emma the beautiful, barely used furniture they had purchased in San Antonio—all except the rocking chair that had been Max's special gift to Jane. Certain she would never have any need for the oak baby bed, chest of drawers and changing table, Emma had demurred. But Max had insisted that they wanted her to have them as a kind of promise for her own future when surely she would find the same happiness they had.

When she had still resisted, Jane had allowed that Emma could always donate the furniture to a church or homeless shelter. Unable to argue with that, Emma had finally acquiesced. Yet she had never made the call to the Salvation Army as she'd planned.

The baby furniture could be doing someone somewhere some good instead of sitting unused in one of her bedrooms. But—foolishly, she knew—she hadn't been able to rid herself of it and the hope it had come to signify.

Jane and Max had overcome enormous odds to find happiness together. And despite every indication that she was wishing for the impossible, Emma wasn't quite ready to let go of her dream.

Maybe when Sam left, she thought, moving down the hallway to her own bedroom. Surely then she would no longer have any reason to delude herself.

Emma completed her tasks with almost fifteen minutes to spare. She used that time to take a quick shower and change into a pair of sunny yellow shorts and a crisp white camp shirt, then drove back to Margaret's house feeling refreshed.

She found Margaret and Sam in the kitchen, bantering playfully as he set the table and she put the finishing touches on the grilled-chicken Caesar salad she had decided to fix for dinner. At Emma's entrance, both of them looked her way, Margaret with a wide, welcoming smile, Sam more warily, though Emma could have sworn she saw a hint of pleasure in his bright blue eyes as they alighted upon her.

He, too, had showered and changed into clean clothes— khaki pants and an olive green cotton crew-neck sweater, the sleeves pushed up to his elbows.

"Talk about perfect timing." Smiling, too, Emma gestured toward the table. "Can I help with anything?"

"Pour the tea, dear," Margaret instructed. "And now that you've finished setting the table, Sam, you can get the French bread out of the oven."

As they ate the simple but tasty meal, Emma answered Margaret's questions about her garden in general and the planting she and Sam had done in particular. Then their talk turned to the weekend ahead and the shopping Margaret wanted to do prior to their departure Friday morning.

Sam offered to go with her the following day since Emma had to work.

"So you're not planning on staying out all night?" his mother asked, arching an eyebrow as she gazed at him steadily.

*Stay out all night?*

Not only surprised but dismayed, as well, Emma turned her head and stared at Sam before she could stop herself.

No wonder he was more dressed up than usual for a quiet dinner at home. He was going out tonight. With someone Margaret had assumed would keep him away until sometime the following day.

Sam glanced at her thoughtfully, then met his mother's gaze again.

"No, I'm not," he replied. Plate and glass in hand, he stood, adding, "But I'd better get on the road if I'm going to make it to San Antonio by eight o'clock."

Certain that he had read her mind, Emma glared at her empty plate as a blush warmed her cheeks. She should be glad he was going out with someone and she should let him know it. But the dull ache deep in her heart made that impossible.

"Oh, yes, you should. I didn't realize it was getting so late," Margaret said.

"Let me help with the dishes first," Sam offered.

"I can do that." Roused at last, Emma stood, too. Forcing herself to smile, she dug Margaret's car keys from her pocket, put them on the table, then took the plate and glass he still held and crossed to the sink. "You just go and have a good time."

"Well, if you insist," he drawled in a tone that set Emma's teeth on edge.

She deposited the plate and glass on the counter none

too gently. Turning back to the table, she saw Sam bend and kiss his mother on the cheek.

"I won't be too late," he murmured, obviously for Margaret's ears only, though Emma heard him, too. As he straightened, he met her gaze. "You two will be all right here on your own, won't you?"

"Of course we will," Margaret answered blithely.

When he still seemed to hesitate, Emma nodded her agreement.

"We'll be just fine."

"See you tomorrow, then."

Directing her attention to the dishes still on the table, Emma heard Sam leave through the back door. As the latch clicked, her shoulders slumped. Beside her, Margaret reached out and touched her hand.

"There's no need to hurry with the dishes unless you have plans for the evening, too," she said in a kindly voice.

"No, I don't." Emma dredged up a smile for her friend. "I just thought I'd get the dishes out of the way. Then we can sit out on the front porch for a while if you want."

"That *would* be nice."

Neither of them said anything more as Margaret put away the leftovers and Emma finished the dishes. But once outside, each of them sitting in a rocking chair, Margaret picked up right about where they had left off.

"It's not what you've been thinking," she began, her words punctuated by the rhythmic creak of her chair runners against the porch's wooden floorboards.

"What isn't?" Emma asked as she stared dully into the falling twilight.

"Sam's going off to San Antonio. He's not meeting a woman, though I imagine that's the impression I gave. Just a couple of fellows he knew at the Air Force Academy passing through Texas on their way to the West Coast. They called right after he got back from your house and asked him to join them for a drink down on the River-walk.''

''Oh, really? How nice. Not that it makes any difference to *me* why he's going there.'' Somehow, she managed to sound nonchalant, though the relief zinging through her was almost palpable.

''That's funny. Loving him the way you do, I could have sworn it would make all the difference in the world.''

Stunned, Emma whirled around and stared at her friend, but in the growing darkness Margaret's expression was un-readable.

''What did you say?'' she asked at last, her voice barely above a whisper.

''You heard me, Emma.''

''But I don't—''

''I'm not blind, dear. Although sometimes I could swear you and Sam are. Blind as bats, the two of you. And stub-born as mules, too.''

''Margaret, don't be ridiculous,'' Emma protested, her face burning with embarrassment once again. ''Sam and I aren't…we can't…''

''No, Emma, you *won't*. Neither one of you. But I hope you will before it's too late,'' Margaret stated cryptically.

The moments of silence that followed were unbearably tense for Emma. But Margaret seemed totally unaffected by the possible repercussions her little speech might have. She rocked placidly, as if she hadn't a care in the world.

Emma, on the other hand, could hardly contain the ques-tions brimming on the tip of her tongue. Questions she dared not ask because she was afraid of what the answers might be.

"Well, it's getting late, and I have a busy day tomorrow. I think I'll go on up to bed," Margaret said, though she made no move to leave her chair.

"Margaret...?" Emma began uncertainly, suddenly realizing that if she didn't speak up now, she might not have another chance.

"You're a courageous young woman, Emma Dalton. You've had to be to overcome the obstacles you have over the years and get to where you are today. But even the bravest among us sometimes fail to act out of fear. Usually fear of making a mistake. Or for the more kindhearted like you—and Sam, too—fear of hurting another. And sadly, that failure to act all too often results in a paralyzing sense of guilt. Guilt that is wholly undeserved.

"Teddy loved you, and I know you loved him, too. But Teddy is dead. Not because of anything you did or didn't do, or because of anything Sam did or didn't do. He was killed in a tragic accident.

"Call me fatalistic, but I have to believe it was simply his time to leave this world. Nothing can change that, and nothing ever will. And Teddy of all people wouldn't want his death to cast a shadow on anyone's future happiness, especially yours and Sam's. And he most certainly would never have wanted the circumstances of his death to keep you apart."

Tears prickling at the backs of her eyes, Emma stood and walked to the porch rail. Crossing her arms over her chest, she drew a ragged breath.

Margaret's quietly spoken words, words filled with undeniable conviction, echoed in her mind as she watched the lights go on in Mr. Bukowski's house across the street.

*Teddy loved you...wouldn't have wanted to cast a shadow...happiness...yours and Sam's...never have wanted to keep you apart...keep you apart...keep you apart....*

"But he's not," she murmured at last, more to herself than to Margaret.

"What's that, dear?" her friend asked, coming up beside her and slipping an arm around her waist.

"Teddy," she began, then paused to take a shaky breath. "He's not...he's not keeping Sam and me apart. Sam doesn't...he isn't...interested." Again, she paused as a sob caught in her throat.

"I can't speak for Sam. It's not my place. And for reasons of his own, Sam isn't quite ready to speak for himself yet. Not in words. But I can assure you that if you listen with your heart, if you trust what you hear and reach out to him, he *will* say what needs to be said. Believe me, he will.

"In the meantime, be brave, Emma. More than that, be *bold*. Don't deny what you want, what you need. Square your shoulders, lift your chin and go after it," Margaret commanded, hugging Emma hard a moment for emphasis.

"But that's just it," Emma countered, brushing at the tears on her cheeks. "I'm not sure what I want, what I need. For years and years, I thought I knew. A home of my own, a place to put down roots, a safe, secure life with a safe, secure man in a safe, secure little town—Serenity...*serenity*...

"I have almost all of that now. All but the safe, secure man. And Sam...Sam is anything but safe and secure. Life with him would be a roller-coaster ride, full of thrills and spills. And going on that ride would mean giving up everything else that's ever mattered to me. Assuming he would even *ask* in the first place."

"Not necessarily," Margaret said. "Sam has changed a

lot over the years, become more himself than the image of his father everyone always insisted he was. Yes, physically, he resembles Caleb, and because of that he's had to battle certain demons that weren't necessarily his own. Demons he had to flee Serenity to leave behind.

"Because of his looks, he was given a part to play by many people, including me. And so was Teddy. Sam was the wild, rebellious one, the one who was supposed to enjoy living on the edge. And Teddy...Teddy was left to play the role of the good son—mild-mannered, unassuming, steady, safe and secure.

"Years too late, I've finally realized what a mistake that was. I think there were many, many times when they would have liked to change places if only they could. I also think Teddy had a streak of wanderlust just like his father's buried deep inside him. And that home and family and even Serenity, Texas, always meant more to Sam than he was ever able to admit.

"Not that he doesn't love flying for the air force. Now, however, he can finally acknowledge that he wants more than that, as he has to me since he's been home."

"But only on *his* terms, of course." The faintest trace of bitterness edged Emma's voice as she remembered her own parents' marriage.

"Years ago, I mistakenly believed that I couldn't be happy anywhere but here. I was born and raised in Serenity, and selfishly, I refused to leave even when I saw that life here was stifling my husband's spirit. Too late, I realized that I could have made a home for us anywhere if only I hadn't allowed my head to block out what my heart was trying to tell me. I got what I thought I wanted. I've lived my entire life in Serenity. But I paid a very high price. I lost the only man I've ever loved.

"I can't tell you what's right for you, Emma. Only you know that. And I'm not suggesting you give up everything that matters to you. Sam certainly wouldn't expect that of you. But compromises are possible. I could have made a home for myself and my family anywhere. I know you could, too. As I've said, you're a courageous woman, and where there's a will, there is always a way.

"Now, I'm going up to bed." She hugged Emma again, then turned to the door.

"Margaret...?"

Emma glanced over her shoulder hesitantly. What could she say? Words of commiseration seemed so lacking. But neither was she ready to make any promises. Much as she wanted to listen to her heart, she couldn't dismiss her past history so easily. Margaret kept insisting she was courageous, but in truth she still feared ending up like her mother.

Yet she didn't want to end up like Margaret, either— alone with what she thought she wanted, yearning for what she really needed.

"Yes, Emma?"

Her friend stood by the door, her hand on the latch, a questioning look in her eyes.

"Thank you," Emma answered at last.

"Why, you're very welcome." Margaret smiled sweetly, then opened the door. "Good night, dear."

"Good night."

Alone on the porch, Emma leaned her head against one of the posts and stared into the night, her thoughts whirling. She had no idea what time it was. Not too late, she supposed. Maybe ten-thirty or eleven. Still, she should go in herself.

It would probably be hours before Sam returned. But just

in case he chose to make an early night of it, she'd rather not run into him. In fact, given a choice, she would rather not be alone with him, day or night, until she'd had a chance to mull over all that Margaret had said.

How much did she know about what had happened between Sam and her four years ago? More than she had let on, Emma ventured to guess. Otherwise, how could she have spoken with such certainty about their feelings for each other?

She had seemed so sure that Sam cared for her. But *did* he, really? And if so, where could that possibly lead? Where did she *want* it to lead? She had to be sure—very, very sure—before she let down her guard and reached out to him as Margaret had urged.

She didn't want to deceive him, and she certainly didn't want to deceive herself.

The unexpected flash of headlights at the top of the quiet street caught Emma by surprise. Like a mouse scampering for a bolt-hole at the approach of a big, hungry cat, she hurried across the porch, opened the door and stepped inside.

All the way up the stairs, she chided herself for being silly. But only when she was safe in her room did she let out the breath she'd been holding.

It couldn't possibly be Sam. He would be out carousing with his friends till the wee hours of the—

The distant sound of an outside door closing, followed shortly by footsteps on the stairs, reached her ears through the solid wood of her bedroom door. Footsteps that slowed in the hallway, then stopped just outside her bedroom door.

Again, Emma held her breath, waiting—for what, she did not dare to name. Long seconds ticked by—one minute, then another passing before Sam finally continued down the hallway.

*Reach out to him...be brave...more than that, be bold...*

Margaret's words replayed in Emma's head, urging her to go after him, to open her door, step out into the hallway and call his name. Instead, hands clenched at her sides, she stood motionless until she heard his bedroom door close. Then, with an odd mixture of relief and regret, she sank onto the edge of her bed and switched on a lamp.

Sighing deeply, she took off her glasses, set them on the nightstand and rubbed her eyes with her fingertips.

"What am I going to do?" she murmured, more confused than she'd ever been in her life. "What on earth am I going to do?"

No answers came immediately to mind. At least none she had the courage to act upon.

Margaret had been wrong. She was a coward, a quaking, quivering coward. Had been and probably always would be—at least where Sam was concerned.

# Chapter Eleven

"I don't know about you and Emma, but if I eat any more seafood, I'm afraid I'm going to start growing gills," Margaret announced from the back seat of her car. "As sorry as I am to see our weekend on the island end, I suppose it's just as well we're leaving in the morning."

"So I guess that means you'd rather not stop for a crab omelet on our way out of town tomorrow," Sam said, his tone teasing as he glanced in the rearview mirror and met his mother's gaze.

Beside him, Emma shifted in the passenger's seat to look his way, her green eyes glinting with amusement.

"I wouldn't try that if I were you," she warned. "Your mother's been talking about the Seaside Café's crab omelets from the moment we arrived."

"All right, all right." Margaret waved a hand at them dismissively. "If you insist, I suppose we can indulge one more time."

"If *we* insist?"

Sam offered his mother a devilish grin, then glanced at Emma. Smiling, too, she shook her head in mock exasperation.

"We can't win, can we?"

"Not often," he agreed.

"About time you realized it, too," Margaret interjected, her voice smug.

Obviously assuming she'd had the last word, she settled back in her seat and looked out the side window. From the corner of his eye, Sam saw Emma's smile widen, but she didn't say any more, either, seeming as content as his mother to gaze at the scenery passing by.

Focusing his attention on the road ahead, Sam thought back over the past few days with a surprising sense of satisfaction. As his mother had predicted, getting away from Serenity seemed to have been good for all of them.

Margaret had thrived on the air of fun-in-the-sun gaiety that imbued the island from one end to the other. They'd hardly had time to deposit their suitcases in the beach house—which had more than lived up to the brochure's promise—before she was busy organizing outings of one kind or another.

At Moody Gardens, they had explored the rain-forest pyramid and viewed both movies offered at the IMAX theater. They had taken an island tour on an old-fashioned tram, rode the passenger ferry to the Bolivar Peninsula, spent an evening at the outdoor amphitheater enjoying a rousing version of the musical *Annie, Get Your Gun,* shopped at the various stores lining the Strand, splashed in the surf and, of course, sampled a wide selection of the seafood offered at the island's many restaurants.

Sam had to admit that the flurry of activity had lightened

his spirits in exactly the way his mother had insisted it would. Though he'd had no real time alone with Emma since they had been together at her house—either back in Serenity or there on the island—he had felt much more relaxed around her.

Though he hadn't delved too deeply into why that had been possible, he couldn't help but believe that busy as he'd been in Galveston, he hadn't had time to allow memories of the past mistakes he'd made to intrude with the same persistence or intensity as they seemed to in Serenity.

At the same time, Emma seemed more at ease in his company, as well. Again, he hadn't sought out a specific reason. He was simply grateful that she had stopped making excuses to leave whenever he entered a room and that when she glanced his way, her look was no longer quite so guarded.

In fact, more often than not over the past couple of days, there had been a warmth in her steady gaze that had stirred the merest flicker of hope in his heart.

Had she, too, been better able to lay the past to rest here? Was she able to look at him as he had been able to look at her—without Teddy's ghostly shadow hovering between them quite so insistently?

They had never been on the island together, the three of them, and so much had changed since he had been there with his brother more than twenty years ago. All the moments he and Emma had shared here with his mother belonged only to them. And with some gentle urging from Margaret, those moments seemed to have drawn them a little closer.

But how long would their new and oh-so-tentative bond last once they returned to Serenity? With the anniversary of Teddy's death only ten days away, neither he nor Emma could avoid being reminded of what had kept them apart all these years. Then, all too easily, they could fall into their old patterns of behavior—patterns that had them fleeing each other's company rather than sharing an indulgent smile at his mother's latest bit of nonsense.

Guiding the Volvo down the two-lane road leading to the beach house, Sam wished their idyll could last forever. Not only because of what he feared would happen between him and Emma once they returned to Serenity. Margaret's appointment with the doctor in Houston loomed ahead of them, as well. Try as he might, Sam couldn't work up much optimism about the final prognosis.

He had read all of the information Emma had gathered, not once but several times over. He had also talked to the doctors his mother had seen—the ones in Serenity, as well as those in Houston. Sadly, he had come to the same conclusions as Emma.

Unless she had gone into remission again, drug therapy of some kind would be necessary to prolong her life. But those very drugs could also produce miserable side effects that would detract from the quality of whatever time she had left. Without the drugs, the disease would progress at such a rate that she probably wouldn't live to see another summer.

For the short time they had been on Galveston Island, Sam had been able to set aside some of his concern about his mother's illness. She had seemed more than ever like the woman he remembered. Her spirits had been high, her appetite for adventure keen. In fact, she had been so full of energy the past few days that he and Emma had been hard-pressed to keep up with her.

Now Sam wondered if she had merely been putting up a good front to allay their worries. He certainly wouldn't put it past her. When she set her mind to something, there had never been any stopping her. She had so obviously wanted their time together on the island to be special.

But had she really been able to overcome the effects of her illness by sheer force of will?

That he would only know after her doctor's appointment the next day.

The sun had begun to drop toward the horizon by the time Sam pulled into the beach house's driveway. Set off by itself at the end of a narrow, sandy road, the multilevel, contemporary, wood-and-glass-and-stone dwelling offered a measure of privacy and peacefulness he had thoroughly enjoyed. Though more heavily used during the day by the families living in the cluster of houses almost half a mile away, the wide strip of beach beyond the dunes fronting the property was nearly deserted just after dawn and again just before sunset. Something Sam knew for a fact since those were the times he had chosen to take his solitary runs.

"It's such a lovely evening," Margaret said as he helped her from the car. "Why don't you and Emma take a last walk along the beach?"

"You, too," Emma urged. "We don't have to go far, and maybe you'll happen upon that elusive sand dollar you've been hoping to find."

Years ago, Margaret had told them, she had found some of the most perfect sand dollars she'd ever seen along this very stretch of beach. She had been determined to add another to her collection during their current stay, but all they had been able to find were bits and broken pieces half-buried in the coarse, dry sand. Too many others searching for shells along *her* beach now, she had grumbled good-naturedly.

"Oh, no, I've given up on that." She smiled placidly,

patting Emma on the arm, then started up the steps to the deck. "I think I'll just sit in a lounge chair and watch the tide roll in or out—whatever." She paused, glanced back at them and made a shooing motion with her hand. "Now go along before the light fades completely."

Sam stood at the foot of the steps, a slight frown tugging at the corners of his mouth, watching as his mother made her way up to the deck. The satisfied smile he'd glimpsed on her face assured him she was all right. At least all right enough to arrange for him and Emma to have some time alone together.

Not that he minded, but Emma might.

Much as he would love having her all to himself for a little while, he didn't want her to feel obligated to keep him company. Just because his mother thought that would be an appropriate way for them to end the evening didn't mean she had to, as well.

"We don't have to take a walk if you'd rather not," he said, eyeing her sideways as he shoved his hands in the side pockets of his tailored navy blue shorts.

"Actually, a walk would be really nice." She glanced up at him, then away, a tinge of pink coloring her cheeks. "But I don't mind going alone if *you* would rather not."

Sam was not only surprised by her response, but also deeply pleased. He had given her the out he thought she might want, but she hadn't taken it. Hadn't even seemed *inclined* to take it.

"No, a walk sounds good to me, too," he assured her, trying not to sound too eager.

He would take whatever time he could have with her, here on the island, as well as back home in Serenity.

Back home...

How long had it been since he'd thought of the small

town in the Texas hill country that way? Not since he had gone off to the Air Force Academy, he admitted.

But now…

Even faced with the possibility that Emma would distance herself from him again once they returned, Sam knew there wasn't anywhere else he would rather be. Had known since Tuesday night, when he'd joined his buddies in San Antonio. Long before he had arrived, he'd already been thinking about how soon he could make his excuses and start the long drive back. Because of Emma…*Emma*…

The memory of her hand on his arm that afternoon, of how she had sensed his anguish and reached out to him, had chased away any desire he might have had to party the night away. Instead, he had wanted only to go home to her. And once he'd arrived…

How great had been the temptation to open her bedroom door, to confront her once and for all with his deepest, darkest desires. Only by reminding himself of the untold truth still hanging over his head had he managed to stop. But he hadn't been able to banish thoughts of what could have been—what could *be*.

Not quite meeting his gaze, Emma nodded. Then with casual ease, she tossed her purse on the bottom step, slipped out of her sandals and started toward the narrow woodplank walkway that formed a bridge across the grassy dunes.

Kicking off his loafers, Sam followed after her, lengthening his stride so they were walking side by side by the time they reached the cool, wet, hard-packed sand where the lick of the gently lapping waves had left a line of froth.

As if by mutual agreement, they turned together, moving along slowly, the setting sun at their backs, Emma with her head bent, eyes scanning the debris tossed ashore and Sam with his gaze locked on the distant horizon.

Though he was no more anxious to speak than she seemed to be, Sam didn't find the silence stretching between them all that comfortable. There was so much he wanted to say to her, so much that *needed* saying, but he hadn't any idea where to begin. Nor could he anticipate where their conversation would lead.

More than likely, some places they would be better off not going just yet. He didn't want to risk spoiling what little time they had left here by dredging up the past. He had waited this long to tell her the truth about Teddy's death. He could—*would*—wait a while longer.

"I wish I could find just one," Emma murmured after a while, pausing to sift through a heap of broken shells and tangled seaweed with her bare toes.

"What's that?" Sam asked as he turned to face her.

"One perfect sand dollar for your mother." The evening breeze tousling her curls and swirling the calf-length hem of her lime green sundress, she met his gaze and smiled wistfully. "As a sort of talisman...for good luck tomorrow."

"You've been concerned about her, too, haven't you?"

"I've tried not to let it show. I didn't want to spoil the weekend for any of us. But yes, I've been very concerned. And I've felt so...helpless."

Looking away, Emma started walking again, and Sam fell into step beside her.

"She's seemed so full of energy and she's been in such a positive frame of mind. I keep wanting to believe the doctors have made some terrible mistake, or that they diagnosed her condition correctly, but by some miracle she's beaten the odds," Sam admitted. "But I've read everything you gave me and I've talked to her doctors myself. I *know* she has leukemia, and I know there's nothing I can do to change that. And I would do *anything* if only I could.''

''So would I, Sam,'' Emma said, her voice thick with unshed tears as she paused again. ''So would I.''

''I know, Emma.''

Touched by her sadness and despair, he reached out for her without thinking. Standing at the water's edge, he put his arm around her shoulders, drawing her close to his side. She hesitated for only the barest moment, then looped her arm around his waist and leaned against him.

''What are we going to do without her?'' she asked.

''I don't know.''

Brushing his cheek against her silky curls, Sam closed his eyes and took a deep, steadying breath. There in the fading light of what had been a beautiful day, he wanted first to rage against fate, then to weep for all the losses he had endured, as well as for those yet ahead. But he had learned long ago to accept with unwavering stoicism those things he knew he could not change.

''It's not fair,'' Emma muttered angrily after a while, butting her head against his chest. ''It's…just…not…*fair*.''

Smiling at her unaccustomed display of petulance, Sam hugged her closer for a long moment, then took a step away and eyed her quizzically.

''So, tell me—who, exactly, guaranteed you life would be fair?'' Slipping a finger under her chin, he tipped her face up so that she had no choice but to meet his gaze.

''Well, nobody.'' She looked at him sheepishly, a hint of a smile playing at the corners of her mouth. ''But aren't we due a break every now and then?''

''One can only hope so,'' he answered fervently.

"Yes, one can only hope so," she agreed, glancing away again.

"It's getting late. We'd better turn back."

His arm still around Emma's shoulders, Sam gestured toward the house, now no more than a dark, distant outline against the lavender hues of early twilight.

"Yes, I guess we—" With a sharp intake of breath, Emma slipped her arm from around Sam's waist, turned slightly, bent and scooped something from the sand at their feet. "Oh...oh, Sam...look."

Grinning broadly, she held out a perfectly formed sand dollar about the size of a fifty-cent piece.

"I can't believe it," she murmured. "Fifteen minutes ago, I was searching so intently, and here it was all along, only a glimpse away, just waiting to be found."

Moved by her whimsical delight in something so simple, Sam smiled, too. Taking the sand dollar from her, handling it gently, he admired its fragile yet amazingly unspoiled beauty. Light as a whisper in the palm of his hand, the shell didn't appear to be as sturdy as it had to have been to survive the roiling waters of the Gulf of Mexico.

Like Emma, he thought, more mindful than ever of her close proximity as the flowing skirt of her sundress, teased by the evening breeze, brushed against his bare legs. She seemed so very fragile, yet he knew how strong she was. And how very, very lovely...

"It's perfect, isn't it?" she asked, tracing a finger over the sand dollar's delicate surface.

"Yes, perfect," Sam agreed, his gaze locked on Emma as he spoke.

"I wish I had something to wrap it in—some way to keep it safe while we walk back to the beach house."

"I just happen to have a clean handkerchief in my back pocket. How about that?"

"Oh, yes."

Emma took the shell from him so he could retrieve the neatly folded square of white cotton. Opening it, he held it out so she could place the sand dollar in the center. Then he refolded it and offered her the little bundle. Almost reverently, she took it from him and tucked it into one of her pockets.

"Now we really should head back," Sam advised, starting off into the deepening twilight.

"Yes, of course." For several moments, she walked along beside him, her steps light. Then she added, "I know you probably think it's silly, but I'm so glad we found the sand dollar."

"I don't think it's silly at all," he assured her quietly. "But..."

Sam hesitated, not wanting to burst her bubble. Yet he couldn't let her pin too much hope on the power of her chosen good-luck charm, either. Her disappointment would be all the harder for her to bear if it didn't work as she seemed to expect it would.

"But what?" she prompted.

"It's my understanding that reports of the sand dollar's mystical properties have, on occasion, been greatly exaggerated," he replied, couching his words in a teasing tone.

"I know," Emma murmured, then startled him by reaching out and taking his hand in hers. "But maybe this won't be one of *those* occasions."

"Maybe not."

Savoring the warmth of Emma's touch, Sam threaded his fingers through hers, bonding them even more tenderly as they walked along unhurriedly in the deepening twilight.

Heartened by the closeness she had initiated, he finally ventured to put into words something he'd had on his mind since she first mentioned it while they were in San Antonio.

"Remember a week ago you said Margaret was the only family you had left?" he asked.

"Yes, I remember. You said the same was true for you, too."

"I did," he acknowledged. "But I've been thinking that doesn't necessarily have to be true. Not if you're open to the possibility of considering me family, too. I know I'm asking a lot. Especially after everything that's happened, but—"

"No, you're not," Emma cut in quickly, her tone emphatic.

Halting, she turned and faced him squarely. Surprising him yet again, she reached up with her free hand and gently touched his cheek.

"I would be honored to consider you family, Sam Griffin, deeply honored," she continued. "But that means you'll have to consider me family, too."

Though her features were barely discernible in the darkness, Sam sensed the sincerity of her softly spoken words.

"Now I'm the one who's honored," he replied, trying with only a modicum of success to keep his voice steady.

"I'll always be here for you, Sam," Emma vowed with a solemnity that made his heart ache.

He told himself she meant it only as a friend. But somewhere deep inside, he clung to the growing seed of hope that something more might be possible for them, after all.

"And I'll always be here for you, Emma," he acknowledged quietly.

"Thank you."

Then, so quickly that later he was afraid he had only

imagined it, she stood on tiptoe and kissed him on the cheek, her lips soft and warm against his skin. Without another word, she started off again, striding ahead almost blithely, tugging him along, her hand still firmly clasped in his.

Dazed, Sam kept pace beside her in silence—a new and different silence—unlike any they had yet to share. A silence softened by the sudden, astonishing glow of expectation.

Just ahead, lights shone in the windows of the beach house, beckoning to them. Once there, he knew they would go their separate ways, to their separate rooms and their solitary beds. But tonight that thought didn't cause him quite the same anguish that it had in the past.

They had bridged a gap tonight, he and Emma. A small one, all things considered. But Sam couldn't deny, *wouldn't* deny, the promise that solitary step brought with it.

Emma hadn't shot him down as he'd feared—actually, quite the contrary. Now all he had to do was find the courage to keep putting one foot in front of the other until all the obstacles still standing between them had been overcome.

As they reached the beach house, Emma gave his hand a last squeeze. Then, letting go, she started up the steps, calling out to his mother.

"Margaret, you'll never guess what Sam and I found on the beach."

"What's that, dear?" Margaret asked, joining Emma as she reached the deck.

"A sand dollar, a *perfect* sand dollar."

"Oh, let me see it."

Climbing the steps more slowly, Sam watched as Emma

pulled his handkerchief from her pocket. Unfolding it, she revealed her treasure.

"I'm hoping it will bring you luck," Emma said.

"I have a feeling it's going to bring us all luck," his mother replied, her eyes meeting his for a long moment before she lifted the fragile shell and, smiling, held it to the light.

## Chapter Twelve

Emma tried not to fidget as she sat on the leather sofa in Dr. Herman Rozan's office. She and Sam had been escorted there by the receptionist at the same time Margaret had been led off to one of the examination rooms. That had been nearly an hour ago—an hour that seemed more like an eternity to Emma.

She had long since taken in every detail of the large, uncluttered room, which was brightened by the sunlight pouring through the floor-to-ceiling windows behind the doctor's French Provincial desk. During the time that had passed, she had come to the conclusion that the artwork hanging on the walls was all original, the oval tray, coffeepot, cream pitcher and sugar bowl on the credenza were Georgian silver and the lush, ruby-toned carpet on the floor was at least a hundred years old.

What she hadn't yet decided was whether the doctor's

pristine desktop—empty except for a modern, multi-buttoned telephone, a leather-bound blotter and a single, strategically placed, rather high-priced fountain pen and matching inkwell—was reassuring or a cause for deep concern.

She thought of asking Sam's opinion, but she didn't want to disturb him with what amounted to a lot of nonsense. What difference did it make if Dr. Rozan was obsessively neat and tidy? He had come highly recommended and had proved to be kind and conscientious. That was all that really mattered.

Talking to Sam would have been such a comfort, though—even about something so mundane. Since early that morning, when they had loaded the car and set out for Houston, he had been quieter than usual. Granted, he'd tried to make a little lighthearted conversation at the Seaside Café, where Margaret had thoroughly enjoyed her crab omelet. But Emma had heard the strain in his voice, and she'd known he had been dreading the hours of uncertainty still ahead of them as much as she had.

It was understandable under the circumstances. But he had also seemed so…distant again. Especially since they had been alone together in the doctor's office. After last night, she had been so sure their newfound closeness—a closeness Sam had been the one to initiate—would continue. Now it seemed she'd been mistaken.

He had asked her to think of him as family, and she had readily agreed. Perhaps too readily, Emma thought, a blush warming her cheeks as she remembered how she'd stood on tiptoe and kissed him on the cheek.

She had made the gesture without thinking, acting in the heat of what she'd considered a very special moment. Now she wondered if she had read more into Sam's invitation than she should have.

She had been so overjoyed at finding the sand dollar. And foolish as it seemed in retrospect, her small discovery had cast a sudden, magical glow on the evening. A glow that could have caused her to assign an altogether different meaning to Sam's words than he had intended.

Her special moment could have simply been Sam doing what he deemed to be his duty. She had been engaged to his brother, after all. And he was too much of a gentleman to leave her feeling totally abandoned.

Last night, lying in her bed, watching the play of moonlight on the walls around her, Emma had truly believed that there might be hope for them yet. Now, shifting restlessly on Dr. Rozan's leather sofa, her gaze drawn to Sam's rigid profile, she was suddenly much less certain.

Just as he had been doing for the past hour, he stood at the bank of windows, hands in his pockets, back turned to her, staring out at only he knew what. Twice already, he had also prowled around the room wordlessly, reminding her of a caged tiger. But even then, his roving gaze hadn't lit upon her once.

Come to me, she had silently begged. Talk to me.

Instead, he had avoided her like the plague, eventually returning to his post by the windows, where he seemed to sink more deeply into his solitary thoughts.

She could go to him, of course. She could cross the lush carpet without him even hearing her. She could put her arms around him, rest her head on his shoulder and ask him to let her share his burden. Could if only she had the courage to risk being rebuffed.

He stood so tall and straight, his shoulders stiff, his jaw clenched, his chin thrust out at a dangerous angle, alone against the world. Would he welcome her commiseration? Or was he so used to facing problems on his own that he would consider it a sign of weakness to reach out and take what she had to offer?

She had vowed to stand by him, and he had vowed to do the same for her. Yet, at that moment, she doubted they could have been further apart if they tried.

*Be brave, Emma. More than that, be bold.* Margaret's words echoed in her mind.

And if not *now,* then *when?* she wondered. Waiting there in the doctor's office for what might prove to be devastating news, they needed each other more than ever.

Making a valiant effort to set aside her fears, Emma rose to her feet slowly. The soles of her sandals glided across the carpet as silently as she'd expected as she crossed the room. Coming up behind him, she slipped her arms around his waist and rested her head against his shoulder.

For just a moment, he tensed, and Emma was sure he would pull away. But then, drawing a ragged breath, he turned and gathered her into his arms.

"Emma…"

He breathed her name on a sigh, rubbing his cheek against her hair and stroking his hands down her back as if to soothe her, and in doing so, soothing himself, as well.

She clung to him without speaking, tears of relief and regret stinging her eyes. She shouldn't have waited so long to go to him, to offer him the comfort she had known in her heart he needed.

"I'm not sure how much longer I'm going to be able to wait here quietly," he said after several moments, his voice rough.

"I know what you mean," Emma agreed, the warmth of his lean, solid body so close to hers reaching into her very soul. "I keep telling myself to hope for the best, then I start imagining the worst."

"I don't suppose there's any chance we can hurry the good doctor along."

"I tried that the last time we were here. The receptionist sent me away with nothing but a cup of coffee and a verbal pat on the head to show for my efforts."

"So you're saying I'm just going to have to be patient."

"Unless you want a cup of coffee and a verbal pat on the head." Drawing back a step, she looked up at him and smiled slightly.

"No, thanks."

He smiled, too, and Emma sensed that some of the strain he'd been under all morning had finally begun to ease.

"Anything interesting out there?" she asked, gesturing toward the windows.

"Sunshine, blue sky, tall buildings, lots of cars on the streets and people on the sidewalks." His arm around her shoulders, still holding her close, he turned to peer out the heavy, faintly tinted glass. "I wasn't really seeing any of it until just now, though. I was remembering...so many things—"

Behind them, the office door opened, sending a rush of cool air toward them. Together, they quickly turned away from the window.

Emma wondered if Sam, too, felt a jolt in the pit of his stomach as Dr. Rozan, nattily dressed in dark gray suit pants, a blue shirt and gray-striped tie, all covered by an immaculate white lab coat, stepped into the room. From the way his arm tightened around her shoulders, she imagined he had.

"Mr. Griffin, Ms. Dalton," the doctor greeted them, his bland expression giving away nothing. "Why don't you have a seat on the sofa. I'd like to talk to you for a few minutes before Mrs. Griffin joins us.''

He waited as they crossed the office and sat on the sofa, side by side, hand in hand. Then he took one of the matching wing chairs across from them.

"How is she?" Sam asked, obviously unwilling to waste time with small talk.

"Surprisingly, she's quite well," Dr. Rozan replied. "From what I could determine from the results of her blood tests, she seems to have gone into remission again."

Her relief almost palpable, Emma slumped against Sam, tears welling in her eyes. Letting go of her hand, he put his arm around her again and hugged her gently.

"Okay?" he asked.

"Yes." She glanced up at him and saw tears in his eyes, as well. "How about you?"

"A hell of a lot better than I was five minutes ago." Smiling, he hugged her again, then turned back to Dr. Rozan. "How long do you think it will last?" he asked.

"That depends on several factors. Your mother has refused to undergo another round of intense chemotherapy, and I can't say I blame her. However, I've recommended she begin taking a new drug that has proved to prolong remissions in cases similar to hers without the more debilitating, and in your mother's case, more life-threatening, side effects. She will probably experience some fatigue and achiness in her joints. As I told her, she'll feel like she has the flu for the first week or so.

"The current course of treatment calls for four weeks on the medication, two weeks off, then another four weeks on, with blood tests weekly to monitor any radical changes in her condition. I've already talked to her doctor at Serenity General Hospital and arranged for him to handle that. Barring any unforeseen difficulties, I'll see her again following the second four-week period.''

"I'm not sure what to say," Sam murmured. "Thank you, Dr. Rozan."

"Don't thank me yet," the doctor warned. "The drug I'm prescribing has had a moderate success rate. However, that doesn't mean your mother's out of the woods yet. I can't offer any guarantees for a permanent recovery. But then, I couldn't do that with a more aggressive form of treatment, either. She's going to have to continue to take it easy, avoid physically and emotionally stressful situations and keep up her strength by eating regular, well-balanced meals. At her age and in her somewhat weakened condition, all those things are imperative.''

"We'll look after her," Emma promised.

"I have every confidence that you will," the doctor assured her. Then he added, "She's a very courageous lady. I'd like to see her have every chance at a full recovery.''

Again, the office door opened, and Margaret, escorted by one of Dr. Rozan's nurses, joined them, her eyes twinkling.

"Talking about me, are you?" she asked.

"Yes, but we're saying only good things," the doctor replied, standing along with Emma and Sam.

"You've given them the good news?''

"Along with instructions to keep you rested and well fed.''

"That used to be *my* job," she grumbled, albeit good-naturedly.

"Not anymore," Dr. Rozan warned, his tone brooking no argument. "You've earned the right to enjoy a little pampering, and that's a right I fully expect you to exercise.''

"Yes, sir." She offered him a mock salute. "Anything else, sir?"

"I'll look forward to seeing you again in September. Make an appointment on your way out," he instructed, smiling as he led them to the door.

They did as he said, then they retrieved the Volvo from the parking garage.

Emma wasn't sure why Margaret and Sam were so quiet as they left the city behind, but *she* was still too stunned to say much of anything. She just wanted to hug the good news to herself and savor it awhile. As the doctor had said, Margaret wasn't out of the woods yet. But there now seemed to be a good chance she would be with them much longer than they had originally been led to believe.

No matter how *cautiously* optimistic Dr. Rozan had advised them to be, she still considered *optimistic* to be the operative word.

"How about a late lunch?" Sam asked once they were well on their way down the I-10 heading west.

"Sounds good to me," Margaret agreed from the back seat. "It's been hours since breakfast, and you two hardly ate a bite then."

"Me, too," Emma said.

She was hungry—*really* hungry—for the first time that day. Like Sam, she had chosen to forego an omelet earlier, nibbling nervously on a slice of toast instead. Hardly a bite, as Margaret had said. But with the worst of her anxiety eased, her appetite had definitely returned.

They stopped at a place that served Texas-style barbecue and gorged on ribs, potato salad, baked beans and corn on the cob, followed by a generous portion of ice-cream-topped peach cobbler they prudently opted to share.

Finally sated, they continued on toward San Antonio, and

from there, to Serenity. In the back seat, Margaret settled back and soon dozed off to sleep.

Her soft snores made Emma smile. Sam's expression softened, too, she noted, glimpsing at him from the corner of her eye.

"She's going to be all right, isn't she?" he murmured as if reading her mind.

"Yes, I think she is," Emma answered, her smile widening as she glanced at him.

For just a moment, he met her gaze and smiled, too. Then he surprised her by reaching out and taking her hand in his.

"I meant to thank you for your...support at the doctor's office."

"Not necessary," she assured him. "We're family, after all."

"Yes, we are."

He threaded his fingers through hers as he'd done on the beach the night before. Warmed by his gesture, Emma looked out the window.

The rolling hill country stretched ahead of them, a sure sign that their journey was almost at an end. Contented as she was, Emma wished they had miles yet to go. She could sit beside Sam forever, her hand clasped in his.

All too soon, the Serenity city-limit sign came into view, and five minutes later, they were pulling into the Griffin's driveway.

"Oh, dear, I didn't mean to sleep so long," Margaret said, stirring behind them. "I wanted to suggest that you take Emma back to her house, Sam." She paused, reaching out to touch Emma on the shoulder. "Not that I'm trying to get rid of you, but after almost a month of playing nurse-maid, I imagine you're more than ready to go home. And with Sam home now, and me on the mend, there's really no need for you to stay on. You have most of your things with you, don't you?'' she added. ''And the rest you can collect whenever time allows.''

''Yes, I have almost everything,'' Emma admitted, trying to hide her dismay.

Talk about being careful what you wish for...

Just days ago, she had been longing to return to her house. The mere thought of living under the same roof as Sam had tied her stomach into knots. She had been so sure they would never find any common ground, that every meeting between the two of them would drive them further apart rather than draw them closer together.

Now just the opposite seemed to be true. They had made such progress, especially last night and again that afternoon. And only by seeing him, being with him, could that progress continue. If she stayed at Margaret's, the opportunities would have been endless. Living in her own home, she would have to make much more of an effort. And in their case—at least for her—making an effort was going to take no small amount of courage.

''Well, then, Sam, why don't you drive over to Emma's house now?''

''Is that all right with you?'' he asked as he turned to look at her.

Still holding her hand, he stroked the inside of her wrist with his thumb. But he was wearing sunglasses, so his expression was hard to read.

Did he really care, one way or another?

Seemingly not, she decided after a few moments. Otherwise, he would have found a reason for her to stay whether he needed her help or not.

Maybe he'd gotten all he wanted from her already. Maybe a little moral support during the most trying moments, now past, was all he'd really intended with his talk of family.

That possibility hurt Emma deeply, but she refused to let it show. Instead, she offered Sam a bright smile as she answered him.

"Yes, of course. That's quite all right with me."

Nodding once, taking her at her word, he let go of her hand, shifted the Volvo into reverse and backed the car out of the driveway.

"I hope you don't feel like we're putting you out, Emma," Margaret ventured. "Having you with me has been a wonderful blessing. I don't want to take advantage of your kindheartedness, though. You've done so much for me, but now it's time you had a break."

"I've enjoyed staying with you," Emma assured her friend, turning to face her. "But I suppose it is time I got back to my own routine. Promise me, though, that you'll let me know if there's anything I can do for you...and Sam."

"I most certainly will. And you'll do the same, won't you?"

"Yes, I promise."

"How about Sunday dinner, then?" Margaret asked, a teasing twinkle in her eyes. "You'll feel like coming over for a visit by then, won't you?"

"I'll jot it down on my calendar the moment I get in the door," Emma replied, her smile no longer quite so forced.

At her house, Sam parked in the driveway, then got out to help with her suitcase. Emma said her goodbyes to Margaret, reminding her again to call if she needed anything.

"And if you need anything, Emma," Margaret said, then paused a moment, her gaze steady, "*you* call."

All too aware that Margaret's idea of *anything* involved

her son, Emma nodded, then gathered her purse and followed Sam to the front porch.

"Thanks a lot," she said, avoiding his gaze as she pulled her keys from her purse and opened the door. "I can manage from here."

"I guess you'll be busy all week." Ignoring her words of dismissal, he picked up her suitcase and shifted it into her entryway before she could do it herself.

"Yes, I will. I have a lot of catching up to do around here as well as at the library."

"Well, then, I guess I'll see you on Sunday."

"Yes, on Sunday."

He hesitated a few moments longer, and Emma thought that he might say something more, might *do* something more. Or maybe he was waiting for her to—

"Emma…?"

"Yes?"

Finally, she glanced up at him, then quickly looked away, her heart pounding. He had left his sunglasses in the car, so there was nothing blocking the sorrow in his eyes. Sorrow edged with a longing that tugged at her heart, making her want to weep.

"Sunday…" he repeated, reaching out and tracing a finger along the line of her jaw.

Sunday… Almost a week away…

She wanted to tell him she couldn't wait that long, that if he took her in his arms this very minute, it wouldn't be nearly soon enough. But she couldn't seem to say the words aloud. Couldn't, *wouldn't*, let him know how much she needed him when he might not really care.

Drawing a deep breath, she nodded once, then slipped through the door.

That night, the peace Emma had always found in her

little house eluded her completely. The silence pressed down around her, echoing off the walls—a silence heavy with heartache and laced with loneliness.

All because of Sam, she told herself as she paced restlessly from one room to another.

She should have never written to him. Should have never asked him to come home. There hadn't really been a need for him to make the trip. Margaret was going to be just fine.

Unfortunately, Emma couldn't say the same about herself. Truth be told, she would probably never be fine again. Sam had come back into her life, stirring in her all sorts of impossible hopes and dreams.

Hopes and dreams she had been foolish to entertain even for a moment. Hopes and dreams that would haunt her long after he had left her once again.

## Chapter Thirteen

As he had every night since their return to Serenity, Sam tossed from side to side on the narrow twin bed in his room. He had slept, eventually, those other nights. Even Sunday after Emma's all too short, all too bright and cheerful visit.

She had breezed in late that afternoon, and had stuck close to his mother the entire time she was there, chattering like a magpie about the blessed lack of side effects Margaret had experienced from the new drug, various happenings at the Serenity Public Library, the state of her garden, the state of his mother's garden. All the while, she had directed little more than an occasional nervous glance his way.

After five days, days during which he'd had to force himself to stay away from her, Sam had been looking forward to her company, to maybe having the opportunity to spend some time alone with her. But he had been disappointed all around.

They had made such progress on Galveston Island. That night on the beach, she had responded so favorably to his overtures. And Monday, at Dr. Rozan's office, when he had been too wrapped up in worry to do more than stare out the window, *she* had reached out to *him* with such tenderness and concern that he'd finally begun to believe she might truly care for him, after all.

But he hadn't wanted to push his luck. Hadn't wanted to come on too strong, and maybe scare her off by voicing his consternation when Margaret sent her home. And evidently, from how eagerly she'd agreed, neither had Emma.

Sam had told himself that perhaps they would be wise to have a little time apart. Time when they could consider, individually, where they should go, where they *could* go next. He hadn't expected her to retreat from him so completely, though. To be honest, he had assumed she would be just as anxious as he was to pick up where they had left off.

He hadn't taken into account the possibility that she didn't want or need any more from him than what he'd already offered her. Or the possibility that she did, but was afraid to let him know it.

Whether intentionally or not, he had rebuffed her in the past—the not too distant past, he reminded himself as he shifted onto his back and stared at the ceiling.

At the coffee bar along the Riverwalk in San Antonio, when she had first spoken of Teddy's death, and again on the stairs here in his mother's house, when she had tripped and fallen into his arms, Emma had not only made *her* feelings known, but had also given him the chance to do the same. But he had held back, as he continued to hold back, because he had yet to be totally honest with her.

Until Emma knew the truth, the *whole* truth, about what

had happened the day his brother died, there was only so far their relationship could go. As long as that particular secret stood between them, they could be friends, rather *reserved* friends, and nothing more.

Which brought Sam back to the present moment. It was now Tuesday night—actually, very early Wednesday morning, and officially the fourth anniversary of Teddy's death.

He should have known better than to think he would be able to sleep, especially here in his mother's house. He had coped much better when he'd been hundreds, sometimes a thousand or more, miles away. Although his method of coping the first two years had more to do with the blissful insensibility he'd found at the bottom of a bottle of booze.

Last year, he'd been in the midst of a grueling seventy-two-hour training mission, so his awareness of the exact date, even the exact time, had been somewhat muddled. This year, however, he'd been able to think of little else from the moment he had come home. And since he'd gone to bed just before midnight—still amazingly sober despite going eye to eye with a bottle of Scotch for several hours after his mother retired for the night—he had been overwhelmed with memories that tore at his heart.

Maybe he shouldn't have been quite so prudent. What could a few drinks hurt, after all? He wasn't on duty and wouldn't be for another ten days. He was in the privacy of his mother's house in the even greater privacy of his own room. No one would know how he'd chosen to ease his pain.

No one but him…

Ready to crawl out of his skin, Sam threw off the quilt and stood up. He had to do something, anything, to work off the tension that was drawing him tight as a bowstring. Anything but start drinking…

He glanced at the clock on the nightstand and saw that it was almost four-thirty. An odd time to be out running, but he doubted anyone would notice.

Swiftly, before he had a chance to change his mind, Sam pulled on a pair of gray knit shorts, a white t-shirt, thick socks and running shoes. He tucked his keys in his pocket, crossed to the bedroom door and opened it as quietly as he could.

He wasn't thrilled with the idea of leaving his mother completely on her own, but she hadn't been having any problems, either with sleeping through the night in general or, in particular, with the medication Dr. Rozan had prescribed for her. And Sam didn't plan to be gone all that long. Not at the pace he intended to set for himself. He should be ready to crawl back to the house, exhausted, in about an hour, maybe an hour and a half max.

He started out of his bedroom, and as he seemed to do each time he found himself in the upper hallway, he glanced at the closed door of Teddy's room. The one place in the house he had avoided for over two weeks now.

Sooner or later, he was going to have to go in there. Sam wasn't sure why. He simply knew that he must. And, he reasoned, now would be as good a time as any.

With his mother asleep, he wouldn't be taking the risk of disturbing her by his intrusion there. She had never indicated that she considered his brother's room to be sacrosanct. But she hadn't opened the door since he had been home, either.

That didn't necessarily mean she intended for him to stay out. She could have just wanted to spare him as many unhappy memories as possible. Still, he would rather do what he had to do without her knowledge.

Before his resolve could waver, Sam reached out and

turned the doorknob. The door swung open easily, he stepped inside the room, then quietly closed the door again. There was just enough light filtering through the slats of the blinds on the windows to guide him to Teddy's desk. He stood beside it, hesitating a few moments, then switched on the lamp, blinking in the sudden, bright glow.

As his eyes became accustomed to the light, he turned slowly, looking around the room, taking in its unaccustomed tidiness. Many of his brother's things still lined the bookshelves. Trophies he had won at swimming competitions and soccer tournaments years ago. Books, too, both fiction and nonfiction, on a vast array of subjects. Many more than Sam had ever owned.

Teddy had always loved to read, anything and everything. Somewhat taken aback, Sam now noted that many of the books were travel and adventure oriented.

There were posters still hanging on the walls, too—all of faraway places: Africa, India, China and Australia. Again, Sam felt an odd jolt of surprise, and then another as his gaze drifted to the bulletin board above Teddy's desk.

It was covered with pictures of Sam in his flight suit, helmet in hand, standing by the jet he flew, as well as the postcards he had sent over the years—postcards from all the places *he* had been.

Sam hadn't spent a lot of time in Teddy's room when he was home, and he hadn't been home that often once he'd gone off to the Air Force Academy. Now he realized how close to the truth his careless comments in the car on the way to the church must have been. He could also understand why Teddy had responded the way he did.

Had Teddy, too, longed for a life somewhere besides Serenity, Texas? But then, why had he come back here and settled down as if it were all he'd ever wanted? Had he done it because he felt that one of them had to stay behind to look after their mother, and Sam had already been long gone?

To Sam's knowledge, his brother had never let on that he considered himself to be under such an obligation. But to whom could Teddy have vented his feelings?

As Sam had just admitted, *he* had been gone for years. And Teddy wouldn't have said anything to worry their mother or upset Emma. Instead, he would have done what he believed to be his duty, quietly and without complaint. Just as he had until Sam gave him the excuse he wanted, *needed,* to escape.

Unwittingly, Sam had offered to take Teddy's place that day four years ago, to take on his responsibilities. And Teddy had jumped at the chance to finally be free. Not because he didn't love his mother or his wife-to-be, but because he'd been dying inside. He had hidden it so well, good son that he'd been, that no one had known it.

Until Sam dangled the ultimate temptation before him in a desperate, last-ditch attempt to once again get what *he* wanted, and everyone else be damned.

"Oh, God, Teddy, I'm so sorry...." Sam muttered, his eyes blurring with tears.

He should have come home more often all those years ago. Surely then he would have realized how stifled his brother had been feeling. And he could have done something to help.

*Shoulda, woulda, coulda...*

"But you didn't. Not until it was much too late, and then only to serve yourself, you bastard."

Unable to look any longer at the evidence of his failure, Sam switched off the lamp and somehow made his way through the darkness to the door. In the hallway, he moved as quietly as he could, stopping only to assure himself his mother still slept before he headed down the staircase.

He let himself out through the front door, locked it carefully, then walked down the porch steps, glad of the lingering predawn darkness. He paused on the sidewalk for a minute or two, swiping at the wet patches on his cheeks as he tried to get his bearings. Finally, he started off at a gentler than anticipated lope, heading in the direction he most often took on his runs through town.

Up to the corner, then left three blocks, and right onto Bay Leaf Lane. To Emma's house, where the windows would more than likely still be dark at this early hour of the morning. He had run past there so many times, late at night or just before dawn, since the day she had given him directions. But never once had he dared to stop. He had simply gone past, blending into the shadows, silently cursing his foolish obsession.

When Sam reached the corner, however, he hesitated, coming to a halt under the street sign. Then, as if pulled by a force he could no longer resist, he turned right instead, setting off on a course he hadn't followed once in the past two and a half weeks. A course that would take him to the north side of town, up past the high school and the hospital, out to where the houses stood farther and farther apart and small yards gave way to fields.

Sam ran steadily, putting one foot in front of the other, pacing himself so that he could go the distance. As the sky lightened to a pale shade of gray and the first faint reddish glow skimmed along the horizon to his right, he finally saw the narrow gravel track he'd been seeking just ahead, marked by a small wooden sign.

His breath coming in gasps, the muscles in his legs burning from exertion, he made the turn, then slowed to a walk.

Around him, shadows seemed to sway and twist as a warm breeze rustled through the oak tress and rippled across the neatly tended lawn. But the place held no fear for him.

Despite the semidarkness, Sam found his way quickly, easily among the headstones, drawn inexorably toward the tall, square, granite monument that bore his brother's name. Leaving the gravel track behind, he started across the grass, his footsteps muffled.

For several heartrending moments, Sam stood before his brother's grave. Then he knelt down, buried his face in his hands and wept.

Not only for all he had done, but for all that he'd only just realized he had failed to do.

# Chapter Fourteen

Emma couldn't say for sure what woke her. Nothing disturbing, she was certain. Not a weird dream—at least, not one she could recall. Nor any strange, scary noises, which would have had her staring into the darkness fearfully, her heart pounding in her chest. She had simply come awake slowly, drifting from sleep to full awareness, her sense of well-being relatively intact.

A glance at the clock on the nightstand told her it was just after five o'clock. Much too early to start the day, considering she'd been up well past midnight.

Unable to fend off the myriad memories—some happy, others incredibly sad—that had sprung to mind as they did each year just prior to the anniversary of Teddy's death, she had been too restless to settle. Only after hours of digging in her garden, pacing through the house, then indulging in an unaccustomed bout of tears, born of regret and remorse, had she dozed off at last.

The rest she'd gotten had been fitful at best, and nothing near refreshing. But she knew that staying in bed wouldn't do her any good. Even if she managed to fall asleep again, the self-reproach that hovered in her soul wouldn't magically disappear.

Today, of all days, she had to face up to the consequences of her selfishness. Today, of all days, she had to acknowledge just how tragically her failure to act had touched the lives of those she had professed to love.

Better to get on with it than to hide under the bedcovers like the coward she had proved herself to be once already. Better to make what peace she could with herself and try to do no more harm in the hours ahead.

She would have to see Margaret and Sam later that morning. They were expecting her to go with them to the special Mass of remembrance at St. Mary's church, then on to the cemetery—a ritual she and Margaret had begun three years ago.

Emma had taken the day off expressly for that purpose, and she had no intention of copping out. But at that moment, she felt a sudden, overwhelming need to go to Teddy's grave...alone.

Maybe there in the predawn darkness she could come to terms with her feelings for Sam once and for all. And maybe there she could finally find the courage to reach out to him, to reveal what was in her heart, or forever hold her peace.

She couldn't go on as she had been, especially the past week, waiting in vain for *him* to come to *her*. He'd had plenty of opportunity, yet he hadn't come anywhere near her. Whether out of his own uncertainty or bland indifference, Emma had no idea. And she'd never been much good at guessing.

Nor could she continue to pretend that his detachment didn't matter to her. Her playacting Sunday afternoon had left her with a roiling stomach, as well as a lashing headache that had lasted well into the following day. She absolutely refused to put herself through anything like that again.

But neither would she let Sam see her torment. She would rather avoid his company altogether, at least after today, than give him a reason to feel sorry for her.

Filled with a sudden sense of determination, Emma rolled out of bed and crossed to the bathroom.

Since she wasn't sure how long she'd be gone, she took a shower, but she didn't bother to dry her hair or put on makeup. Her curls would spring to life on their own in the morning breeze, and any attempt to hide the dark circles under her eyes would have been futile anyway. She dressed in a long, slim, denim skirt and a pale blue T-shirt, slipped her feet into sandals, grabbed her purse and went down to the kitchen.

There she walked over to the refrigerator and retrieved the bouquet of pale yellow roses she'd cut last night. She had planned to take them to the cemetery when she went with Margaret and Sam, but she didn't want to wait that long. She wanted Teddy to have the roses now, her personal gift to him.

She had loved him—would always love him in a way that would forever be unique. She could only hope he had known that, especially in his last moments.

The drive to little Mount Grace Cemetery took only a few minutes. In the pale gray predawn light, the streets were mostly deserted.

Only when she turned onto the gravel track leading to the grave sites, did Emma suffer a momentary pang of misgiving. While Serenity had always been a fairly safe place, the cemetery was somewhat off the beaten path, and she was there alone. But Teddy's grave was just a few steps off the gravel track. She could always scurry back to her car if anything seemed to be amiss. Although *who* would be lurking about, up to no good, when it was almost daylight anyway, she had no idea.

Chiding herself for being silly, Emma switched off the engine, doused the headlights and let her car roll to a stop a few yards from the tree beneath which Teddy was buried. The headstone was still in deep shadow, but she was no longer hesitant to leave her car and walk the short distance to where it stood.

Not bothering with her purse, she picked up the flowers, opened the car door and started across the lush, dew-damp grass, head bent, watching where she was going so she wouldn't trip over a fallen tree branch or stumble into a hole. Only when she was almost to the headstone did she finally look up.

With an audible gasp, she skidded to a halt, her heart hammering in her chest as she spied the hunched figure of a man sitting with his back against the granite monument. Her mouth dry, she stood perfectly still, staring at him wordlessly for several seconds, wondering who on earth—

Slowly, the man raised his head, and immediately Emma recognized him.

"Sam…" she began, her initial reaction one of relief. She took a step toward him, but something in his expression stopped her at almost the same instant his voice cut her off.

"Go away, Emma," he ordered, his tone harsh. "Just…go…away."

Making no move to get up, he met her gaze unwaveringly. His pale face was streaked with tears, his eyes were bleak, his jaw set at a brook-no-argument angle. He was dressed in shorts and a T-shirt, both wet with perspiration, and his blond hair, also damp, stood away from his head in spikes. The way he sat, his forearms braced on his bent knees, there was an air of exhaustion about him—exhaustion and defeat.

Obviously, he had run all the way to the cemetery. Taking into account the things he'd said in the past, as well as the reasons for her own pilgrimage, Emma could understand why. He, too, had demons to face. He'd revealed that much the afternoon they'd been together in San Antonio.

That day, he had insisted her apology wasn't necessary. But why? He had claimed he was responsible for Teddy's death. How could that be true when he hadn't been the one to cause the accident? She hadn't been able to follow his reasoning then. But there had been no doubt in her mind that Sam believed it was true.

As he still must, she thought.

His current demeanor was all the evidence she needed. The miles he'd run to the cemetery had been meant as a kind of penance. Yet he still hadn't been able to give himself absolution.

For what? she wondered once again.

"Didn't you hear me, Emma? I said, *go away*," he repeated angrily, glaring at her.

Crushed by his tone, she was tempted to obey him. But there had been a faint catch in his voice, an underlying, unmistakable wavering that drew her in spite of everything still standing between them.

Did he really want her to leave or was he silently, subconsciously willing her to stay?

*Listen with your heart...trust what you hear,* Margaret

had told her. *If you reach out to him, he* will *say what needs to be said....*

*Be brave...more than that, be bold....*

Emma drew a deep breath, bracing herself for whatever was to come, and continued toward him.

"I heard you just fine, Sam," she answered mildly. "But I'm not ready to leave yet."

In the instant before he turned his face away, Emma saw a flash of panic in his eyes. She fully expected him to stand and try to stalk past her. *Try* being the operative word, since she was fully prepared to stick out her foot and trip him up short if that was what it took to keep him from running away again.

To her relief, however, Sam stayed where he was. Of course, he seemed determined not to look at her, or acknowledge her in any other way. But that she could deal with.

In fact, as far as she was concerned, he could pretend to be part of the headstone as long as he wanted. She intended to talk to him, regardless. Responsive or not, he wouldn't have any choice but to hear what she had to say.

Clutching the bouquet of roses in one hand, she rested the other on the headstone for balance and sat down next to him. He glanced at her, his lips narrowed in a grim line, then turned his head away again.

"Remember that day in San Antonio when I tried to apologize for the things I said to you at the hospital after Teddy died?" she began, searching desperately for the right words, words that might rip open their wounds but in the process also allow them to finally begin to heal.

Sam said nothing, but sitting so close to him, Emma sensed his sudden tension.

"You told me not to berate myself," she pressed on.

"Well, I think it's time *you* stopped berating *yourself,* too. You were not the one responsible for Teddy's death. You just happened to be driving the car—"

"I did a hell of a lot more than *just drive the car,*" Sam snarled.

The fierceness of his tone caught Emma totally off guard, slamming into her with an almost palpable force. And when he faced her, the blazing pain in his eyes tore at her heart.

Suddenly, she found herself rethinking the wisdom of ripping open old wounds, then realized it was already much too late. She had started something Sam now seemed determined to finish.

"I was supposed to be taking my brother to the church. He suggested we go the long way. I didn't put up any argument. I wasn't in a hurry to get there myself. I hated the thought of watching you walk up the aisle and into *his* arms. I started teasing him. At least that's what I tried to tell myself I was doing."

He looked away for a long moment, his hands clenched into fists, his jaw working convulsively.

"Sam, you don't have to—"

"I asked him if he was sure he wanted to tie himself down to a wife and family without ever having gone anywhere or done anything except teach high-school English in his hometown," Sam continued as if she hadn't spoken. "Then *he* asked *me* what I expected him to do—leave you standing at the altar? And I…I told him I could always take his place.

"All of a sudden, I wasn't kidding around anymore and Teddy realized it. Realized I wanted you even though I had no right. You were his fiancée. You loved *him* and *he* loved you, and I knew it. But after that kiss…

"Even though you never said or did anything to lead me

to believe it mattered to you the way it did to me...I just couldn't leave well enough alone. And Teddy...oh, God, Teddy unbuckled his seat belt. He told me to let him out of the car just past the intersection. He said he could catch a ride back to the house, clear out his stuff and be gone before the service was over.''

Pausing again, Sam drew a deep, sobbing breath.

Too stunned by his revelations to speak, Emma simply stared at him.

''I told him not to be silly. I told him that you loved *him*. And then...and then...''

Unable to finish, Sam tipped his head back and closed his eyes as fresh tears trickled down his cheeks.

No wonder he had blamed himself all these years, Emma thought, her heart aching for him. He had thought that his teasing had been the ultimate cause of Teddy's death. Teasing he had initiated not out of malice toward his brother, but because of his feelings for *her*.

But there were so many other factors involved. A drunk driver roaring through a stoplight. The obvious ambivalence Teddy had had about marrying her—an ambivalence she had always suspected but never mentioned to anyone. And, of course, her own failure to speak up.

Teddy would have never been in the car with Sam in the first place if she'd had the courage to follow her heart, and Sam had a right to know it.

All these years, he had believed he hadn't had a valid reason for teasing Teddy. He'd thought the kiss they'd shared hadn't meant anything to her. And he had suffered for it in ways she was only just beginning to realize.

But no more, she vowed, setting aside the bouquet of roses and scooting closer to him.

''Sam, listen to me,'' she said softly as she reached out

and traced the curve of his cheek with her fingertips. "There's something you need to know."

He flinched from her touch and tried to pull away.

"Emma, please, how many times do I have to ask you to go?" he demanded, his voice ragged. "You wanted answers. Now you've got them. So just...go away and leave me alone."

"I'm not going anywhere until you hear what I have to say." Taking his chin in her hand, she forced him to look at her. When he finally did so, his eyes were cold and distant, but she refused to let him put her off. "I loved Teddy deeply. But I didn't want to marry him any more than he wanted to marry me. Unfortunately, we couldn't admit it to anyone, including each other. We were the best of friends and occasionally we were lovers. But the physical part of our relationship never seemed to be that important to him, and it certainly wasn't ever that important to me.

"I'm not sure about Teddy, but being with him was comfortable for me. He made me feel safe and secure. I didn't want to give that up. Even after you kissed me and I couldn't deny any longer that...that *you* were the one who made me feel the way a bride was supposed to feel about her groom.

"I should have called off the wedding that afternoon, but I was too afraid. I didn't want to give up the kind of life I thought I could have with Teddy for something so much more...uncertain."

Tears blurring her eyes now, Emma clasped her hands in her lap and bent her head. She had seen the flicker of surprise in Sam's eyes, and then she'd seen dismay. He had every right to despise her; she certainly despised herself.

But she couldn't bear to see him look at her with the scorn she deserved.

"I should have stopped the wedding," she repeated quietly. "Then you and Teddy would have never been in the car to start with. So, you see, it all comes back to me, not you. If only I'd had the courage to speak up, he would still be alive today...."

Blinking rapidly, Emma tried to hold back her tears, but still they spilled onto her cheeks.

"Emma, please...don't..." Sam murmured.

His arms went around her, shifting her, lifting her onto his lap, and she clung to him, weeping as she had never allowed herself to weep—for all the pain she had caused, for the dreams she had crushed, for the best friend she had loved and lost forever and for the man who held her now, rocking her gently, stroking her hair as he soothed her with tender words and kisses light as a butterfly's wings.

After what seemed like a very long time, Emma's tears finally began to subside, but she still hung on to him as the sky lightened and the birds started twittering in the trees. She didn't know what else she could say, and the mere thought of leaving the shelter of his arms was more than she could contemplate.

"We didn't really know him, did we?" Sam asked, brushing his lips against her forehead. "At least not the way we thought we did."

"Maybe because he tried so hard to be what others thought he *should* be. Your mother said once that neither you nor Teddy had any real choice about the roles you played in the family, and she blamed herself for it."

"That could have been true when we were younger," Sam admitted. "But if Teddy was so unhappy, why didn't he speak up? Once he finished college, he could have done anything he wanted. My mother wouldn't have stood in his way, and I don't think you would have, either.''

"He never said anything to me, ever, about wanting a different kind of life someplace else. Maybe leaving Serenity was as hard for him to consider as staying was for you.''

"The hell of it is, he always *seemed* so content to me. Of course, I wasn't around all that much, so there's a good chance I was mistaken. I only just realized how many books he had about traveling to foreign countries—posters, too, plus all the postcards I sent him from the places I've been.''

"He seemed content to me, too, and I was *always* around,'' Emma replied, as much at a loss as Sam seemed to be.

"Could we have only imagined that?''

"I hope not. His life was so short, and he was so good-hearted. He truly deserved to be happy during the time he had here.''

"Speaking of good-hearted, he would probably be pretty upset if he could see us now, tearing ourselves apart over him,'' Sam said, slipping a finger under her chin and tipping her face up so that she met his searching gaze.

"You're right,'' Emma agreed, a gentle smile lifting the corners of her mouth as she remembered just how sweet and kind and how very careful of others' feelings Teddy had always been. "He would have been appalled at the agony we've caused ourselves all these years.''

"I'm not proud of what I did, but I never meant him any harm, Emma.''

Still holding her gaze, Sam cradled her face in his hands, his thumbs stroking away the last of her tears.

"I know, Sam. I didn't, either. But we lost him anyway.''

"And each other..." he murmured, his eyes shadowed with sorrow.

"For a while, at least." Reaching up, she touched his cheek.

"Yes, for a while."

Putting his arms around her, he drew her close again, and Emma nestled against his chest gratefully.

"Poor Teddy. He must be sitting up in heaven, shaking his head at the two of us," Sam continued.

"Actually, knowing Teddy, he's probably wishing he could knock our heads together—just to get our attention so he could tell us to get on with our lives," Emma said, smiling once again. "He never did have any patience with people who insisted on wallowing in regret."

"Do you think we can?" Sam asked, his arms tightening around her almost imperceptibly. "Do you think we can get on with our lives after everything that's happened?"

"I think we owe it to Teddy to at least give it a try. He wouldn't begrudge us finding a little happiness."

"Together...?" Sam murmured hesitantly.

Leaning against him, Emma felt the way he tensed as he spoke the single word. He seemed almost afraid to voice that particular thought aloud. As if he were still unsure of her feelings for him despite all she'd said.

Of course, she *had* used the past tense when she'd admitted that she'd refused to follow her heart four years ago. Maybe he thought she had stopped loving him during the time that had passed since then.

Sitting back so she could meet his gaze, Emma put her hand on his cheek again.

"I would like that, Sam," she said. "I would like very much for us to be together."

Threading her fingers through his hair, she urged him

closer and brushed her lips lightly over his. He hesitated a moment more, his eyes searching hers. Then he bent his head and kissed her, his mouth claiming hers only briefly, but with such passion he took her breath away.

When he raised his head again, he hugged her to him for several long seconds, murmuring her name, a lingering hint of disbelief in his gruff voice. Finally, his reluctance evident, he loosened his hold on her.

"I should go back," he said. "I didn't expect to be gone so long, so I didn't leave a note for my mother. She'll be up and around soon, if she's not already, and I don't want her to worry."

Suddenly aware of her surroundings once again, Emma realized that the sun had begun its climb over the eastern horizon. The full light of a new day would be upon them soon. A day that brought with it the chance to hope and dream anew.

"Want a lift? Or would you rather jog back?" she asked, glancing up at him teasingly.

"A lift would be nice. As long it's not too far out of your way," he teased back, helping her to her feet with a minimum of awkwardness, then standing, too.

"Not at all." She brushed a few bits of grass off her skirt and ran a hand through her hair in a vain attempt to smooth her errant curls. "Why don't you give me a minute and I'll be right there. The car's open."

With a nod of understanding, Sam left her alone by Teddy's grave. She watched for a moment as he retreated, then turned back to the headstone. Kneeling again, she picked up the abandoned bouquet of roses and put it in the small metal container embedded in the grass. Against the dark gray granite, the pale yellow blooms looked radiant.

Emma smiled sadly, missing her friend as much as she

ever had. She and Teddy had shared so many joyous moments, moments that would always remain dear to her
heart.

But they had also made their fair share of mistakes. Sam,
too, for that matter. Understandable—since they'd only
been human—and unchangeable. What was done was done.
As she'd told Sam, however, Teddy would have wanted
them to get on with their lives, to finally find a little happiness.

"I love you, Teddy, and no matter what, I always will,"
Emma whispered.

Overhead, a gust of wind rustled through the tree
branches, and a single oak leaf, fresh and green, drifted
down to land in her lap. Smiling, she picked it up, then
glanced skyward.

"Thanks, friend. I needed that."

Feeling as though a great weight had been lifted from
her heart, she rose again, tucked the leaf in her pocket and
turned to join Sam where he waited by the car.

"Are you okay?" he asked, his concern for her obvious.

"Yes." She went to him, and without the slightest hesitation, put her arms around him. "I'm just fine."

"Good." He drew her close, holding her quietly for a
few moments before adding, "Ready to go home, then?"

"Ready."

They made the drive to Margaret's house in a compan-
ionable silence Emma appreciated. They had said so much,
*shared* so much, at the cemetery. She needed a little time
to collect herself, and she imagined Sam did, too.

Together, they had laid to rest the demons from their
past, and together, they had expressed their hopes for the
future. Hopes that seemed similar. But were they really?
she wondered. She supposed only time would tell.

Emma had intended to drop Sam off, then go back to her house. But when she pulled into the driveway, he turned to her and, reaching out, tucked a curl behind her ear.

"Can you stay?" he asked.

She didn't question why he wanted her there. Just knowing that having her nearby was important to him was all the reason she needed to agree.

"Sure. I'll put on a pot of coffee while you go up and take a shower."

"I think my mother has already beat you to it."

He gestured toward the porch where Margaret stood, smiling indulgently, a steaming mug in her hand.

"I see you two have been up and about for a while," she said as they joined her.

"We sort of...happened upon each other," Emma explained, giving her a hug.

She refused to go into any great detail. The time she and Sam had spent together at the cemetery was too personal to discuss. But then, from the knowing look in her friend's eyes, she probably didn't have to. She had a feeling Margaret knew exactly where they'd been and why, and that she understood.

"Yeah, we did," Sam echoed, hugging his mother, too.

"And not a moment too soon, I'd wager," she stated, her smile widening. "Now, Sam, you'd better take a shower. And, Emma, you run up to my bathroom and wash your face, then come back down and help me put breakfast on the table. We can eat as soon as Sam's ready, and after that, the three of us can choose some flowers from the garden to take to the cemetery after Mass. How does that sound?"

"Just fine," they replied in unison, then traded self-conscious smiles.

''Well, then, go on,'' she chided, shooing them toward the door. ''Time's a-wasting...''

Together, they slipped into the house and started up the stairs. Halfway up, Sam reached out and took her hand. They continued on that way until they paused outside his mother's bedroom. Then Sam gave her hand a squeeze, bent and kissed her cheek and whispered, ''Later...''

Her breath catching in her throat, Emma nodded, and reluctantly let him go.

*Chapter Fifteen*

"Do you have any plans for this evening?" Margaret asked as she took another dish from the drainer on the kitchen counter and wiped it dry with a blue-and-white-striped towel.

Standing at the sink Thursday night, rinsing the pot he had just scrubbed, Sam felt the heat of a blush climb his cheeks.

Oh, if his mother only knew, he mused, thinking of the trip to the drugstore he'd taken early that afternoon and the purchase he'd made while he was there—condoms—now tucked away in his back pocket.

Actually, she probably had a pretty good idea of what he had in mind for the hours ahead. She was no dummy. Not where he and Emma were concerned. She had proved that already.

Granted, she hadn't commented on the changes in his or

Emma's demeanor when they'd been together yesterday. But she was too savvy not to have noticed the new affinity that had sprung up between them as they'd stood together during the Mass of remembrance and again, at the cemetery, as well as later in the day, when they sat with her on the porch, recalling their fondest memories of his brother.

As if by mutual, albeit unspoken, agreement, out of respect for Teddy and the somberness of the day, they hadn't done anything...overt—no holding hands or kissing in her presence. But they had sought each other out at every turn, exchanging long, lingering, often poignant looks that she would have had to have been blind not to see.

Of course, she had all but thrown them together every chance she'd gotten the past three weeks, making her approval known, at least to him, and giving her blessing in the bargain. From the self-satisfied smile he glimpsed on her face, she had already begun to congratulate herself on a job well done.

Sam wasn't quite as certain of what the future held for him and Emma. There was no guarantee they would live happily ever after. Not with the obstacles that still stood in the way. Now, however, he had hope where none had been before, and the firm belief that nothing was impossible between two people who loved each other as they did.

"Nothing special," he answered as casually as he could, setting the pot in the drainer and washing the sudsy residue from the sink. "I thought I'd go for a walk. Maybe stop by Emma's house. Want to come along?"

"*Maybe* stop by Emma's house?" Her eyes twinkling merrily, Margaret handed him a fresh towel so he could dry his hands.

"All right, I'm *definitely* stopping by Emma's house,"

he admitted, his face warming even more. "Do you want to come along or not?"

"Not tonight, Sam. I have plans of my own already, and to be honest, I was hoping you did, too. I've invited several of my friends to come over at seven for a little penny-ante poker, and you know how rowdy we old girls can get after a few hands. I thought you'd have a much more enjoyable evening somewhere else. So you go on over to Emma's and stay as long as you want."

She winked at him mischievously as she patted him on the arm, eliciting a low groan on his part. There were times when she could be so subtle, but this didn't seem to be one of them.

"I'm not planning to be out late," he said, turning away to hang his towel on the rack alongside the counter.

"Of course you won't be *out*. You'll be at Emma's. Does she know you're coming?"

"We didn't discuss anything specific," Sam admitted.

When Emma had left last evening, her exhaustion had been evident. The day had taken as much of an emotional toll on her as it had on him. Both of them had needed a good night's sleep before they could contemplate anything further—even a few hours alone in each other's company. He hadn't wanted to press her about it then, and she'd had to work all day today. Now he felt he could finally go to her, and he was.

"She's probably home, but if she isn't expecting you, she might be out in the backyard. Sometimes she goes out to the gazebo to read in the evening, but usually she just works in the garden until it gets too dark to see. Anyway, don't worry if she doesn't answer the front door, and don't go off thinking she's not there. Check the backyard first."

"Any other instructions?" Sam asked, offering her a wry smile as he faced her again.

"Nothing I care to spell out in plain language right this minute. I'm assuming that you'll know exactly what to do once you see her, and I'm trusting that you'll do it with the consideration she deserves.

"Not all of us are lucky enough to get a second chance when it comes to love lost," she added. "Now that you've found each other again, don't let her slip away out of fear or uncertainty. As I've told Emma often enough, listen to your heart."

"I'll give it my best shot," he replied, feeling acutely uncomfortable under her penetrating gaze.

He hadn't expected her to respond quite so succinctly to what he'd meant as a teasing question. Yet he knew that everything she'd said was true.

He and Emma had been given another chance to find happiness together. While he meant to go carefully, he wasn't about to hold back completely. He had hidden his feelings for her as long as he could. Foolhardy and perhaps even painful as it might turn out to be, he was fully prepared to put his heart on the line.

Emma already knew that he cared for her. He'd told her as much yesterday morning. Tonight he hoped she would finally let him show her just how deeply. He truly believed they belonged together. Now all he had to do was convince her of it, too.

Thinking back to something *she* had said to him, as he had found himself doing at the oddest moments, he didn't think it would be difficult. *You were the one who made me feel the way a bride should feel about her groom....*

"I know you will." His mother patted his arm again, interrupting his reverie, then made a shooing motion with her hands. "Now go on and get out of here. I've got a few things to do before my guests arrive, and frankly, you're in my way."

"I guess that means you don't need my help with anything first?"

"None at all, but thanks, anyway."

"I'll see you later, then."

She eyed him askance, then shook her head with mock resignation.

"Obviously, you haven't heard a word I've been saying."

"I heard you just fine, especially the part about showing Emma consideration. In case you've forgotten, Serenity is a relatively small town."

"Well, all right. But if you come home before my guests leave, I'm afraid we're going to have to have another talk, and I'm going to be forced to use plain language, after all."

"Fair enough."

Sam gave his mother a hug, then headed out the back door, his spirits lighter than he could remember them being in a very long time.

The evening was about as fine and fair a one as could be had in the Texas hill country at the end of June. The sun had only just begun its dip toward the western horizon, giving them several hours of light yet. The heat of the day lingered, as well, but without the humidity that would make even the nights oppressive on toward August.

Dressed in shorts and a T-shirt, Sam was comfortable, even walking briskly as he was. Around him, the scent of grilling meat, the splash of sprinklers on lawns, the occasional barking of a dog or whoosh of a child whizzing by on a bike emphasized the peacefulness of his hometown in ways he could only now begin to appreciate.

He had run from there once, thinking the place had nothing to offer him, never imagining that one day it would hold everything he could ever want.

Granted, his job would take him away again eventually—take *them* away once he and Emma were married. Not far, at first, however. For which he was especially thankful.

He had been assigned temporarily to a squadron at one of the air bases outside San Antonio. That would give Emma time to adjust to life as a military wife while she was still close to home. Time, too, for her to realize that *he* wasn't as wild or irresponsible as her father and *she* wasn't as weak or cowardly as her mother.

Serenity would always be a place they'd return to. He would never ask Emma to give that up completely. But he hoped she would gradually see that wherever he came to her at the end of a day when his duties allowed—wherever they were together—was their real home.

He would plant the gardens with her, help her put down the roots she needed. And he would tend the plants as lovingly as she did so that she knew he understood. Starting with the little house he would find for her in San Antonio just as soon as she agreed to marry him.

He was going to be asking so much of her since she would be giving up her job, as well. But in return, he could vow that she'd never want for anything. He intended to be loving, faithful and true to her until the day he died, and he meant for her to know it from now on.

With his mother's admonition in mind, Sam was fully prepared for the ringing of Emma's front doorbell to go unheeded, and it did. Her car was in the driveway, though, and thanks to Margaret, he knew exactly where to seek her out.

She wasn't sitting in the gazebo, reading. Nor was she weeding one of the flower beds. Rather, she was walking slowly along the perimeter of the rose garden where they had worked together the first time he'd come to her house. With her head bent and her hands tucked in the pockets of her flowing yellow skirt, she looked oddly disconsolate.

She had her back to the gate opening into the yard, so she didn't see him come in. And lost in thought as she seemed to be, she didn't hear him as he walked toward her across the grass.

"Hey..." he called out quietly when he was still several yards away, trying, unsuccessfully, not to startle her.

She spun around to face him, her surprise evident, and then her pleasure, as well, when she smiled up at him.

"Sam..." she murmured, crossing the distance still separating them, her steps swift and light.

His heart swelling with love, he opened his arms to her, gathering her into his embrace and holding on tight, his momentary concern for her abating somewhat as she clung to him happily.

"How are you doing tonight?" he asked.

"Better now that you're here. I wasn't sure..."

Her voice trailed away, and she shook her head as if dismissing whatever she'd been about to say.

"You weren't sure about what?"

Putting his hands on her shoulders, Sam eased her back a couple of steps so he could see her face. He didn't want any uncertainty—however small or seemingly inconsequential—to come between them again.

They had bared their souls to each other yesterday, laying the first blocks in the foundation upon which he hoped they'd be able to build a lifetime. But that wouldn't be possible without the mortar of their mutual trust and honesty.

She looked up at him, smiled crookedly, shrugged and shook her head again.

"I wasn't sure you would come here tonight," she admitted at last. "And I wasn't sure you would be pleased if I came to you. After yesterday, I thought maybe you might need a little...breathing space."

"For a while last night I did. To make my final peace with the past. But from the moment I woke up this morning, all I could think about was how soon I could see you again. I almost went to the library this afternoon when I was out running errands. In fact, I had to make myself stay away. The way I was feeling, I wouldn't have been able to stop myself from stealing off with you. No matter how you protested..."

"Do you really think I would have protested?" she asked, grinning at him audaciously, obviously delighted by his revelation.

"Not the way you're looking at me now," he replied.

"You can steal me away anytime, Sam Griffin. I promise not to make a fuss."

"Are you absolutely sure? Because there's a very good chance I'm going to be tempted fairly often in the future."

"Absolutely sure."

Putting her hands on his chest, she stood on tiptoe and kissed him lightly on the chin.

That was all the encouragement Sam needed to make the first move toward assuaging his growing hunger for her. With a low moan, he bent his head, captured her luscious mouth with his and pulled her hard against him in a way that could have left no doubt in her mind of just how much he wanted her.

Sighing softly, Emma put her arms around his neck and opened her mouth for him, her tongue swirling over his, teasing him, tempting him, as she arched against him, her desire seeming to match his own.

He couldn't seem to get enough of her, standing there in the garden. He moved his hands down her back, then cupped her bottom, pressing her more firmly to him as he went on and on and on, plundering her mouth like a starving man feasting at a banquet. Nor did she hold back anything, giving and taking equally.

When he finally raised his head to gulp a breath of air, she gazed at him, a stunned look on her face.

"Why…why did you stop?" she asked after a moment, her voice unsteady.

"I was running out of oxygen, not to mention self-control," he muttered, brushing her curls away from her face. "Just in case you hadn't noticed, we're out in the middle of your backyard, it's still daylight and I'm about sixty seconds away from tumbling you onto the grass, stripping you naked and having my wicked way with you."

"Oh…" She blinked once, then again, looked around quickly as if just coming awake after a long sleep and blushed a wild shade of crimson. "Oh, Sam, maybe we'd better go in the house."

"Are you sure that's what you want, Emma? Because once we're in the house, I'm taking you straight to bed. I want to make love to you—more than I've ever wanted anything. But I don't want you to feel…rushed. If you have any doubts at all, any objections of any kind, say so now and I'll leave."

Wordlessly, she stepped out of his arms, hesitated, looked away.

For a few agonizing seconds, Sam feared he had, indeed,

pushed her too far, too fast. That with the heat of the moment passing, she was having second thoughts. Just as she had every right to do. She deserved to be wooed and courted in a gentlemanly fashion, not ravished by a man on the verge of losing all control.

But then, she met his gaze again, smiled slowly, reached out and took his hand in hers.

"I want to make love to you, too, Sam," she said, her voice whisper soft, yet filled with undeniable certainty.

Tugging on his hand, she backed toward the house a few steps, and he started after her, his heart swelling with love for her—a love he would never again have to hide.

As he came up beside her, she turned and walked more quickly across the lawn, pausing only to open, then close and lock, the back door to her house. Together, they walked through the kitchen and down the hallway, past the living room and dining room to the staircase in the entryway.

There he couldn't hold back any longer. Pulling her up short, he gathered her into his arms again and kissed her fiercely. Then, with a growl of triumph, he swept her off her feet and started up the stairs, his determined footsteps echoing in the cool, dim quiet of the house she had made her home.

## Chapter Sixteen

Emma clung to Sam as he climbed the steps, her arms around his neck, her head nestled against his shoulder, her heart fluttering in her chest with anticipation.

She had been afraid this moment would never come. Even after all that Sam had said to her at the cemetery, she hadn't believed, unequivocally, that the feelings he had confessed to having for her four years ago had survived the time and distance that had come between them since.

As the hours had passed, yesterday and again today, their odd, unplanned encounter by Teddy's grave had begun to take on an air of unreality in her mind. Gradually, she had found herself wondering if Sam's idea of *together* really was the same as hers.

Now she knew in her heart that he wanted to be with her as much as she wanted to be with him. Not necessarily forever. She had already come to terms with the impossibility of that given the differences in the kind of lives they lived—hers rooted in Serenity, his wherever duty called.

But at this moment, there was nothing to keep them apart, and that was good enough for her. They had dealt with the past, they were here together now and she refused to contemplate the future, at least for the time being.

At the top of the stairs, Sam hesitated, glancing at her questioningly.

"First doorway on the left," Emma directed, her heart-beat accelerating.

Calling herself a hopeless romantic, she had put fresh sheets on her bed and a vase of flowers on the nightstand before she left for the library that morning. She was glad she'd made the effort.

While she doubted she would have had the presence of mind to protest if Sam had tumbled her onto the grass and taken her there, she much preferred their first time to be as special as it would be in the privacy of her bedroom. The bedroom she had made ready just for him.

Enough light still filtered through the wide-slatted blinds on the windows to bathe the room in a golden glow. But as Sam stood her gently by the bed and pulled back the quilt, Emma experienced a moment of excruciating shyness that made her wish for total darkness. She wouldn't be able to hide anything from him when they made love, and she was sadly unsophisticated when it came to sexual relations.

"What?" he asked quietly, feathering a kiss on her fore-head as if he sensed her sudden hesitation.

"There's…" she began, then shrugged, not meeting his gaze. "There's so much light in here."

"All the better to see you with, my dear," he teased, nuzzling her neck as he began to unbutton her blouse. "And I want to see you, Emma. I want to see every inch of your beautiful body. More than that, I want to see the look in your eyes when I'm buried deep inside you.''

The reverence she heard in his voice chased away the last of her lingering fear. He wanted her just the way she was. And, oh, how she wanted him....

Now that they were in her bedroom, however, he didn't seem to be in quite as much of a hurry as he had out in the yard. As if he wanted to savor these moments as much as she did, he took his time unbuttoning her blouse, kissing her neck, his open mouth hot and wet against her skin. Slowly, he moved lower, trailing his lips over the swell of her breasts as he pulled her blouse wide, then laving her nipples through the silken fabric of her bra until her knees began to buckle.

Hands braced on his shoulders, she arched toward his clever mouth, her breathing ragged. Down low, deep within her, the pulsing was almost painful, yet she was sure she could never get enough of his tender ministrations. Little did she know that he had only just begun to pleasure her.

Kneeling in front of her, he rested his head against her belly. With almost maddening care, he slid his hands over her hips, down along the backs of her legs, then up again, even more slowly, under her skirt to the juncture of her thighs.

She shivered violently as his fingers found her through the chaste cotton of her panties, rubbing her, then sliding under the elastic band and gently probing. Barely able to stand, she cried out as a wave of desire sliced through her.

In an instant, Sam pulled his hand away and stood again. Hushing her murmured protest with a deep, drugging kiss, he finally made good on his promise to strip her naked, then lifted her onto the bed. His eyes hooded, his expression unreadable, he looked down at her for several long moments, his gaze skimming over her. Reaching out, he brushed her tangled curls away from her face, then smiling slowly, seductively, removed her gold-rimmed glasses and set them on the nightstand.

Quickly, he dealt with his own clothes, pausing only to take a foil packet from the back pocket of his khaki shorts.

Her vision hazy without her glasses—though not too hazy to see and appreciate the masculine beauty of Sam's body—Emma lay against the pillows, staring at him unashamedly. And when, at last, he turned back to her, she opened her arms and welcomed him into her embrace.

Again, he seemed to have regained a measure of his self-control.

"You're beautiful," he said, obviously content—at least for the moment—just to look at her.

"You, too." Smiling, she ran her hands over his chest, delighting in the play of his muscles under the satin smoothness of his bare skin.

Closing his eyes, he sighed under her touch, and with a boldness she would have never imagined she possessed, Emma reached down and traced her fingertips along the hard, throbbing length of him. She heard his breath catch in his throat an instant before his eyes opened, and then he rolled on top of her, pressing her against the mattress, his mouth claiming hers as his hands once again teased over her body.

Within a few short minutes, he had her writhing under him, panting and begging almost incoherently for the release she needed—the release only he could give her.

"Please, Sam, now," she moaned.

"Yes, *now*."

He turned from her just long enough to put on a condom, then eased himself between her legs. Braced on his forearms, his hands in her hair, he gazed down at her, his eyes holding hers. Slowly, gently, he entered her, watching her face with an intensity that touched her soul as he buried himself deep inside her.

Seeing the look in his eyes as he went still, just holding her so they could savor the pulsating heat of their union, Emma was glad for the light, after all.

"I love you, Emma," he murmured.

"And I love you, Sam."

At last, he began to move inside her, his thrusts slow and gentle at first, then faster, harder, deeper, turning almost savage as he took her higher and higher, until she finally flew over the edge.

With a soft cry that blended with Sam's guttural moan, Emma climaxed on an explosive wave of pleasure made all the more complete by Sam's own wondrously powerful release.

They lay together, legs tangled in the sheets, breathing hard for several minutes. Then, murmuring an apology, Sam shifted onto his side. Unwilling to be separated from him so soon, Emma curled against him. He pulled the bedcovers up over them and held her close.

Unexpectedly, a rush of tears burned at the backs of her eyes as she clung to him.

She loved him so much, and he had said that *he* loved *her*. More than that, he had shown her the true depth of his tenderness and regard, not only delighting her senses, but taking pleasure in it, as well. Suddenly, she found herself wanting forever, after all…forever in his arms.

But how could she have it without giving up everything else that was important to her? Was she strong enough to make a home for herself and Sam wherever the air force sent them? Did she have the courage to even try?

If, in fact, Sam asked her to. She had made her feelings about leaving Serenity pretty plain to him already....

"You're awfully quiet," he said, stroking her hair with his hand. "Not having any regrets, are you?"

Touched by the concern she heard in his voice, Emma snuggled against him more closely.

"None at all," she assured him. "What about you?"

"Being here with you makes me feel complete. I don't know exactly how to explain it, but the emptiness I've had inside me for longer than I can remember is gone now. Because of you, Emma."

"I feel that way, too, Sam."

Levering up on her elbow, she trailed kisses along the side of his neck, then nibbled at his ear, her longing for the tantalizing touch of his hands and the tempting tease of his mouth almost more than she could contain.

Only minutes ago, she had thought herself well and truly sated. Yet she was pawing him like an avaricious hussy. Luckily, he didn't seem to mind. Putting his hands on her arms, he pulled her up so he could kiss her hard on the mouth.

"Hold that thought," he muttered when he finally broke away. "I'll be right back."

Good as his word, he ducked into the bathroom and out again in under two minutes. Not long after that, he had his head between her legs, doing things with his lips and teeth and tongue she had never even begun to imagine. Things that had her bucking and moaning and crying out his name long before he was anywhere near finished with her.

Afterward, her body feeling like a mass of molten honey, she dozed in a state of giddy dissipation. And when she awoke in the darkness, she gave back to him in kind, tasting him the way he had tasted her, making *him* buck and moan and cry out *her* name.

"I'd better go," Sam said just after midnight.

When she had finished having her way with him, he had carried her into the bathroom and stood her in the shower, where they had proceeded to play all sorts of deliciously silly games involving a very sudsy bar of soap. Clean and dry, after more monkey business with the towels, they had finally gone back to her bed, snuggled close and fallen fast asleep—at least *she* had.

Sam seemed to be wide-awake. He also seemed intent on leaving her.

"Why?" Emma asked.

Her mind still muzzy, she made no move to shift the arm she'd wrapped around his waist.

"Because Serenity is a small town, and half the people on your street saw me arrive earlier. I don't want any of those same people to see me leave again in the morning."

"I don't care about that," she muttered.

"Well, I do. I don't want to give anyone a reason to disparage you in any way. Believe me, sweetheart, I don't *want* to go, but people in small towns like to gossip. You're going to be living here until I can find a home for us in San Antonio."

*A home for them in San Antonio…?*

Emma took in his last comment with an odd mixture of emotions. Joy first, because he wanted her with him when he took up his new assignment at the air base in San Antonio, followed by terror for exactly the same reason. He wanted her with him—which meant giving up her home here in Serenity to live in a strange place.

Well, not necessarily *strange,* and certainly not some

godforsaken hole-in-the-wall halfway around the world. But he could end up being transferred somewhere like that at any time.

"I don't want you to have to put up with any nonsense about why we married so quickly," he added, then pulled her closer and kissed her soundly. "You will marry me, won't you, Emma? Just as soon as possible?"

She looked up at him wordlessly, hoping he couldn't see her expression in the darkness. She had never had an easy time hiding her emotions, and at that moment, she was experiencing equal measures of shock and dismay.

"I…I don't know, Sam…." she stammered, easing away from him. "Marriage is a big step to take. We've only just found each other again…."

"I'm sorry. I didn't mean to rush you, talking about marriage—practically out of the blue," he said, contrition evident in his tone. "But I love you, and I want to be with you. I want to go to sleep at night holding you in my arms, and I want to wake up in the morning with you right there beside me. God, I've wanted that for so damned long, I guess I got a little carried away.

"You're right, though. We should take it slow, talk about it. Talk about a lot of things like we've never had a chance to do. But at least say you'll think about my proposal, Emma. Please…"

"I don't imagine I'm going to be able to think about anything else," she admitted ruefully.

"Good."

He kissed her again, then slipped out of bed, switched on a lamp and gathered his clothes from the floor. He pulled on his briefs and stepped into his shorts, then glanced at her and asked, "Are you working tomorrow?"

"No, I'm off. Marion has something to do Saturday, so I traded days with her."

Lying back against her pillow, Emma watched Sam dress with a growing sense of sadness. She didn't want him to leave her. But the only way they could be together the way she wanted was if she married him. Then her whole life would be turned upside down.

Just as her mother's had been...

"Do you have any plans?"

"I thought I'd mow the lawn."

"How about if I come over and give you a hand?"

"All right," she agreed, focusing on the here and now.

She had over a week before Sam had to report for duty in San Antonio. He wouldn't expect an answer from her before that. In fact, she would probably be able to put him off even longer. He wasn't going to be all that far away. He would be able to come home whenever he had a few days off. They could be together then.

He had already admitted that she deserved time to consider his proposal, and she intended to take as much as she needed. She had to be sure of what she needed, as well as what she wanted.

She *wanted* Sam in her life, *wanted* to plan a future with him, make a home and have a family. But she *needed* Serenity and the security it had afforded her almost from the first day she'd arrived. And as far as she could see, she couldn't at the same time have what she wanted and what she still believed she needed.

"Do you have a back-door key I can borrow so I can lock up on my way out?"

Now fully dressed, Sam sat down beside her on the bed again.

"I have a back-door key you can keep," she replied,

modestly holding the quilt over her bare breasts as she sat up. "It's in the glass tray on top of the dresser. Feel free to come visit anytime."

"I'd rather be more than a visitor." He offered her a lopsided grin, then leaned toward her, threaded his fingers through her hair and kissed her on the cheek.

"You *are*, Sam," she insisted, capturing his face in her hands and brushing her lips over his. "Much, much more."

"I hope I am, and always will be." He hugged her close, then stood again. "What time tomorrow?"

"About eight o'clock. We can't fire up the lawn mower before then or the neighbors will complain. But if we wait any later, it'll be blazing hot before we're even half finished."

"I'll be here at eight, then."

With obvious reluctance, he turned and started toward the door.

Emma had to fight the urge to call him back. He would come. She had no doubt of that. But it wouldn't be fair to him. He was willing to give her time. In return, she was going to have to live with the distance he had every right to impose.

He paused in the doorway and glanced back at her, but said nothing more. A few moments later, she heard his footsteps on the stairs, and a few moments after that, the sound of the back door closing.

Switching off the bedside lamp, she slid under the bedcovers and reached for the pillow Sam had used. Cradling it in her arms, she closed her eyes and breathed in his scent. She could almost imagine he was still there.

Except imagining wasn't good enough anymore....

## Chapter Seventeen

Six weeks, Sam thought as he guided his newly purchased car along the all too familiar road that connected San Antonio to Serenity, Texas. Six weeks and Emma had yet to accept his proposal, much less set a wedding date.

He was growing more and more hesitant to give her an ultimatum, too. He was afraid she would turn him down flat and he'd lose her for good.

The way things were, he could have a few days with her whenever he was off duty. And she was still willing to discuss possibilities.

She had even come to San Antonio twice since he'd been there. Once so he could show her around the air base and introduce her to some of his fellow officers and their wives, and again just two weeks ago to look at three houses he had found in one of the nice neighbourhoods that featured older homes with larger, lovely yards and gardens. One house in particular had seemed to catch her fancy, but he had sensed that she was holding back, not yet ready to take what would amount to the first step toward a permanent commitment.

While Sam couldn't honestly say Emma seemed any happier with their current situation than he was, she did seem content to let things ride. And since he had jumped the gun once already the first night they'd made love, obviously spooking the hell out of her, he had schooled himself to be patient.

He would never forget the look of terror that had flashed in her eyes as he laid out his plans for them. In a giddy rush of excitement and anticipation, he'd been so eager to make her his bride. He had completely disallowed the tragic unhappiness of her childhood and her resulting need for the kind of security she had found only when she'd put down roots in Serenity.

Mistakenly, he had believed that after the way she'd made love with him, giving all of herself with such joyous abandon, she would be as anxious as he was to take the next step. A step that would bind them together not only as friends and lovers, but also as husband and wife.

He hadn't factored in the reservations she would have— reservations so ingrained after years of fending for herself that setting them aside for love alone might not be possible for her to do.

Emma loved him. Sam believed that with all his heart, whether she said the words aloud or not. And she *did* say the words—every chance she had, with a fervency he couldn't deny.

Trusting him was another matter altogether, though, and trust was the one thing she had in all too short supply. Considering the kind of life she had been forced to lead before she landed in a foster home in Serenity, Sam could understand why. Unfortunately, cognizance hadn't helped him much when it came to finding a solution to the problem.

How could he convince her that he wasn't like her father if she wouldn't give him the chance? Yet why would she give him the chance when it meant giving up everything else that seemed to matter to her?

Only by risking the eventual abandonment she seemed to fear most would she finally come to realize he'd never leave her willingly. There was no other way he could prove that to her. Not as far as he could see.

Talk about being caught in a conundrum...

He couldn't guarantee he would always be there for her. He was a major in the United States Air Force, and as such, he might not always have the choice. Training, war games and peacekeeping missions around the world could take him away at the most inopportune times, often with little advance warning. With saber rattling starting up in eastern Europe again, such a possibility loomed ahead of him that very moment.

What he *could* guarantee was that, until the day he died, she would be the most important person in his life, and he would come home to her—wherever their home happened to be—every possible chance that he could.

He wasn't shiftless or wild. Contrary to popular opinion, he never really had been. And he'd slaked any thirst he'd had for daredevil adventuring long ago. He wanted and needed safety and security, too. The kind of safety and security he found each and every time Emma put her arms around him and held him close.

Sadly, he'd begun to think that—short of giving up his

career—convincing her of his true nature was going to be almost impossible.

Sam had considered leaving the air force more than once over the past few weeks. But what other kind of work could he do that would be any different? He was a highly trained military aviator. All he knew was flying, and any job piloting a plane, whether for an airline or a cargo company, would take him away from Serenity.

Turning his back on his military commitment only to fly commercially didn't make sense to him. First and foremost, he had a duty to repay the investment the government had made in him. He couldn't walk away from that just yet. And, in all honesty, he loved flying for the air force. He was damned good at it, and his skills were sorely needed.

Five years from now, he'd be eligible for retirement. Maybe then he could contemplate a change. But even that he couldn't promise Emma in good conscience.

Heaving a sigh of utter frustration, Sam drove past the Serenity city-limit sign and turned toward his mother's house. He had been later than he'd anticipated getting away from the air base that Friday evening so he had already missed dinner with her and Emma. In fact, late as it was, Emma had more than likely gone back to her house by now.

Driving into town, he was partly tempted to go straight to Bay Leaf Lane and lose himself in her arms. Margaret would understand, probably even approve. But for the first time since he'd moved to San Antonio, he was also oddly reluctant.

He needed Emma's love to make him feel complete. But he also needed her trust, and though he knew why she was unable to give it to him just yet, that inability had also begun to take an emotional toll on him.

Sam wasn't sure how much longer he could go on the

way he had, leaving her bed halfway through the night—
on the *few* nights they actually had together. He had always
prided himself on being an honorable man. Lately, however, there had been times when he'd felt downright con-
temptible as he'd crept out of her house and scurried away
in the dark.

Emma *had* gone back to her house, but letting himself
in the front door, Sam saw his mother waiting for him in
the living room. Already dressed for bed in a nightgown
and robe, she sat on the sofa, a book open in her lap. As
he crossed the room, she stood and greeted him with a
warm hug and a cheerful smile.

She had just begun the second four-week round of the
drug treatment Dr. Rozan had prescribed, and so far, all her
blood tests had come back negative, indicating her leukemia was still in remission. She had also gained a little
weight, and her energy levels were up—both encouraging
signs.

"I wasn't sure you'd stop by here first," she said. "Are
you hungry? I've got fried chicken and potato salad, left
over from dinner, in the refrigerator."

"Thanks, but I grabbed a sandwich on my way out of
town."

"Well, then, I suppose you're anxious to see Emma."

Sam shrugged, then slumped on the sofa, avoiding her
inquisitive gaze.

"What's wrong?" she prodded, getting straight to the
point, as always.

He shrugged again, tossing his keys from hand to hand,
unsure exactly how to respond. He didn't want to burden
her with his problems. He was a grown man, after all. He
should be capable of finding his own solutions. But her

wisdom and guidance had gotten him through a lot of tough times in the past.

"Something to do with those so-called freedom fighters in eastern Europe stirring up trouble again?" she continued. "On the news tonight there was talk of putting on another show of military force to send them scampering back to their respective holes."

Sam eyed her in surprise. She was right. His concern about his relationship with Emma had increased in intensity as the political upheaval in eastern Europe had escalated over the past few days. There was a good possibility he could be reassigned to his former squadron and on his way back to Italy at a moment's notice.

With Emma here in Serenity, he could be forced to say goodbye to her over the telephone. There would be no telling when he would be back, and when he finally did return, he would have to start all over again, trying to gain her trust. Only by then, it would be even more difficult. He would have already abandoned her in just the way she feared most.

"How did you guess?" he asked at last.

"After the news report ended, Emma looked just like you do now. She went outside for a while, and although she insisted she was all right when she came in again, I could tell she'd been crying."

"You know, I've been racking my brain, trying to find a way to convince her to marry me, but maybe I should just let it go. Much as I hate to admit it, I have to be the last man on earth she needs in her life." The thought of her weeping at the mere possibility he'd be called to combat duty was almost more than Sam could bear. Standing, he paced across the room, paused and angrily eyed the silver-framed photographs on the mantel. "She needs somebody like Teddy. Somebody who won't just up and leave her—''

"Oh, piddle," Margaret cut in, her tone equally harsh. "If memory serves, your brother was prepared to up and leave her—more prepared, I'll wager, than *you* will ever be.

"Emma doesn't need a man like that. She needs the man she loves—the same man who loves her enough to tear himself apart at the thought of causing her pain. She needs *you,* Sam Griffin, and don't you ever doubt it."

"But not enough to trust me. She looks at me, sees her no-good father and remembers what he did to her mother."

"So you're going to let *that* keep you apart? I would have thought you'd be all the more determined to prove to her you're not the fickle type. That you, of anyone, would have the persistence to gain her confidence. That no matter how often she retreats, you would keep on advancing, slowly but surely, heart in hand, until she stops turning away.

"Of course, if you don't really love her as much as I suspect... Well, then, yes...by all means, go ahead and give up on her."

Was that what he wanted? To give up on Emma?

He would never be able to see her again. Never be able to hold her or touch her. Never hear her laughter or see her smile or—God help him—kiss away her tears. Never plant another rosebush with her. And never, ever put their baby down to sleep in the crib she kept hidden away...

"No," he muttered, raking a hand through his hair. "I can't do that. Can't...give up on her."

"I didn't think so."

"I...I think I'll go on over to her house now."

"You do that, son."

Coming up beside him, she patted his arm consolingly.

"Any plans for tomorrow?" he asked, smiling down at her as he slipped an arm around her shoulders.

"I thought maybe we could drive up to Inks Lake in the afternoon and have a picnic supper," she replied, walking with him to the front door. "It's been years since I've been there. I hear they have canoes for rent now. Very romantic—canoeing across a lake on a summer evening."

"Sounds good to me. See you in the morning."

Drawing back, she eyed him critically.

"Not before noon."

"All right. Not before noon," he agreed, smiling at *her* persistence.

Sam walked to Emma's as he always did, but tonight he did so with renewed faith. He had waited so long for her already, and he had never been a quitter. He would wear her down eventually in the best way he knew how—by coming back to her again and again and again until she no longer doubted the integrity of his purpose.

He saw that her house was dark as he headed down her street. She had probably given up on him and gone to bed already. That was fine with him. He liked the idea of crawling under the quilt with her and kissing her awake—liked it quite a lot.

He was so deeply into his fantasy of rousing her—all warm and soft and sleepy—that he started with surprise when he stepped into her kitchen and saw her sitting in the alcove.

"Sam…?" she murmured as she stood.

"I thought you'd gone to bed."

"No…"

She hesitated a moment longer, then flew across the room, into his waiting arms.

"I...I was afraid you wouldn't come tonight," she said, her voice choked with tears.

"Emma, sweetheart, don't cry," he soothed, cursing himself for the worry he'd caused her. "It took me longer to get away than I expected it would when I called earlier. Then I stopped by my mother's house. She was still up, and we talked a while. But I'm here now."

"I missed you so much the past ten days."

"I missed you, too."

"Make love to me, Sam. Right here, right now," she pleaded, her hands fumbling with the snap of his jeans.

"Oh, no." He caught her hands in his, stilling them, then swung her into his arms. "I've waited ten impossibly long, impossibly lonely nights to be with you again. I intend to take my time with you, upstairs, in our bed."

Making good on his word, Sam did just that, showing Emma—in ways she couldn't deny even if she tried—just how much she meant to him.

When at last they were both completely sated and their breathing had finally returned to normal, Sam drew the bedcovers up over them and curled around her protectively.

"You said *our* bed," she ventured into the silence after a while.

"Mmm, yes. Any objections?"

"No..." She nestled closer to him, her bottom tucked up against him, spoon style, and covered the hand he'd splayed over her belly with one of her own. "Are you going to sleep?"

"Not if you don't want me to." Smiling, he nuzzled the back of her neck with his lips.

"What I...what I want...is for you to stay with me tonight," she murmured. "I don't care who knows. I want to wake up with you in the morning."

"I don't know, Emma," he teased gently. "That could be habit forming."

"I know," she acknowledged, her voice soft as a whisper. "So...will you?"

"Well, if you insist..."

"Mmm, I most certainly do."

Sam had tried to be a gentleman, but it hadn't worked in his favor. In fact, leaving Emma in the middle of the night could very well have reinforced her basic fear. Now he was ready to pull out all the stops.

He wanted her to see just how good it could be between them—tonight, tomorrow and always. He wanted her to be able to turn to him in the darkness, to reach out and know that he was there.

He had her love, but he was also determined to win her trust. As far as he was concerned, anything less would be unacceptable.

## Chapter Eighteen

The telephone on Emma's desk rang late on a Thursday afternoon, almost two weeks after Sam's most recent trip to Serenity. Reaching over a stack of books and a scattering of papers, she grabbed the receiver. Her attention still on the requisition form she was filling out, she issued a brisk, businesslike greeting.

"Good afternoon. Serenity Public Library. Emma Dalton speaking."

"Emma, it's Sam."

Startled, she dropped her pen and clutched the receiver more tightly, a sudden, inexplicable sense of dread pooling in the pit of her stomach. Sam never called her at the library. At least, he never had until today.

Her first thought was of his mother. Had something happened to her? But surely, if that were the case, *she* would have been contacted before Sam. Not only was she right there in town, but most people in Serenity were also aware of her special relationship with Margaret Griffin.

Then Emma thought of the nightly news reports detailing possible military deployments to help curb the upheaval in eastern Europe, and the odd, almost detached way in which Sam had spoken. As if he'd already braced himself to deliver bad news.

Dread turned to ice-cold, numbing fear as she drew a shaky breath. She knew why he had called—knew with painful certainty what he had to tell her. He had tried to prepare her for the possibility when they'd been together, but she hadn't wanted to listen to what he'd had to say.

Hadn't wanted to believe that he would leave her, after all…

"Still there?" he asked, reminding her of how long she'd gone without acknowledging him.

"Yes, I'm here," she said, her voice quavering. "Is…is something wrong?"

"I'm sorry, Emma," he began. "Sorry I have to tell you over the telephone. I'm being sent back to Italy. We're flying out tonight."

"Tonight…?"

Bad enough that he was leaving her, but how could he do it on such short notice? Again, she admitted that he'd tried to warn of that possibility, as well, and again, she had refused to pay attention.

"I'm not going to have time to come to Serenity. I'm going to be in briefings until early evening. Then I have to pack my gear." He paused, drew an audibly ragged breath. "God, I wish you were here.…"

She could be, Emma realized, glancing at the clock on the wall. She could jump in her car, drive like crazy and be waiting for him at his apartment. He'd given her a key. She could let herself inside and...what?

Watch him pack his bags and go?

How many times had she and her mother watched her father do just that?

Too many times for her to want to go through a repeat performance now.

"Well, I'm not," she answered, sounding so matter-of-fact that she surprised herself.

"Believe me, Emma, I don't want to leave you like this, but it's—"

"Your job?" she finished for him. "I know that, Sam, and I understand."

"Do you?" he demanded, anger now underlying his tone. "Do you honestly understand why I have to go? Or do you think I'm simply running out on you, just like your father ran out on your mother?"

She hesitated a moment, surprised by how close he'd come to the truth. He knew her so well. But then, she'd told him her worst fears, hadn't she? Now he was throwing them back in her face.

"Have you talked to *your* mother yet?" she asked, refusing to acknowledge his gibe.

He didn't respond for several seconds. Then, in a tone just as terse as hers, he said, "I'm going to call her now, but I'd really appreciate it if you'd look in on her later, as well. That is, if it's not too much trouble."

"Of course it isn't any trouble," she hastened to assure him. Suddenly feeling mollified, she added, "I...I don't suppose you know how long you'll...you'll be gone."

"No idea at all. Goodbye, Emma. Take care."

Before she could say anything more, Emma heard a sharp click followed closely by the insistent beep-beep-

beep of the dial tone. With a mixture of shock and outrage, she stared at the receiver, slowly realizing that Sam had hung up on her.

"Well, fine. Be that way," she muttered darkly as she cradled the offending instrument.

Riding high on the crest of her seemingly righteous indignation, she made it through the rest of the day, though she would have been hard-pressed to say exactly what she accomplished had anyone asked. All she really remembered doing was shuffling papers and thumbing through books rather mindlessly.

By the time she climbed into her hot, sticky car at six-thirty, however, she was beginning to experience the first stirring of bitter regret.

She loved Sam. Loved him with all her heart and soul. But she hadn't bothered to tell him. Instead, she had treated him like her worst enemy, blaming him for something that wasn't his fault.

She had reacted in a childish, stupid way, giving up a chance to see him one more time before he left simply *because* he was leaving. She had totally disregarded the fact that he wasn't taking off on a whim. Nor was he bored with her or indifferent to her needs.

He had a job to do—a job that gave him a sense of pride and fulfillment. And he was going off to do it. Reluctantly, because *he* loved *her.* Yet more dutifully than a lesser man would.

She should have been proud of him, and she should have taken the chance she'd had to let him know it. Had she not been so angry, so spiteful, she could have been there with him. She could have held him in her arms and kissed him so that when he finally left, it was with the taste of her on his mouth.

At Margaret's house, Emma parked in the driveway, trudged up to the front porch and rang the bell. Her friend came to the door almost immediately.

"I was sure you'd change your mind and go to San Antonio, after all," she said by way of greeting.

"No." Emma moved past her slowly. "I should have, but I…" She sat on the sofa and stared at her hands. "I really blew it," she finished at last.

"Well, yes, it does seem that way. Happens to the best of us, though."

"So what do I do now?"

"As I see it, you have two choices. You can wallow in self-pity or you can set about making things right between you and Sam before he gets on that transport plane tonight. Unfortunately, he called again about fifteen minutes ago. He's leaving earlier than originally planned, so you'll have to do it over the phone. Not the best way to make amends, but better than nothing."

"I'm not sure he'll even listen to me now."

"Maybe not, but don't you think it's worth a try?"

"Yes…yes, I do," Emma admitted. Standing again, she started toward the door. "I'd rather call from home, but I can come back…after…"

"Don't worry about me, dear. I'll be all right. You take care of your needs tonight—yours and Sam's. I'll talk to you again tomorrow."

At her house, Emma headed straight for the telephone. She dialed the number of Sam's apartment from memory, her hands shaking, her heart pounding with anxiety.

He had every right to be furious with her, and no doubt, he was. But she couldn't let him go thinking she cared so little for him—

The fourth ring was cut off by the answering machine.

Emma frowned uncertainly, tempted to hang up. Was it possible he'd already been there and gone again? She hadn't thought to ask Margaret exactly when his flight was due to leave, but it was almost seven now.

She had so much to say to him. How could she do it in a sixty-second message—a message he might not get for weeks? Of course, he might not have made it home yet. Or he might actually be there now, but unable to come to the phone.

At the sound of the beep, Emma drew a quick, steadying breath.

"Sam, it's Emma. It's seven o'clock Thursday night. I'm home, and I...I really need to talk to you, to tell you how...sorry I am for the way I behaved earlier. So...please call me...if you can. I love you."

She hung up the receiver and hurried upstairs to change out of her skirt and blouse. Eyeing the telephone on the nightstand as if that alone would make it ring, she pulled on shorts and a T-shirt.

In the kitchen again, she opened the refrigerator door and stared at the half-empty shelves. She had planned to stop at the grocery store on her way home to stock up for the weekend when Sam would be there. Now that wouldn't be necessary.

She risked a glance at the clock on the wall—7:25. Where was he? Already on the transport plane? Or at the apartment, packing his gear, still too angry to talk to her?

Crossing to the pantry, she pulled out a bag of chips, then put them back, her roiling stomach rebelling at the idea of eating anything.

She eyed the phone on the counter, glanced at the clock again—7:40 now—then paced to the alcove and sat in one of the chairs by the table, for all of two minutes. Up again, she moved to the sink, took a glass from the cabinet, ran water into it.

As she shut off the faucet, the sudden, shrill ring of the telephone jolted through her. She dropped the glass in the sink, luckily without breaking it. Her heart racing, she spun around and ran across the kitchen, her bare feet slapping against the linoleum.

She grabbed the receiver on the third ring, then nearly dropped it.

"Hello," she said at last, a catch in her voice.

"Emma, are you all right?"

*Sam...thank God...it was Sam.*

"I...I was just running to...to get the phone," she stammered. "I didn't want to...didn't want to..." Unexpectedly, her eyes filled with tears, and she paused to swallow a sob. "Sam, I'm so sorry. I should have been there with you. I *could* have been there if only I hadn't been so foolish."

"Emma, sweetheart, it's all right."

"No, it's not," she insisted. "I acted like you were committing some kind of horrible crime when all you were doing was your job. But I couldn't face the thought of you going away. You were right. I was thinking of my father, but you're not like him. You're a decent, honorable man. I love you and I'm going to miss you so much, but I didn't even bother to tell you—"

"Tell me now, Emma," he cut in, his tone firm yet gentle.

"I love you, Sam. I love you with all my heart. And I'm going to miss you so much."

"I love you, too. And I'm going to miss you every hour of every day until I'm home again. You'll be waiting for me, won't you, Emma? Because I *am* coming home to you just as soon as possible.''

"Yes, Sam, I'll be waiting for you."

"I'll be in touch once I get settled in my quarters at the air base. You have Internet access and E-mail on that fancy computer of yours at the library, don't you?''

"Yes," she admitted, frowning thoughtfully.

"Good. So do I. Got a pen handy?''

He gave her his E-mail address, then jotted down hers.

"We'll be able to talk every day," she said, smiling for the first time that evening.

No matter where in the world Sam went, linked as they would be by the magic of cyberspace, it wouldn't seem like he was quite so far away.

"It won't be as nice as hearing your voice, but it will most definitely be the next-best thing.''

"Yes, it will," she agreed.

"Well, I'd better get going," he advised with obvious reluctance. "My flight is scheduled to depart in about an hour.''

"I love you," she said, wanting to be sure, one more time, that he knew it. "So very much…''

"And I love you," he, too, repeated, a noticeable catch in his voice. "See you soon.''

"Yes, soon…''


For a day or so after Sam left, Emma moped around the house, generally feeling sorry for herself. But then, she found the first of what would be many E-mail messages from him waiting for her when she logged on to the Internet.

He had arrived safely at the air base in northern Italy, he missed her more than ever and oh, by the way, would she mind going over to San Antonio every now and then while he was away, maybe with Margaret, to check on his apartment and take his car out for a drive? There was an extra set of car keys in a kitchen drawer. He'd appreciate it so much.

Emma had assured him she didn't mind at all. In fact, she was glad he'd asked. With one reason to go to San Antonio, others soon came to mind.

Gradually, as one week became two, then three, she found herself thinking more and more of how she wanted her life to be when Sam returned, and began taking steps— albeit *baby* steps—toward that end.

The first weekend she drove to San Antonio, Margaret went with her. They had planned to stay only one night, but ended up staying two nights instead. Taking Sam's car, they went exploring one afternoon, ending up in the neighborhood where she and Sam had looked at houses earlier in the summer.

The one Emma had liked was no longer on the market, but she saw another with a For Lease sign that looked equally promising. Without examining her motives too closely, she pulled over to the curb and jotted down the number of the real-estate agency listing the property while Margaret nodded her approval.

The following day, they stopped at a nearby nursery and bought a variety of indoor and outdoor plants to liven up the interior of Sam's rather sterile furnished apartment, as well as the bare balcony.

Nesting, Emma thought, without any great surprise. Maybe she had some sort of natural instinct for turning a house, or a barren apartment, into a home. Considering the kind of future she now had in mind, she certainly hoped so.

On her second trip to San Antonio, this time on her own, since Margaret had already made plans with several of her friends, Emma took along some of her favorite coffee mugs, a few books and CDs, and a brightly colored quilt for Sam's bed. On that trip, she also looked at houses again, venturing into a couple of other neighborhoods the real-estate agent recommended.

Prior to her third trip—made over a couple of weekdays since she had to work over the weekend—she called one of the officers' wives she had met through Sam. At Emma's suggestion, they met for lunch, along with several of the other wives. Their candid conversation about life "in the military" was fascinating, as well as a bit frightening.

They all seemed to be surviving quite nicely, though, their good humor and their years-long marriages intact. Their overall camaraderie and their obvious concern for each other's well-being, especially while their husbands were away, was reassuring, as well.

Emma realized that there would always be other women nearby who would not only understand what she was going through, but also offer their support whenever Sam couldn't be there for her.

On that third trip, Emma also checked out job prospects at the various libraries around town. Several positions were currently available and others would be opening up in the near future. She shouldn't have any trouble finding work if she wanted it, and that, too, was reassuring.

During the time Sam was away, Margaret also had her scheduled appointment with Dr. Rozan. There was more good news from him. Margaret's leukemia remained in re-mission. She could go off the drug she'd been taking for two months, then the doctor would see her again and decide if further treatment was necessary.

On the drive back to Serenity, Emma was elated. Margaret, too, seemed very pleased. Yet she had also prepared for less-heartening news in a way meant to lessen any burden on Emma and Sam.

"I want you to know that I've found someone who can come and stay with me in the event I take a turn for the worse," she announced in a matter-of-fact tone. "You and Sam are going to have enough adjusting to do without worrying about me. I know I can count on you in a crisis, but when minor problems arise, I want to be able to manage on my own without depending on your help."

"But—" Emma began, ready to protest.

"No *but*s, Emma. Callie Miller is just the person to enable me to do that. She's a retired nurse who's recently lost her husband. I met her at one of the senior socials at St. Mary's a few months ago, and we got to talking—found out we had a lot in common. Occasionally, she does some private nursing to supplement her income, and I can certainly afford to pay her."

Aware of how determined Margaret was to give her and Sam the opportunity to be together wherever he was stationed, Emma didn't argue with her.

As had been expected, political pressure from neighboring countries, combined with an increased threat of military strikes, brought the crisis in eastern Europe to a reasonably swift conclusion. To Emma's relief, use of deadly force proved to be unnecessary. Not a single U.S. serviceman was killed, and six weeks after Sam's departure, his return seemed imminent.

For the most part, Emma was prepared.

She had tentatively given notice at the library, recommending Marion Cole for her position. Since her husband had found work in Serenity, they would be staying in town, after all.

Emma had also talked to Father Langley at St. Mary's. She couldn't set an exact date for her and Sam to be married yet, but she had put the kindly old priest on alert. His obvious happiness for them had truly warmed her heart.

All she had left to do was make a decision about her house. Selling it outright was hard for her to contemplate. She and Sam wouldn't be buying a house of their own for a while yet. His assignment in San Antonio had come about as a result of a request he'd made because of Margaret's illness, and would be temporary at best.

They didn't need the money a sale would bring for a down payment on another property. But hanging on to her house, especially if she couldn't find a dependable tenant, could end up being more trouble than it was worth.

Her dilemma was solved by chance. A letter arrived from Megan Cahill. She, too, had lived in the same foster home as Emma and Jane, and like Jane, had left years ago, never to return. The last Emma had heard from her, almost a year ago, she had been living in San Diego with her husband and young son.

Now it seemed Megan was returning to Serenity, alone, and was in need of a house to rent. While worry for her old friend's misfortune—though Megan hadn't elaborated, she and her husband were separating—Emma saw a solution to her own problem.

Megan could live in *her* house for a nominal rent, giving Emma and Sam time to decide on a final means of disposition sometime in the future.

Sam called at last, early on a Monday morning, with the news Emma had been longing to hear.

"I'm scheduled to depart on a flight out tomorrow morning. Actually, late tonight your time,'' he advised without preamble.

''I'll be waiting for you,'' she promised, her voice husky.

''Flight time is about fourteen hours, so I probably won't be able to make it to Serenity until sometime Wednesday afternoon. I'll have to stop by the apartment first, get cleaned up...''

''No problem.''

Smiling sleepily, she thought of how surprised he was going to be when he got to the apartment. She hadn't told him half of what she'd been up to in his absence.

''I'd better go,'' he said. ''Love you.''

''Me, too. See you soon.''

Her smile widening, Emma hung up the receiver, then tossed the bedcovers aside, ready to set in motion her own very special plan for Sam's welcome home.

## Chapter Nineteen

By the time Sam collected his gear and caught a ride to his apartment, it was almost three in the morning. He had managed to doze, off and on, during the interminably long flight, but never for any extended period of time. He'd kept having erotic dreams about Emma—dreams that brought him awake in a painful state of arousal.

Maybe after a hot shower and something to eat—he *did* have canned soup and crackers in a cabinet at the apartment, didn't he?—he would be able to get a few hours' sleep before he headed for Serenity. Tired as he was, he didn't dare get on the road just yet.

From the outside, his apartment looked deserted—the front windows dark, the blinds closed. But as Sam let himself in the door, he paused uncertainly. Even though his key had fit the lock, he glanced at the number on the door, just to be sure he hadn't wandered into the wrong place by mistake.

A lamp burned in the living room, casting a warm, welcoming glow over what had been a basically characterless room when he'd left six weeks ago. Now a vase of fresh flowers and a scattering of books and magazines graced the coffee table. A quilt he'd never seen before had been tucked over the back of the sofa, and there were several silver-framed photographs on the end table.

Someone had been there while he was gone, and he had a good idea who. But where was she now?

Down off the hallway to his right, he could see that another lamp had been left burning in his bedroom. Quietly, he closed the door and locked it, set his bags on the floor, then started down the hallway, his heartbeat quickening with sudden anticipation.

She was lying on his bed, sound asleep, her glasses and an open book beside her, another quilt, similar to the one on the sofa, tucked around her. She wore a pale yellow sleeveless nightgown that nearly matched the roses in the bowl on the nightstand, and her red curls tumbled over the white-linen-and-lace pillowcase—another new addition—in a silky, begging-to-be-touched tangle.

Sam leaned against the doorjamb and closed his eyes, overwhelmed by what she had done for him. With her own distinctive touches, she had made a home for him, and she had come there to wait for him just as she'd promised.

Despite their constant communication while he had been gone, he'd had some reservations about how she'd greet his homecoming. He had been fully prepared to start again, building up her confidence in him. Now that seemed wholly unnecessary.

Straightening, he moved across the carpeted floor as silently as he could. He didn't want to disturb her until he'd had a chance to clean up. Then he intended to wake her slowly, gently, lovingly....

Sam should have known the sound of the shower running, even muffled as it was by the closed bathroom door, would probably wake Emma, and she wouldn't hesitate to join him.

Still, the slide of the glass shower door caught him off guard. Startled, he turned away from the steaming spray as she stepped into the narrow enclosure, wearing nothing but a smile, and suddenly, she was in his arms, clinging to him, kissing him fiercely.

In those first passionate moments, Sam thought of nothing but their mating, raw and wild. As he lifted her up, her legs wrapped around his waist, and he entered her with one swift, deep thrust. She uttered a soft cry, burying her face against his neck, and moved convulsively.

Unable to hold back, Sam drove into her hard, fast, finding his release at almost the same instant Emma found hers. Still holding her locked to him, he sagged against the tile wall, breathing hard as he shut off the water.

"Welcome home," she murmured, her lips moving deliciously against his earlobe.

"Oh, yeah," he growled. "You can say that again."

"What I'd really like is to *do* it again."

"In bed, this time. Slow and sweet and gentle, the way I planned originally."

Only when they were snuggled close under the bedcovers did Sam realize he hadn't even *thought* about protection.

"You know," he began hesitantly, "I didn't have a condom handy in there."

"I know," she answered much too blithely.

"How do you feel about the possibility of an unplanned pregnancy?"

"I'm open to it, although the timing's not quite right," she answered without seeming to have to think twice. "What about you?"

"I'd like for us to be married first."

"Me, too."

"When?" he pressed, holding his breath.

"I've talked to Father Langley. He'll marry us whenever we're ready. All I have to do is give him a day and time."

"What about you, Emma? Are you sure *you're* ready?"

"Well, I've had my dress for over a week now, I've given my notice at the Serenity Public Library and I've found a house for lease I think you'll like." She paused, frowning slightly, and levered up on an elbow. "I'm not rushing you, am I?" she asked.

"Rushing me?" Sam laughed out loud, then grabbed her and hugged her hard. "Have I told you how much I love you?"

"Not since you've been home."

"I love you, Emma Dalton, with all my heart and soul."

Almost two weeks later, on a crisp, clear Saturday morning in late October, Sam left his mother's house, his heart filled with anticipation. Wearing his dress uniform, he climbed into his car and started toward St. Mary's Church. At the corner, however, he turned in another direction. He had plenty of time before the ceremony was scheduled to begin, and there was somewhere he needed to go first.

There was little activity at Mount Grace Cemetery that morning. A few others were out, putting flowers on graves, but no one glanced his way as he drove past.

Sam parked the car and walked the short distance to Teddy's grave. Immediately, he saw the flowers at the base of the granite headstone. Chrysanthemums from Emma's garden, he realized. Blooms of bronze and gold and buttery yellow tied with a wide ivory satin ribbon.

She must have come earlier, he realized, his heart swelling with love for her. Today of all days, she would remember Teddy, just as he was.

He stood quietly for several moments, his thoughts skimming from past tragedy, to present happiness, to the future stretching ahead, bright and full of promise.

"I wish you could be with us today," Sam said at last. "I know how happy you'd be that we're together...."

He took a step back, tears burning his eyes. Then, straightening his shoulders and standing at attention, he saluted smartly, turned on his heel and walked back to the car.

A short while later, Sam stood at the altar, his gaze roving over the people filling the church pews. His mother beamed at him proudly, as did her many friends. Emma's co-workers from the library and some of his fellow officers and their families were there, as well. Even Jane and Max Hamilton, along with their son, Blair, and their butler, Calvin Kerner, had come to celebrate the day with them.

Somehow, their small, intimate wedding had grown out of all proportion, but he didn't mind. He'd have Emma all to himself soon enough.

Emma...

At the sound of the organ's first triumphant notes, Sam looked toward the back of the church. Slowly, she started down the aisle toward him, her lovely ivory satin dress, simple yet elegant, swirling around her ankles, her lustrous curls caught up in a gold-and-pearl clip.

She met his gaze unwaveringly, her eyes luminous, her smile wide and radiant.

Emma...*his* Emma...for now and always...

## Chapter Twenty

"Here's a nice one, Maggie," Emma said, bending forward and snipping a delicate, long-stemmed, pink rose from the bush she and Sam had planted almost two years ago when they'd moved into this house in North Carolina.

"A *really* nice one, Mommy," Maggie crowed, holding out the basket she carried. "Now we have *three*. That's how many I am—*three*."

"Yes, you are. Three years old already." Beaming at her young daughter, her paternal grandmother's namesake, Emma ruffled her silky red curls. "What a big girl."

"And a big *sister*," the child added, patting Emma's expanding tummy. "In *three* months." She giggled as she danced along beside Emma. "How much longer is that, Mommy?"

"Not too much longer, sweetie."

"Grandma's coming then, isn't she? I can't wait."

"Yes, Grandma's coming then."

"Well, ladies, pillaging in my garden again...?"

"Daddy!" Maggie shrieked, dropping her basket as she spun around. "Mommy, Daddy's home."

Turning, Emma watched as Sam strode across the lawn toward them, a smile lighting his handsome face. Maggie ran to meet him, leaping into his arms and hugging his neck. No longer quite as coordinated as she'd like to be, thanks to her wider girth, Emma followed more slowly.

"You're home early," she said, stepping into the welcoming curve of his arm. "Not that I'm complaining. You-know-who is about due for a you-know-what."

"No nap, Mommy. I'm a big girl now."

"Just a short one, Mags?" Sam suggested, charming his daughter with a gentle tickle under her chin.

"Okay, Daddy. Just a short one," she agreed with another giggle.

Turning to Emma, he smiled conspiratorially.

"Why don't you wait out here while I put her down?" he suggested.

She nodded agreeably, settled into one of the chairs by the patio table, and tipped her face up, savoring the warmth of the March sun.

She had a pretty good idea of why her husband had come home so early on a weekday afternoon. He'd shown up unexpectedly, just like this, a look of excitement and anticipation on his face, twice already in the four years they'd been married. Once just before they'd moved to California and again just before their move to North Carolina.

Her major was now a lieutenant-colonel, and his career was on the rise. She was very, very proud of him, and almost as excited as he about what the air force had in store for him next.

Moving from place to place hadn't been nearly as traumatic as Emma had feared. Not with Sam smoothing the way for her, and Margaret, still blessedly healthy, lending a helping hand whenever possible.

She had also found that she had a knack for making new friends and fitting in wherever they went. The other officers' wives had become a kind of extended family for her. And now that she had Maggie and another baby on the way, her life seemed complete. So complete, Emma had accepted Megan's offer to buy her house in Serenity without the slightest hesitation.

Joining her on the patio again, Sam pulled up a chair beside her and eyed her expectantly.

"Well, where to?" she asked, offering him a smile.

"How does Colorado Springs sound?"

"Very nice," she admitted.

"I'm glad you think so. I've been asked to take over as head of the flight-training program at the Air Force Academy."

"Oh, Sam, that's wonderful."

He had talked about wanting to teach at the academy if a suitable position opened up. Now, it seemed, one had.

"We won't have to move until after the baby comes, and we'll probably be there awhile. The job can be as permanent as we want it to be, and I think I'd like a little more permanence now that we're a growing family."

"We already have the kind of permanence that's most important—our love for each other," Emma reminded him gently. "But I could get used to living in one place longer than two years—just as long as you're happy."

"I'm happy whenever we are, as long as we're together." Standing, he took her by the hand and pulled her to her feet, his smile turning seductive. ''Come on, let's go celebrate while the imp's asleep.''

''Better hurry. Her idea of *short* is thirty minutes or less, and her clock's already ticking.''

''No problem, sweetheart,'' he growled, dragging her, giggling all the way, down the hallway to their bedroom. ''No problem at all...''

\* \* \* \* \*

**Silhouette Romance proudly presents an all-new, original series...**

**Six friends dream of marrying their bosses in this delightful new series**

Come see how each month, office romances lead to happily-ever-after for six friends.

In January 1999—
**THE BOSS AND THE BEAUTY** by Donna Clayton

In February 1999—
**THE NIGHT BEFORE BABY** by Karen Rose Smith

In March 1999—
**HUSBAND FROM 9 to 5** by Susan Meier

In April 1999—
**THE EXECUTIVE'S BABY** by Robin Wells

In May 1999—
**THE MARRIAGE MERGER** by Vivian Leiber

In June 1999—
**I MARRIED THE BOSS** by Laura Anthony

Only from

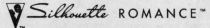

Available wherever Silhouette books are sold.

If you enjoyed what you just read,
then we've got an offer you can't resist!

# Take 2 bestselling love stories FREE!

# Plus get a FREE surprise gift!

---

**Clip this page and mail it to Silhouette Reader Service™**

| **IN U.S.A.** | **IN CANADA** |
|---|---|
| 3010 Walden Ave. | P.O. Box 609 |
| P.O. Box 1867 | Fort Erie, Ontario |
| Buffalo, N.Y. 14240-1867 | L2A 5X3 |

**YES!** Please send me 2 free Silhouette Special Edition® novels and my free surprise gift. Then send me 6 brand-new novels every month, which I will receive months before they're available in stores. In the U.S.A., bill me at the bargain price of $3.57 plus 25¢ delivery per book and applicable sales tax, if any*. In Canada, bill me at the bargain price of $3.96 plus 25¢ delivery per book and applicable taxes**. That's the complete price and a savings of over 10% off the cover prices—what a great deal! I understand that accepting the 2 free books and gift places me under no obligation ever to buy any books. I can always return a shipment and cancel at any time. Even if I never buy another book from Silhouette, the 2 free books and gift are mine to keep forever. So why not take us up on our invitation. You'll be glad you did!

235 SEN CNFD
335 SEN CNFE

| | |
|---|---|
| Name | (PLEASE PRINT) |
| Address | Apt.# |
| City | State/Prov.      Zip/Postal Code |

\* Terms and prices subject to change without notice. Sales tax applicable in N.Y.
\** Canadian residents will be charged applicable provincial taxes and GST.
  All orders subject to approval. Offer limited to one per household.
  ® are registered trademarks of Harlequin Enterprises Limited.

SPED99                   ©1998 Harlequin Enterprises Limited

# This March Silhouette is proud to present

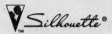

# SENSATIONAL

## MAGGIE SHAYNE
## BARBARA BOSWELL
## SUSAN MALLERY
## MARIE FERRARELLA

This is a special collection of four complete novels for one low price, featuring a novel from each line: Silhouette Intimate Moments, Silhouette Desire, Silhouette Special Edition and Silhouette Romance.

*Available at your favorite retail outlet.*

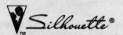

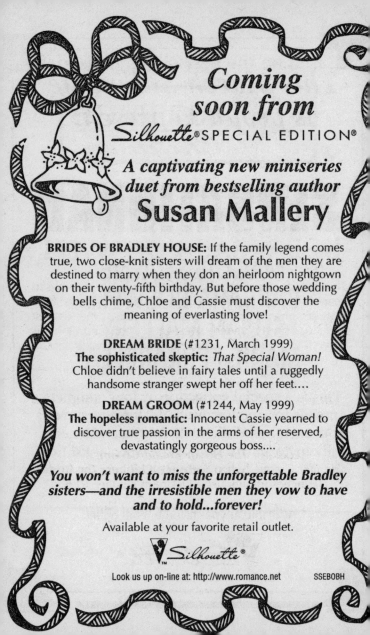

# Coming soon from

## *Silhouette* ® SPECIAL EDITION ®

### *A captivating new miniseries duet from bestselling author*
# Susan Mallery

**BRIDES OF BRADLEY HOUSE:** If the family legend comes true, two close-knit sisters will dream of the men they are destined to marry when they don an heirloom nightgown on their twenty-fifth birthday. But before those wedding bells chime, Chloe and Cassie must discover the meaning of everlasting love!

**DREAM BRIDE** (#1231, March 1999)
**The sophisticated skeptic:** *That Special Woman!*
Chloe didn't believe in fairy tales until a ruggedly handsome stranger swept her off her feet....

**DREAM GROOM** (#1244, May 1999)
**The hopeless romantic:** Innocent Cassie yearned to discover true passion in the arms of her reserved, devastatingly gorgeous boss....

*You won't want to miss the unforgettable Bradley sisters—and the irresistible men they vow to have and to hold...forever!*

Available at your favorite retail outlet.

*Silhouette* ®

## Based on the bestselling miniseries

## A FORTUNE'S CHILDREN *Wedding:*
### *THE HOODWINKED BRIDE*

# by BARBARA BOSWELL

This March, the Fortune family discovers a twenty-six-year-old secret—beautiful Angelica Carroll *Fortune!* Kate Fortune hires Flynt Corrigan to protect the newest Fortune, and this jaded investigator soon finds this his most tantalizing—and tormenting—assignment to date....

Barbara Boswell's single title is just one of the captivating romances in Silhouette's exciting new miniseries, **Fortune's Children: The Brides,** featuring six special women who perpetuate a family legacy that is greater than mere riches!

Look for *The Honor Bound Groom,* by Jennifer Greene, when **Fortune's Children: The Brides** launches in Silhouette Desire in January 1999!

Available at your favorite retail outlet.

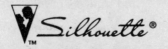

*Silhouette*

SPECIAL EDITION®

™

*That's My Baby!*

*Don't miss these poignant stories coming to*
**THAT'S MY BABY!**—only from
*Silhouette Special Edition!*

## December 1998  THEIR CHILD
### by Penny Richards (SE# 1213)
Drew McShane married Kim Campion to give her baby a name. Could their daughter unite them in love?

## February 1999  BABY, OUR BABY!
### by Patricia Thayer (SE# 1225)
Her baby girl would always remind Ali Pierce of her night of love with Jake Hawkins. Now he was back—and proposing marriage!

## April 1999  A FATHER FOR HER BABY
### by Celeste Hamilton (SE #1237)
When Jarrett McMullen located his long-lost runaway bride, could he convince the amnesiac, expectant mother-to-be he wanted her for always?

**THAT'S MY BABY!**
*Sometimes bringing up baby can bring surprises...
and showers of love.*

Available at your favorite retail outlet.

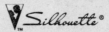

™ *Silhouette*®

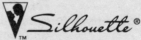

**Silhouette®**

SPECIAL EDITION™

# COMING NEXT MONTH

**#1231 DREAM BRIDE—Susan Mallery**
*That Special Woman!/Brides of Bradley House*
According to family legend, Chloe Wright was destined to dream of her future husband on her twenty-fifth birthday. The self-proclaimed pragmatist didn't believe in fairy tales…until enigmatic Arizona Smith mysteriously entered Chloe's life—and passionately swept her off her feet.

**#1232 THE PERFECT NEIGHBOR—Nora Roberts**
*The MacGregors*
Brooding loner Preston McQuinn was determined never to love again. But he could hardly resist his vivacious neighbor Cybil Campbell, who was determined to win his stubborn heart. Would the matchmaking Daniel MacGregor see his granddaughter happily married to the man she adored?

**#1233 HUSBAND IN TRAINING—Christine Rimmer**
Nick DeSalvo wanted to trade in his bachelor ways for his very own family. And who better than Jenny Brown—his best friend's nurturing widow—to give him lessons on how to be a model husband? But how long would it take the smitten, reformed heartbreaker to realize he wanted *Jenny* as his wife?

**#1234 THE COWBOY AND HIS WAYWARD BRIDE—Sherryl Woods**
*And Baby Makes Three: The Next Generation*
Rancher Harlan Patrick Adams was fit to be tied! The only woman who'd ever mattered to him had secretly given birth to *his* baby girl. And he couldn't bear to be apart from his family for another second. Could the driven father convince fiercely independent Laurie Jensen to be his bride?

**#1235 MARRYING AN OLDER MAN—Arlene James**
She was young, innocent and madly in love with her much older boss. Trouble was, no matter how much Caroline Moncton enticed him, gorgeous cowboy Jesse Wagner insisted she'd set her sights on the wrong guy. But she refused to quit tempting this hardheaded man down the wedding aisle!

**#1236 A HERO AT HEART—Ann Howard White**
When Nathan Garner returned to Thunder Ridge, Georgia, he was enveloped in bittersweet memories of Rachel Holcomb. Walking away from her gentle tenderness hadn't been easy, but it had been necessary. Could he reclaim Rachel's wary heart—and bring his beloved back into his waiting arms?